"I need to remember everything about us...." Cole said

"Everything?"

"How we met, what you wore, how our first kiss tasted."

As Cole's lips angled downward, Holly realized she'd better start talking. So she told him they'd met at a Christmas party, near a vat of hot apple cider spiced with cinnamon. They danced to soft carols, her white-gloved hands resting on his lapels, her red velvet gown swirling. Long after the music ended, they kept dancing. And later, inside an open sleigh with snowflakes glistening in their hair, Cole held her close, kissing her for the first time.

"Right then," Holly finished, "we knew we belonged together. It was as if we'd met before and loved each other forever...."

It was so romantic, Holly thought.

But of course, every word was a lie.

Dear Reader,

Every year—no matter where I happen to be at Christmastime—I travel home to the place where I was born. I lose my city self, don my old rubber boots and flannel shirts and spend time hiking the snow-covered hills of our farm, visiting extended family, playing with countless nieces and nephews, relaxing by the fire. While I know that Christmas is everywhere—in every place and inside the human heart—my own would never feel complete without this time-honored ritual of homecoming.

Cole in My Stocking came directly out of my love of country Christmases. It also came from many of my other preoccupations: nature's ability to transform us and affirm life, a belief in simple gifts and everyday miracles, searching for the path of one's truest self and following it, and making peace with the past. It's a story about single mom Holly Hawkes and her two adorable kids who are struggling to bloom and find love where they've been planted. And it's about Cole Rayburn, a larger-than-life hero who's been living a lie and who—after he loses his memory—is reborn and restored to his true self on Christmas.

What Cole and Holly find is my wish for you this season: I hope you will also find one small, quiet moment of grace and remember the awe and wonder you felt as a child on a holiday morning. And I hope for that one moment—wherever you happen to be—you'll feel like you've just come home.

Happy Holiday,

Jule McBride

JULE McBRIDE
COLE IN MY STOCKING

Harlequin Books

TORONTO • NEW YORK • LONDON
AMSTERDAM • PARIS • SYDNEY • HAMBURG
STOCKHOLM • ATHENS • TOKYO • MILAN
MADRID • WARSAW • BUDAPEST • AUCKLAND

For John and Helen Hegedus, in memory. Especially for
Helen who never saw more than she wanted to and who
created memories that were so much better than reality:
You'll never be forgotten.

And also for the wonderful Anne Stuart who said this
book was good enough.

ISBN 0-373-16658-3

COLE IN MY STOCKING

Copyright © 1996 by Julianne Randolph Moore.

Prologue

On a Christmas Eve Past...

"Ho, ho, ho, hooray!" A blustery wind gusted through Joe's Stardust Bar in Weller's Falls, New York, and right before the door slammed shut, a departing patron boomed, "Yes, indeed, I do believe in Santa Claus!"

Cole Rayburn slung a bar towel over his shoulder and winced—as much at the comment as at the festive atmosphere inside Joe's. Was Cole the only lonely soul who'd noticed that 1986 was the worst damn holiday season in history?

He glanced around, his heart sinking. Merry red and green lights blinked from every corner of the homey, neighborhood bar, and bright yellow paper stars were affixed to the jukebox, which was now playing "Rudolph the Red-Nosed Reindeer." Joe had even rigged the cash register, so each time the drawer cha-chinged open, a cardboard Santa tipped his hat. And written across the bar's mirror, in scripty snowflake lettering, were the words Joe's Stardust Bar Hopes You'll Find the Magic Spirit of Christmas!

Bah humbug.

Every last light, ornament and snowflake in the joint was depressing Cole. Even worse, his sixth sense was telling him that the woman at the end of the bar, an out-of-place business type who'd introduced herself as Glennis Gaynes, wanted something from him. She'd been nursing the same scotch-rocks for an hour—and calmly staring Cole down.

"C'mon, Cole," someone called. "Let's see another one of your magic tricks."

"Vatch," Cole said in a feigned German accent. "Vatch very carefully." In the next instant, a great flourish of his bar towel distracted the customers, while, with a lightning fast sleight of hand, he made his most recent tip vanish from the old oak bar.

The trick won Cole a hearty round of applause. But why was Glennis Gaynes watching him so intently? She seemed about Cole's age, which was twenty-three, but he could swear he'd never laid eyes on her before.

At first, she'd just stood on the icy sidewalk outside Joe's, studiously staring through the window at Cole and occasionally stamping her high heels against the cold. From the corner of his eye, Cole had watched blowing flurries spiral wildly around her, settling on the upturned collar of the camel hair steamer coat that draped down her long frame. In spite of the subzero temperature, she was wearing whisper-thin white stockings and a flimsy red silk scarf—and she didn't even bother to shiver much. The forty-mile-an-hour winds hadn't mussed her blond French twist, either.

Finally, she'd whisked herself inside the bar—in a gala swirl of snow flurries and floral perfume—just as someone plunked another quarter in the juke and the Andrews Sisters started singing "White Christmas."

Cole—who had no family, nowhere to go this Christmas—and no woman to keep him warm on this coldest of cold winter nights—just wished Glennis Gaynes had turned out to be his type. But he liked country girls, the kind who wore down-filled jackets and no makeup. And Glennis had *city* written all over her.

With perfect grace, she'd slid onto a stool at the far end of the bar, away from the other customers. Cole had watched her remove her coat, exposing the crisp, elfin green business suit beneath. Then she'd ordered the scotch-rocks as if it were her middle name and introduced herself. She'd told Cole she worked in Manhattan, and that she'd come upstate to visit her folks for the holidays.

Now Joe squeezed past Cole, slapped a new 1987 calendar against the mirror behind the bar and taped it into place. "This one's on the house, folks!" Joe shouted jovially. "Last call till we reopen for New Year's."

Last call. Already, as Cole made his way down the bar replenishing drinks, he could see the footprints Joe's customers would leave in the snow as they headed home to lit fires and cozy families, hot toddies and cool eggnog, warm beds and warmer kisses. In his twenty-three years, Cole had heard enough goodbyes to last any man a lifetime. Now, he steeled himself against those that would be said tonight.

Grow up, Cole. It's just one Christmas alone.

Still, he'd been staying at the Sleep Inn down the road for the past week, and he hardly relished the thought of waking there tomorrow, alone on Christmas morning.

He reminded himself that he'd be heading out of town at first light—toward a logging job he'd found up north. Maybe he'd meet a girl there he could marry. Build a house in the mountains by a lake where he could fish. Settle down. Raise a family.

And then he'd never be alone on Christmas again.

When he reached Glennis Gaynes, Cole raised an eyebrow. "Another scotch-rocks? It's on Joe."

"No, thanks." She shook her head, leaned forward and lowered her voice conspiratorially. "But I do have a proposition for you."

Cole wasn't that surprised. Even he knew he'd been blessed with more than average good looks. *Let her down easy, Cole.* Somehow, he managed to chuckle. "Sorry, but if I took you up on it, it might ruin all my plans for a lonely holiday."

Glennis's green eyes widened. "Not that kind of proposition!"

Then what did the woman want? "No?"

"Look. Could you just tell me something about yourself?"

Cole merely squinted at her. But then something— maybe her insistent contralto voice or the interested intensity of her eyes—loosened his tongue. And he wound up telling her everything.

Cole told her how his mother had died years ago, and how he'd lost his dad back in October. Cole had sold Rayburn and Son, the family-run garage where he'd apprenticed under his father as a mechanic, and just last week, he'd sold the house where he'd grown up. Now all his dad's medical bills were paid in full. While he'd been waiting for a logging job to come through, Cole had been biding his time in Weller's Falls, selling Christmas trees and tending bar. Tonight was his last night in town.

He wrapped up his life story with a wry grin. "And I thought I was the bartender."

"Cole Rayburn..." Glennis reached forward and firmly shook his hand. "Your luck's about to change."

"Don't tell me." His dry chuckle floated across the bar. "You're one of Santa's helpers, here to offer me all the magic of Christmas."

"Well..." Glennis drew in a sharp, seemingly invigorating breath. "Sort of."

Cole's mouth quirked. "You're an elf?"

"No, I'm an assistant producer at the cable station where I work." Glennis lowered her voice another notch. "And I want to make you a star."

"Out of what?" he couldn't help but tease.

"I mean it," she said in a hushed tone. "I want to make you famous. I'm twenty-five and I'm already an assistant producer, but I need one big discovery of my own...."

Trying not to look too interested, Cole leaned back and casually poured himself the draught Joe had been offering him all night. He took a sip, foam tickling his upper lip. "Come again?"

The next thing he knew, Glennis was talking a mile a minute. She'd known he was "star material" the second she'd seen him, which was why she'd been watching him. She was impressed by his magic tricks and the patter he used with the patrons.

"German. Irish. Japanese. You don't look like you've traveled," she said. "Where did you learn all those accents?"

"From TV." Cole shrugged. "Infomercials, mostly."

"With your command of accents," Glennis said breathlessly, "you could pretend to be anyone!"

Cole said nothing. That the woman seemed on the level was downright disconcerting. A small spiral notepad appeared from somewhere, and she slapped it onto the bar. Clicking a tiny gold pen, she asked a string of rapid-fire questions: Did Cole know any flashier tricks? Did he have any ideas for big sets?

Finally, she said, "Do you like kids?"

He shrugged. "Sure."

"Feel passionately about magic?"

"Absolutely."

At the word, years dropped away and Cole recalled that long-ago Christmas when he'd received his first magic set. Inside a small blue attaché-style case, he'd found a wand, a star-studded cap, and a set of star-printed curtains. Hinged poles were included. They snapped outward and the curtains hung from them, creating a makeshift stage. There was a book, too, full of magical words like *abracadabra, alakazam* and *open sesame.*

Cole was seven, and it was his first Christmas since his mother had passed on. How had his father known that a magic set could make a motherless little boy feel as though he'd suddenly gained control of the world again?

But it had. Within a week, Cole was palming coins and cards and making small household objects disappear at will. Later, when Cole was in high school and working at his dad's garage, he discovered he loved cars nearly as much as magic. When things were slow at work, he'd use his newfound mechanical knowledge to create diagrams of large-scale magic tricks—sketches of complicated boxes, trunks designed for great escapes and systems of lights that would make vanishing veils shimmer like stardust.

"Yeah," Cole repeated. "I've definitely got a passion for magic." *Maybe because magicians control the world they create.*

Glennis shrugged. "Well, frankly, even if you didn't, research teams could come up with the stunts. The main thing you've got to offer is charisma."

Cole grunted noncommittally. After all, he'd heard more pipe dreams in his brief stint at Joe's bar than he could ever recount.

But what if this was a real opportunity? He was only twenty-three and he no longer had ties here. Since Weller's Falls wasn't exactly a boomtown, most of his high school friends had already moved away. Whimsically, Cole thought that maybe there was a Santa. Or maybe Glennis really was an elf.

Glennis sighed. "You don't completely fit the profile."

"Profile?"

"I've done a lot of research and everybody wants the next hot TV magician. They want a man who can command a crowd the way you do. Physically, you're perfect—tall, dark hair and blue-black eyes. Self-possessed. Muscular but lean. Suave."

Suave? Now, that was pushing it. Cole glanced pointedly down at his faded jeans and hiking boots.

"You'd need a suit," Glennis said. "Or to wear all black. And you'd have to be...more Ivy League. A hint of a British accent would be good. Your name would have to go."

Cole's eyes narrowed. "You want me to change my identity?"

She groaned. "Don't be such a purist. Half the biographies in Hollywood are fiction. And you know what my motto is?"

Cole hadn't a clue, though he was slowly realizing Glennis was probably a real shark at the office. He shook his head.

"What the public wants, the public gets." Glennis slid a business card across the bar. "You could come to New York City with me tomorrow—or you could think it over and give me a call."

She sure didn't waste any time. Cole glanced down at the card. When he recognized the name of the station, his mind started running wild. Could his life really change this way? All of a sudden . . . without warning? On a night so cold his soul felt frozen? On a lonely, snowy Christmas Eve night at a place called Joe's Stardust Bar?

"No one but us could ever know your life is really a PR fabrication," Glennis warned.

Cole glanced at a television that was mounted in a corner with the sound muted, then toward the customers at the other end of the bar. "Don't you think people would recognize me?"

"Not after I make you over."

"A magician who is, himself, living out an illusion . . ." Cole murmured. Somehow, the idea appealed to him.

His eyes stole to the window, where Joe's neon sign blinked against the glass. Farther away, the white steeple of the local church rose high above the rooftops, disappearing into the starry night sky. Inside the many modest homes, people stoked fires and warm smoke poured from chimneys. And from all directions, Christmas lights were burning bright. For an instant, Weller's Falls seemed to appear to Cole in miniature, as if it were inside a snow globe. And then, as if Cole had picked up his whole hometown and given it one hardy shake, the snow outside began to fall in earnest.

Could I live a lie if the trade-off was fame, fortune, and the ability to perform my magic the way I've always dreamed?

"A long time ago," Cole finally found himself saying, "when I found out there wasn't really a Santa Claus, I asked my father why he'd lied to me all those years. And you know what he said?"

Glennis shook her head.

Cole leaned closer. "He said that sometimes we have to lie in order to tell the truth."

Glennis looked confused. "What truth are you going to tell by pretending to be someone else?"

"The truth of the magic," Cole returned softly.

And that's how, on one cold, lonely Christmas Eve, a bartender named Cole Rayburn mysteriously vanished into thin air, and the world's most famous magician—Joe Ray Stardust—was born.

Chapter One

Ten years later, the present...

If only Joe Ray Stardust had never been born, Holly Hawkes fumed. It scarcely seemed possible, but there was a slight chance she'd lose her kids—and all because of a sexy magician she'd only seen on television.

"Don't worry, Holly," Danice Jacobs assured her. "Judge Selsa won't give your in-laws custody of the kids, especially not the week before Christmas."

Holly's grateful glance flicked over Danice's coffee-and-cream skin and trim navy suit. Impulsively, she squeezed her court-appointed attorney's hand. "I know you're doing everything you can."

But Holly's ex-in-laws were so rich, so powerful, and so intent on getting the children. Both Jessica and Robert Samuels, Senior were seated behind a table in the near-empty courtroom, looking the very picture of poised professionalism. Holly smoothed her long, wavy chestnut hair, then her simple cream skirt and sweater set. *For all practical purposes, you've been completely self-reliant for the past seven years,* she reminded herself. *So, don't worry. You can take care of this.*

"Mrs. Samuels," Judge Selsa intoned, "you feel that Benjamin and Theresa, ages four and five respectively, should be placed with you, rather than with their mother, Ms. Holly Hawkes?"

"She's a Samuels now!" Jessica tossed her head, making her elegant auburn bob swirl around her shoulders. "And so are those children!"

Holly didn't bother to rein in her temper. "The first thing I did when I divorced your son, Jessica," she returned hotly, "was to take back my maiden name."

Jessica sniffed. "And see how rude she is!"

Holly gasped. "I'm rude! You're trying to take away the kids!"

Judge Selsa sighed. "Please calm yourselves."

Jessica ignored him. "We own the Express Mall downtown," she continued imperiously. "And we could provide so many more opportunities for Benji and Treasure..."

Watching Jessica wring her bejeweled, manicured hands, Holly almost exploded again. Holly wouldn't make much money at her new receptionist job, but the kids had everything they needed—including the love their father had never given them.

Poor Benji, Holly thought. A five-year-old at day care had been picking on him because he didn't have a dad, and when Benji had concocted an imaginary father, it had only made matters worse. Now her four-year-old was sporting his first black eye. She shook her head. For the past year she'd been working sporadically and living on her savings, so she could stay home with the kids. Now she had no choice but to start working full-time.

Judge Selsa continued addressing the Samuelses. "You maintain that Ms. Hawkes urged your son, Bobby, to take a job as a roadie with the Joe Ray Stardust Show two years ago?''

"Yes." Robert Samuels ran a hand through his thick, silver hair, then he leaned on a hand-carved cane he carried for show. "I strongly believe that job ruined my son. Bobby was a good boy before he met her—"

"Good *boy?*" Holly shrieked. "That *boy* of yours is thirty-three years old!"

"Please control your temper, Ms. Hawkes," Judge Selsa reminded.

At that moment, a fortyish man in a gray suit scurried into the courtroom, approached the bench and began conferring with Judge Selsa.

Holly's jaw set with angry determination. Why wouldn't the judge just listen to her? She'd begged Bobby not to take that job. She'd wanted him home with her and the kids, not traveling with some infernal magic show.

But Bobby had said the job was his dream come true. Because Joe Ray Stardust only toured during the summers and for Christmas benefit performances, Bobby would be in New York City most of the year, working at the cable station where the weekly segments of Joe Ray's popular Thursday night show were shot.

Once Holly agreed to move, the rest was history. Bobby rarely came home after that. If he wasn't traveling, he claimed he was working late at the studio. And Holly was left alone, caring for the kids in a large city where she knew no one.

Then last Christmas season, Holly had been invited to attend the holiday bash for Joe Ray Stardust's crew. Bobby had even promised to introduce her to the famous magician. Instead, she'd lost track of Bobby—and found him later, just in time to hear Joe Ray Stardust fire him. Stunned, she'd merely listened from the shadows. Joe Ray said Bobby couldn't handle the fast track. He was partying, sleeping around....

Oh, she'd suspected it. Even known it. But hearing someone say it aloud cut through her denial. She'd pulled on her red velvet cape and fled the fancy party immediately, with Joe Ray Stardust's deep, melodious bass voice and upper-crust British accent still ringing in her ears. The day after Christmas she'd filed for divorce. And within the week she and the kids were headed out of New York City and back home to the freedom and clean air of the West Virginia mountains. They'd settled in Belle, right outside of Charleston.

"I'm sorry, but something's come up," Judge Selsa said, as the man who'd interrupted the proceedings hurried from the courtroom again. "We'll have to adjourn for a few days."

"I want this settled now!" Jessica Samuels burst out. "We're here because this woman ruined my son's life!"

Holly whirled around in her seat. "You had your chance to raise a son, Jessica. And I definitely don't want you raising mine, especially not given the way Bobby turned out!"

"Pipe down, Holly." Danice's soft-spoken warning implied that Holly's righteous indignation could get her into trouble.

This really is all Joe Ray Stardust's fault, Holly thought. She might no longer love her two-timing ex, but she pitied him. After Joe Ray fired Bobby, Bobby had gone right off the deep end.

Even worse, the magician was performing a Christmas benefit matinee in Charleston this afternoon—and Holly had to go. Her elderly neighbors, Irma Garvin and Stella Lewis, had offered Holly free tickets right in front of the kids. If Holly had said no, Benji and Treasure would never

speak to her again. Fortunately, her new employer had
been kind enough to give her the latter part of the afternoon off. Glancing down at her watch, Holly hoped he was
as understanding about this long lunch hour.

Judge Selsa cleared his throat. "We'll resume this hearing on December twenty-fourth, at 3:00 p.m.."

"The twenty-fourth?" Holly murmured. "On Christmas Eve?" She was so shocked, she didn't even see her in-
laws leave the courtroom.

"Don't fret," Danice said to Holly. "You're employed
and as long as your life proceeds as it is now, you won't
have any trouble. You might go ahead and pay your January rent early, though."

Holly gulped. She'd gotten a little behind and December wasn't yet paid.

"Find yourself some character references, too," Danice added. "Just to be on the safe side."

Holly nodded, feeling suddenly numb. She'd been so
intent on handling this herself that she hadn't told a single
soul what was happening. Not even her parents. They were
retired, and Holly simply couldn't allow Jessica and Robert Samuels to disturb their Christmas. Benji and Treasure didn't know, either. Or her new employer. And Holly
already felt she'd imposed on her neighbors so much....

Danice shot her a quick smile. "C'mon, Holly. What
could go wrong in a week?"

"Who knows?" Holly returned dryly. "Maybe I'll kill
Joe Ray Stardust."

JOE RAY KEPT HIS POWERFUL body still. With a mere flick
of his wrist, he waved his wand, making red and green veils
dance in circles around the last bunny that remained on
stage.

"Watch—" The few strands of premature silver in his black hair shone under the hot stage lights, and his deep bass voice, twinged with hints of an English accent, mesmerized the hushed crowd. "Watch carefully, boys and girls."

All night, in the darkness of the packed theater, Joe Ray had watched the faces of the children while he'd made rabbits hop through pine wreaths and elves vanish in puffs of smoke. Then, in a shower of golden glitter that served as stardust, he'd even made Santa appear. Wrapped gifts—plastic wands and decks of cards—had been dispensed to the kids. Now, as soon as this last bunny was gone, Joe Ray would vanish, too.

And maybe this time, I won't come back.

He imagined disappearing for good—cleaning out his hefty bank accounts, heading to some forgotten island and leaving the world to whisper about what had really become of him.

But how could he vanish when the kids stared at him with such wide-eyed wonder? Those little faces were so honest, so incapable of lies. Somehow, they always kept Joe Ray going—to the next taping, the next benefit, the next signing of his new book, *One Magic Christmas.*

As the red and green veils circled ever more quickly around the bunny, Joe Ray's mouth curled into a mysterious smile. "Are you watching me now?"

Not a soul said a word, but the response of the children was as clear as Christmas bells. *Yes, Joe Ray, we're watching.*

"I think this bunny might like to go home for the holidays," he said. And with a tap of his wand, the bunny disappeared. As the veils floated slowly to the floor, a murmur of childrens' voices sounded, then the rapid clapping of tiny hands.

Holding his arms wide apart, Joe Ray bowed, then began to turn in circles. Once again, the red and green veils rose magically from the floor—and once again Joe Ray wished he really could vanish.

Lately, his mind kept returning to that lonely Christmas Eve ten years ago in Joe's Stardust Bar. What had really happened that fateful night? Had Glennis brought him a Christmas miracle—or had he merely sold out, trading in his true identity for fame and fortune? Only one thing was certain: ten years ago, he'd had no idea what he was giving up.

As the veils rose around him, he realized he ached for a woman to love tonight. He shut his eyes and imagined the silken touch of her winter-pale skin and the hot-honey flavor of her wild kisses—until his heart and body burned for her. But he couldn't quench the raging fire because the entire world thought he was a happily married man.

His wife and their two preschoolers supposedly lived in a private Connecticut suburb on the Stardust Estate, which Glennis had bought back in 1987. Even though the huge stone mansion remained unoccupied, Glennis periodically redecorated it according to her taste. It was hidden behind high security fences and wooded grounds; house lights and sprinklers ran on an elaborate system of timers.

Yes, Joe Ray Stardust was a man to be envied. Every single ingredient of his life now fit Glennis's researched recipe for success—the wife, the kids, the privileged background and the touch of an English accent.

But it was all a lie.

And beyond the pleasant illusions and eye-catching tricks, Joe Ray still craved the reality of love. For how could there be magic if there was no one to share it with?

As the veils thickened around him, circling and hiding him from the audience, years dropped away. For an instant, he almost thought another Christmas miracle had occurred, and as he vanished to a round of applause, he felt like Cole Rayburn again, that regular guy from upstate New York who liked to fish and hike, build fires in winter and make love.

Backstage, a pay phone receiver dangled toward the floor.

"It's Glennis," someone said.

Joe Ray reached for the phone, bracing himself for what he knew was coming. "Sorry, Glenn, but I've only got a minute. I need to take my final bow."

Glennis started in, as if they were already in midconversation. "But, Joe, all we have to do is generate new PR material. We could pretend you got a divorce, then we could date, and if things worked out between us, we could move to the Connecticut estate. After all these years, I—I love you."

No you don't. But recently, she'd become fixated on him for some reason. Lowering his voice, he said, "You know I'm not the right guy for you."

Maybe not for anyone. For years, he'd tried to forget about love. How could he have an honest relationship when women always assumed he was two-timing his wife? And how could he talk about wanting kids when he supposedly already had them?

Only Glennis knew his true identity—and shared his fear that celebrity hounds might dig up the long-lost Cole Rayburn and expose him. She was the only woman in the world with whom he could be himself.

But Joe Ray didn't love her.

"Look," he said. "I'm on a flight within a few hours. When I get to New York, we'll talk about this. Glennis, we're better off as friends."

"Can I pick you up at the airport?"

"Of course."

Hanging up the phone, he felt like the victim of one of his own magic tricks. Cole Rayburn had vanished—and over the years, the memory of him had become as elusive as the tricky scarves Joe Ray Stardust pulled from his top hats. For a fleeting moment, he considered blowing his own cover. He wanted his life back. And he wanted to fall in love.

Then he thought of the children.

He knew what he represented to them. He was like Santa Claus. Full of magic. Kind and trustworthy. Definitely not a liar.

So, with applause still ringing in his ears, he forced himself to forget about winter-pale skin and kisses in the dark and lasting love. And forcing a smile, he headed for the stage to take his final bow for the children.

"WELL, I GOT THROUGH that entire show without killing Joe Ray Stardust." And now winds from the nearby Kanawha and Elk rivers were chilling Holly to the bone. Waving her old red umbrella, she dodged wet snowflakes while her feet sought purchase on the sheet of ice that coated the pavement. She was so upset, she barely noticed she was muttering. "That man's just awful!"

But so...charismatic. During the performance, Joe Ray Stardust's arresting midnight eyes had captured the attention of everyone in the Charleston Civic Center. Television just didn't do him justice. The instant Holly had heard his faint English accent and bass chuckle, she'd felt compelled to rise from her seat and—

"Destroy his perfect life," she said firmly, unwilling to admit that the man's in-the-flesh good looks had seriously affected her. "Just the way he destroyed mine."

Her green jalopy, which she'd left near an unused stage door to avoid parking fees, was the only car in sight. Glancing around nervously, she felt glad Irma, Stella and the kids were waiting inside the warm safety of the Civic Center. It was only five, but fully dark. Street lamps on this isolated lot weren't even lit, although Christmas bulbs gleamed hazily from the faraway Express Mall.

The Samuelses' mall. Holly heaved a heartfelt sigh. If only court had been the worst of it.

But no-ooo.

It was only the beginning. She'd returned late to her office and had gotten fired.

Now she slipped—and slid right into her car. Hoping to find Benji's extra sweater, she opened the spacious trunk and tossed her umbrella inside. Her eyes scanned over a wool plaid coverlet and some gifts: a croquet set the kids had wanted even though they couldn't play in winter, the mallets of which she'd already tied with bright red bows, a Barbie outfit, and *One Magic Christmas* by Joe Ray Stardust.

Benji had begged for the book, which was full of coin and card tricks. From its glossy front cover, Joe Ray Stardust surveyed Holly. She glared back at the squarish, clean-shaven, handsomely chiseled face of the man who'd ruined her life.

"Car trouble?"

When Holly's chin snapped up, her forehead narrowly missed the raised trunk lid. Belatedly ducking, she slipped on the ice again. Her flailing hands—so clumsy in their knitted gloves—merely slapped against the trunk's ledge as someone snatched a fistful of her green down jacket.

She sputtered, "What—what do you think you're—"

Before she could finish, a strong male hand had pulled her to her feet. When it dropped her sleeve, she slid, and arms quickly circled her waist, forcing her against the dark woolly wall of a broad, sweater-clad chest.

Holly's heart pounded with pure panic. Self-defense maneuvers riffled through her mind, but it was so icy that even the most popular trick—one swift kick to the groin— would most likely leave the stranger unharmed and land her on her behind.

She groped madly behind herself, her hand dunking inside the trunk, her fingers crawling over the interior and closing around the stem of a croquet mallet. As she moved, she glimpsed the man's expensive wool slacks, lean muscular legs and stylish work boots. His open coat brushed her cheek, feeling so soft it had to be made of cashmere. Trying to ignore the smell of his pine-scented soap, she emitted a breathless, flustered sigh and checked her shaky footing. Then, she quickly shoved his chest. Clutching the mallet, she swung it from the trunk. Her head snapped up—and she gasped in horror.

"Hey there." A deep bass chuckle was whisked away by the evening's biting wind. "I'm Joe Ray Stardust."

It was enough to make Holly break down and cry. Instead, her fingers tightened instinctively on the mallet. "This just isn't my day," she muttered under her breath.

He leaned toward her inquiringly. "Excuse me?"

She merely glared back at him in the darkness. Was she supposed to be pleased about the fact that he'd wrapped her in a bear hug? Outside, the air was below freezing, but the instant her cheek had touched his sweater, her internal temperature had shot up to boiling. Now, confronted with his dark-haired, dark-eyed good looks, the pulse in her throat started ticking wildly. If she got one degree warmer, the ice beneath her feet would actually melt.

Tamping down her rising hysteria, she assured herself that her body's dangerous reaction to the man was due to fury, not desire. "Joe Ray who?" she asked sweetly.

And then she tried not to stare. Was it her imagination or did Joe Ray's knowing, seductive smile suggest he was thinking about capturing her in his arms again? Against her will, her mallet-free hand shot nervously to her throat, and she fumbled senselessly with her jacket zipper. Oh, why did these down coats have to be so darn warm?

Joe Ray Stardust glanced inside her open trunk pointedly and nodded at *One Magic Christmas*. Sure enough, his picture was still right there on the book's cover. Holly took a frantic inventory. *Strong square jaw and straight nose; wavy, silver-threaded raven hair that licked his earlobes; eyes the color of a clear winter's night*. It was him, all right. And when he looked at her again, she felt awfully stupid.

As well as downright faint. Her eyes settled on the powerful chest she'd been crushed against. Gulping, she lifted her chin—and wished she hadn't. Lord knew, she never went looking for trouble. But in Joe Ray Stardust, she'd sure found it.

Each look at him transported her. The parking lot vanished and she found herself nowhere but in extremely hot water. Not to mention drowning in the depths of those blue-black eyes. Haunting and inescapable, they dared her to look elsewhere, and yet told her to run away.

But she couldn't move. For what seemed like an eternity, she simply stood there, watching heavy white snowflakes catch in his long jet eyelashes. The way they sparkled was so positively enchanting that Holly found herself almost believing in things like Christmas miracles and gift-bearing Santas.

He glanced at the book in the trunk again. "*That* Joe Ray Stardust," he finally said.

She'd almost forgotten. But his smug tone reminded her she had a score to settle. Should she confront him? Tell him how much she hated him for what he'd done to Bobby? Call him a home wrecker right to his face?

"Joe Ray Stardust?" Her legs felt oddly rubbery, but she raised her chin another determined notch and fought the urge to lean against the trunk for support. "Am I supposed to faint?"

"The way you nearly hit the pavement when you saw me—" Joe Ray's mouth quirked in a faint smile "—I thought you might."

"You thought wrong."

His lips twitched. "I can see that now."

At his clear amusement, her cheeks grew warm in spite of the cold. Even worse, his frankly assessing gaze made her fingers itch to smooth her disheveled hair. She even wished she'd worn a longer coat, since her thigh-length down jacket didn't exactly do her skirt justice. "Well, excuse me," she managed to say dismissively, her piqued breaths fogging the air. "But I'm sure you're accustomed to having people fall all over you."

She had the distinct impression that she'd said something wrong. And that Joe Ray Stardust was definitely a force to be reckoned with. His eyes narrowed and his gaze became so penetrating that she had to fight not to back away.

"I guess I do have a few fans."

What an understatement. The man was world famous. She tried, but failed to disguise her venom. "Then shouldn't you be basking in the limelight, instead of creeping around in the dark, scaring lone women to death?"

At first, he didn't bother to respond. His potent gaze drifted over her with torturous slowness and his lips parted ever so slightly in what might have been surprise. When Holly realized he didn't know quite what to make of her, she felt a rush of satisfaction, the first she'd felt all day. Unfortunately, at the haughty toss of her head, strands of her hair caught the whipping wind and stung her cheeks as if in censure.

Joe Ray's voice was only mildly curious. "So, are you still planning to attack me with that croquet stick?"

As much as she wanted to get rid of the weapon, his eyes pinned her where she stood and her fingers froze around the wood. In order to save face, she said, "Maybe."

He lazily raised an eyebrow, as if acknowledging she might attempt him bodily harm and saying it didn't concern him much. Then his attention shifted to her second-hand sedan. The green paint was chipped, the back fender dented. No doubt, a limo was about to pull around for Mr. Fabulous. Holly watched him trace a line along the ledge of her trunk. His fingers were a magician's fingers—long and nimble, strong and quick.

"Wouldn't she start?" he asked.

The man was determined to help her in spite of her rudeness, and his unmistakable pity was the last straw. "She starts just fine," Holly snapped. "And I'm not having trouble. So why don't you get lost?"

He didn't budge. Her anger didn't seem to ruffle him. Nor did the cold. And the damnable man hadn't so much as put his ungloved hands in his pockets for warmth. By degrees, his eyes were turning darker. "Guess you didn't enjoy my show."

"Maybe I didn't."

But she had. His enchanting tricks and charming illusions had held her spellbound. Tonight, watching him perform, she'd recaptured a sense of magic she hadn't felt in years. Maybe she'd even feared she'd lost it forever. The way the kids' faces had beamed with pleasure meant the world to her, too.

Not that she'd share that with him.

"But you *were* at the show," he said.

Holly swallowed hard. If she'd wanted to put him on edge, she guessed she'd succeeded. But why should he care where a nobody like herself had spent the afternoon? Reminding herself she wasn't supposed to willingly risk hypothermia just so she could chat with him, she crept backward an inch.

His eyes narrowed another fraction. "Were you at the show?"

"Don't you know?" she couldn't help but say. "Why, when you guessed what all the kids wanted for Christmas, I just assumed you were really telepathic."

His voice was deathly calm. "Of course."

All at once, Holly realized her eyes were caressing his hair again. Darn it, each time she looked at him, waves of forgetfulness washed over her. *Concentrate. Remember Bobby. Don't forget that your rent's unpaid, you lost your job and the kids don't have a Christmas tree yet.* "If you're so telepathic," she suddenly burst out, "then I guess you can read *my* mind."

He shot her a frankly insinuating gaze. "I guess I can."

She tried to ignore the innuendo, but fresh color rose to her cheeks. "Then you know I'm hoping you'll do what you do best—and vanish."

"What did I ever do to you?"

"You'd be amazed," she retorted.

"Do we know each other?"

Holly caught glimmers of emotion in his eyes—caution, secrecy, watchfulness. Her imagination ran wild. Did he fear she was some forgotten woman from his past?

Don't be a fool, Holly. The man was wealthier than Croesus. According to the bio in his book, he lived on a Connecticut estate with his wife. He had kids the same ages as Benji and Treasure.

Recognition sparked in his eyes and his voice seemed to carry a warning. "Have we met before or not?"

"Never." Technically, it was the truth...unless he'd seen her in the shadows a year ago, when she'd surreptitiously listened to him fire Bobby.

Suddenly, with the lightning speed of his profession, he grasped her elbow and covered the scant space between them. His touch communicated instant heat and raw power, nerves of steel and sinewy strength. He was in perfect shape. Daring escapes from chains and ropes and trunks no doubt demanded it. Feeling his close physical proximity, Holly was once again seized by panic. Especially when he pulled her so close that their foggy breaths mingled together on the night air.

"Please—" His low seductive whisper was tinged with that heavenly British accent. "Just tell me who you are."

"Suffice it to say you ruined my life."

His eyes—assessing and analytical, critical and dispassionate—roved over her face. She could almost see the wheels of his mind whirring as he attempted to recall their meeting. His breath fanned across her skin, warming her cheeks and making her whole body tingle. "How could I ruin your life if we've never even met?"

His silken voice made her heart flutter like the wings of a nervous butterfly. They were so alone out here, and the already thick air was getting foggier by the minute. Just who in the world did Joe Ray Stardust think she was?

Holly mustered her brightest tone. "Look, I'm sure somebody must be wondering where you are by now. As nice as it was for you to try to help me, I somehow doubt you actually possess skills as a car mechanic."

She'd said the wrong thing. His grip on her elbow tightened. "Were you a customer at the...garage?"

"Garage?" Somehow, she disengaged herself and backed away a fraction. Carefully shifting the croquet mallet from one hand to the other, she started to reach inside the trunk, so she could grab Benji's sweater and get the heck out of here.

His voice stopped her. "Where do you think you're going?"

"I'm getting my son's sweater," she said with the strained calm she reserved for maniacs. "And then I'm going to shut my trunk and get in my car." *And leave you in the dust.*

"Sorry," he said gruffly, "but I've got a few more questions."

This was, she decided, the strangest exchange she'd ever had in her life. "Excuse me?" she said shakily.

"I'm not through talking to you."

Pure fury coursed through her. She didn't care how rich and famous he was, no man talked to her that way. "Look, my kids and two elderly neighbors are waiting for me. So I suggest you start talking. You have two seconds." She glanced down at her wrist, only belatedly realizing she wasn't wearing a watch.

"You have kids?"

Was he afraid she was some woman he'd met on the road, had an affair with—and then made pregnant? The mere thought made her traitorous body feel a little woozy. Should she deny it outright, in order to dispel him of the insane notion?

She shook her head as if to clear it of confusion. "Look, I don't know where you think you know me from but—"

"Quit playing games. Are you...from upstate New York?"

Lord, probably the man *had* had an affair. Bobby had. Wasn't there one faithful man left in the universe? Her eyes skated toward Joe Ray Stardust's ring finger. But a simple gold band was firmly in place.

Unfortunately, Joe Ray grabbed her elbow again. And this time he pulled her right against his chest. "Last chance," he said. "Who are you?"

"No one!"

"Did one of the newspapers send you?"

With the force of a revelation, she realized that Joe Ray Stardust had a secret to hide. "If you don't let me go, I'm going to fight. And," she added with far more bravado than she felt, "when I fight, I fight dirty."

"I'll just bet you do."

"You may have ruined my life," she snapped, "but I am not—I repeat, am not—going to stand here freezing to death while you maul me! I don't owe you anything, least of all explanations for my feelings about you."

With that, her jaw set. As sinful as it was, she half hoped he drove himself crazy wondering who she was. Because she'd be long gone. She didn't intend to examine her motives regarding this encounter too closely, either. Call it pride, but she suddenly didn't want Joe Ray Stardust to know she'd been foolish enough to marry a two-timer. *Especially not when he might be one himself.*

During her speech, the man hadn't moved a muscle. He was still pinning her with his hypnotic gaze. Far off, inside the warm auditorium, her kids, Irma and Stella were waiting, no doubt wondering what had happened to her. But here, the powerful arms of this magic man had wrapped her in a near embrace. Against her will, she recalled how very, very long it had been since she'd been held by a man in the dark.

Their lips were mere inches apart; their cloudy breaths warmed the frigid air that circulated between them. She knew she couldn't entertain her feelings, not even for a moment. But who could have foretold that she'd feel so powerless to move away from this stranger...this man who'd touched—and ruined—her life from afar?

He's thinking about kissing me.

She felt it in her bones. Saw it in his eyes. Then his sensuous lips parted as if he hadn't kissed a woman in years.

Get out of here! Run for the car! Run for your life!

But it was too late.

His lips locked over hers, his hungry mouth claiming a kiss that was as ravenously greedy as it was self-assured. For a stunned minute, she couldn't move. Heartfelt longing arrowed through her like darts dipped in liquid desire, dousing her anger, replacing it with new heat that burned through her veins.

But she couldn't stand for this! She wasn't some loose woman a married man met on the road and kissed—or worse. Gripping her mallet, she grabbed a rough handful of Joe Ray's sweater. His kiss was heavenly, but she shoved him away with all her earthly might.

Then everything happened in a heartbeat.

They both slid. She fought to regain her balance on the ice, but her arm swung wild and the clublike end of the mallet walloped Joe Ray's forehead. At the contact, a dull crack sounded. Then with a great whoosh, his feet flew from beneath him, his arms snatched at the air and he thudded hard on the pavement.

Holly's first thought was that he'd gotten just exactly what he deserved.

Then all the blood drained from her face.

Because Joe Ray Stardust didn't get up. *This simply can't be happening!* She'd never felt so close to true hysteria in her whole life. Holly gulped and dropped the mallet into the trunk. During the melee, the red bow had come untied and her fingers—so accustomed to dressing the kids—itched to retie it, as if that might restore some sense of normalcy.

Staring down at Joe Ray's perfectly formed, if immobile body, she mustered all her mental energies and willed him to move.

He didn't. Had she merely hurt him? She gulped again. Or killed him? Suddenly coming out of shock, she sprang into action, flinging herself to the ice, kneeling beside him. As she grabbed his hands, he emitted a long groan.

"Oh, thank you," she whispered, her eyes raising heavenward. "C'mon," she crooned in a voice she usually used to coax the children. "Now, let's just get you up...."

But now he seemed twice her size. With a surge of adrenaline, Holly gripped his waist in a bear hug, then rose with superhuman force. Valiantly, she pulled him to his feet—but then realized she had no place to put him. Her eyes darted around frantically. Staggering on the ice, she felt sure her back would break beneath his weight. Just as her knees buckled, she managed to lunge toward the trunk.

Thankfully, he slumped safely inside. But any relief she felt was short-lived. Because Joe Ray Stardust looked as if he meant to settle in for a nice, long nap. He pulled his feet into the trunk, curling his long legs around her spare tire, then he nestled his cheek on Benji's sweater and wedged his shoulder against her lug wrench.

"Mr. Stardust?" she whispered.

He muttered something that sounded like, "Leave me the hell alone."

His words were slurred, but otherwise he sounded fine. Her eyes scanned the parking lot. Quickly tucking the plaid coverlet in the trunk around Joe Ray to keep him warm, she started sliding over the ice toward the stage door in the distance.

She'd barely gone two perilous paces before the door swung open wide. The roadie who appeared was wearing a Joe Ray Stardust jacket. Of navy, gold and white leather, it was just like the one Bobby used to own. From this distance, the man could have *been* Bobby.

Holly stopped uncertainly in her tracks, the truth of her situation sinking in. *I've assaulted a major television personality.* She inhaled sharply as Judge Selsa's courtroom swam before her eyes. If the Samuelses got wind of this, she might loose Benji and Treasure.

"You seen a guy out here?" the roadie yelled.

"No!" She shouted the word before she thought it through.

Inching back toward the trunk, she checked the ledge for fingers and toes. Then with a nervous jump, she slammed the trunk shut.

I can't believe I just did that.

"Well, thanks," the roadie yelled jovially.

Holly felt sure she was losing her mind. "You betcha!"

Moving on sheer hysteria, she circled her car and hopped inside. Her fingers shook so badly that she could barely start the engine. When it sputtered to life, she didn't exactly feel better.

Her quivering foot gently depressed the gas pedal. *I love my parents and I love my kids. I'd give a neighbor in need the shirt off my own back. I'm a good person.*

But would anybody believe her?

So far tonight, she'd kissed a world-famous married man, clubbed him over the head and she was now driving around on a solid sheet of ice with him locked in her trunk. "Don't panic," she whispered. "Just don't panic."

Chapter Two

"Where's my sweater, Mommy?" Benji asked.

In the trunk! The words danced in Holly's head like a nonsensical nursery rhyme. *In the trunk with the hunk!*

Her eyes shot wildly to the rearview mirror, piercing the car's interior, scrutinizing her passengers. Irma was in the front. Tiny, birdlike Stella was in the back, staring out the window through delicate eyeglasses perched on the tip of her nose. Bundled in the back seat with Stella, the kids' dark brown hair and eyes peeked from beneath identical knit hats. Holly's gaze caught Benji's and she winced at his black eye.

"Sorry, Benji, I—" Her thin, high-pitched voice was quavering, but she couldn't steady it. "I just forgot to get your sweater from the *trunk,* honey bunch!"

Had the way she'd said "trunk" called undue attention to the word? "Besides, your trunk—" One of Holly's hands shot from the steering wheel and clamped down hard over her mouth. "I mean er—*coat,*" she continued, "really should be warm enough." She quickly reached forward and cranked up the heat.

Benji groaned in consternation. "Why'd you forget?"

Because the sexiest married man alive is in our trunk, Benji, Holly thought hysterically. *Not only is he famous*

and a great kisser, but he's also using your little blue
sweater for a pillow. Now don't you want to be a nice boy
and share it with Mr. Joe Ray Stardust?

"Mommy, you're talking funny," Treasure commented
tartly.

Holly gasped. Her voice was a dead giveaway! And her
heart was racing. Her hand returned to the wheel, and her
trembling fingers froze around it. Should she pull over and
confess to Irma and Stella? As senior citizens, could they
offer a more mature perspective on her situation?

"Holly..." Irma grunted and turned her large girth toward Holly. She ran a hand through her short, iron-gray
hair, then stared at Holly through her bifocals. "Did you
just hear something?"

"No!" One of Holly's shaking hands shot from the
steering wheel to the radio. With lightning speed, she
flicked it on and turned up the volume. A holiday carol
filled the car.

"I could swear I heard something thump," Irma clari-
fied.

"Trunk?" Holly echoed in horror.

Irma squinted at her. *"Thump,"* she corrected. "And,
Holly, if you'd turn down that darn radio, you could hear
better."

"Mommy!" Treasure shouted in censure, covering her
ears with mittened hands as if to make Irma's point. "That
radio's loud!"

Holly barely heard her. Her mind was spinning. Had Joe
Ray awakened? Was he pounding on the trunk's interior?
But no, Irma must have heard something else.

She forced herself to turn down the radio—but only a
smidgen. Unfortunately, the melodious strains of the particular Christmas carol were soft and soothing—not nearly

loud enough—and they included the refrain, "Peace on earth, goodwill to men."

Goodwill to men, Holly thought with renewed panic. The only man she'd touched in a year she'd clubbed with a mallet. And now he was lying prone in her trunk—and she was kidnapping him.

Somehow she needed to tamp down her rising apprehension and get ahold of herself. *But he's so famous. Surely, people are searching for him! Oh, Holly, you're in trouble.* The image of a nameless, faceless state trooper, complete with a bloodhound, popped into her mind.

An oblivious Irma started pointing out sights on Kanawha Boulevard: the red and green lights that illuminated the columns of the state capitol, the decorations at the governor's mansion. When "Santa Claus is Coming to Town" started to play, Irma bellowed, "Now, c'mon everybody, sing along!"

The next thing Holly knew, the kids and Irma were crooning at the tops of their lungs—and such raw-boned terror seized her that she almost stopped the car. She felt so jumpy she was sure she'd involuntarily eject from her own seat. Everything was jumbling in her head, seeming surreal. In the parking lot with Joe Ray, she must have been in shock. Her senses had undergone total, numbing shutdown. She'd thought of her kids first and acted on pure instinct.

But now, every blessed detail of the crazy events crowded into her consciousness: the demanding pressure of the magician's mouth, the rough wool of his sweater grazing her cheek and the heavenly softness of his cashmere coat. She smelled his pine scent and saw herself slip...saw the hard wood of the mallet whack the man.

The mallet, she thought shakily. Oh Lord, she couldn't possibly give that croquet mallet to the kids for Christmas

now. How could this be happening? For a fleeting instant, she tried to convince herself that this was all just a
very bad dream. Then she embraced reality again.
Hunching over the wheel and punching up her high beams,
she forced herself to squint into the falling snow.

"You'd better not shout," the kids and Irma were singing now, "you'd better not pout."

And you'd better not wreck! Holly admonished.

She'd never even had a fender bender—her used car had
come with the dents—but if she was going to wreck, now
would definitely be the time. *Just like Jimmy Stewart in* It's
a Wonderful Life, *I'll probably wreck right into a tree.*

Oh, she could just see it—a kind state trooper helping
Irma, Stella and the kids from the car, then asking her for
the keys to her trunk. She'd turn and run, she decided,
head into the dark West Virginia woods, escaping the scene
of the crime just as the trooper found Joe Ray.

Yes, Holly's arms would wave crazily in the air and
she'd have that wild, insane look in her eyes, just as Jimmy
Stewart had when he'd run away from his beloved wife
Mary at the library because she didn't even recognize him.
The poor woman had completely forgotten who her hus-
band was and—

Stop it! With an abrupt movement, Holly switched on
the windshield wipers.

"Holly?"

Her head snapped toward Irma. The large seventyish
woman was staring at her oddly.

"Santa Claus is coming to town!" the kids shouted.

"Both of you sit back down in that seat and put on your
seat belts," Holly managed to say. The kids giggled but
promptly complied.

"Is our singing too loud, Mommy?" Benji asked with
a grin.

Holly thought of Joe Ray. "You sing as loud as you want, honey bunch."

Irma was still staring at her. "Are you okay, Holly?"

Why, sure, Irma, she imagined herself saying brightly. *I'm fine. I just wish we weren't driving around with a hunk in our trunk.*

"I'm right as rain," Holly said aloud.

Irma looked unconvinced. "Well, good. I was just saying that it was awful nice of you to bring me dinner all this past week when you took Stella hers...."

As Irma started gossiping about their neighbors at the Pine Cottage Estates, Holly's nerves calmed some. She even glanced in the back seat at Stella again. Even though Stella still worked for a dry cleaning establishment, she lacked Irma's robust energy. Especially since last Christmas, when she'd had a fight with her only son, Jonathan. The two hadn't spoken all year, and now the holiday was depressing Stella. After Thanksgiving, she'd refused to eat unless Holly and the kids took her a hot plate.

"Holly?" Irma said.

"Hmm?" Holly's guilty glance slid toward the rearview mirror—and the trunk.

Irma's eyes narrowed in concern. "I just said that for all you've done for Zeke and Mr. Berry, those two fools ought to knock some money off your rent."

Holly had enough on her mind without contemplating the manager and owner of the Pine Cottage Estates—or the unpaid rent.

"Mommy—"

Holly felt grateful for Benji's intrusion, until he continued.

"Daddy's comin' home for Chris'mis, right?"

Before Holly could respond, Treasure picked up the thread. "And he's gonna give Mr. Harden an' Mr. Berry lots of money."

"And get us a Chris'mis tree," Benji added. "An' if Santa don't bring my puppy, then daddy'll do it."

For an instant Holly forgot Joe Ray Stardust and wished her son had fallen in love with a mutt, instead of a pedigreed pup. The long-haired dachshund, whom Benji had already named Hot Dog, was in the window of Pretty Pets, near the day care center. For weeks, Holly had been begging Mr. Warring, the owner, to keep the puppy until she could pay for him.

Treasure giggled. "Daddy'll bring presents!"

Benji reached over the seat and tugged Irma's shoulder. "My daddy knows magic and looks like Joe Ray Stardust!"

Holly's whole world turned topsy-turvy again. How could she have forgotten that characteristic of Benji's imaginary father? The kids, of course, had short memories, had rarely seen Bobby, and only knew their father had worked for the magician they idolized. *The magician in your trunk!* Holly's pulse was off and running again.

Irma lowered her voice. "Holly, I know you're awfully independent and that you don't talk about whatever happened between you and their father, but... Well, maybe you shouldn't let the kids go on like that, as if their daddy's coming home for the holidays."

Before Holly could respond, Benji said, "My daddy's even better than Joe Ray Stardust 'cause—"

Thankfully, Treasure cut him off by bursting into "Have a Holly Jolly Christmas." Stella remained moodily silent, but Irma and Benji joined in the song. Holly turned a corner and her headlights swept over a bus kiosk and a large sign that said Pine Cottage Estates. The green script letters were faded, and only one unbroken floodlight illuminated them.

"C'mon," Holly whispered to the car, hoping her clutch didn't stick.

As she drove up the hill, the Pine Cottage Estates, which were anything but estates, popped into view. Scattered across a mountainside that was thick with untended pines, the tumbledown cottages were arranged around Mr. Berry's home, a white-painted, brick colonial with a wide porch and columns. Overshadowed by a towering blue spruce, the once stately house had long ago fallen into disrepair.

As Holly passed her own cottage and headed farther up the hill toward Stella and Irma's, she tried to calm her nerves enough to make a rational plan about how to—

Deal with the body.

She gulped hard. *I'll get Joe Ray out of the trunk, sneak him inside and then I...I'll beg, that's what I'll do.*

Somehow, she'd make him understand. Irma was right—she was independent, probably to a fault—but she'd tell Joe Ray everything. She'd mention Bobby, the loss of her job and the custody battle. She'd talk very respectfully. She wouldn't even chastise him for that adulterous kiss. And then she'd assure Mr. Stardust that she'd do anything—absolutely anything—if only he'd forget that any of this ever happened.

"Tell me no," Holly whispered.

Her ears had to be deceiving her. She'd come outside as soon as she settled the kids. Now, she tugged down her hat and with two quick jerks of her head checked to make sure no one had seen her. Or noticed that singing was emanating from deep inside her closed trunk.

She jogged from her porch to the car, her boots crunching on the packed snow, her keys jingling from a finger. In spite of the wet flakes tickling her lips, her mouth went bone dry when she reached the driveway.

Tilting her head, she strained to make out the song Joe Ray was singing, but the words remained muffled. His voice had turned edgy and there was something very strange about it that she couldn't quite put her finger on.

Wincing, she gingerly inserted the key into the trunk lock and turned it. Just as she did so, the singing stopped. Taking a deep breath, she swung the lid upward and stared down, her whole body tensing for fight or flight.

"Santa Claus is co-ming tooo town!" Joe Ray sang.

It was the last thing she expected.

In the darkness, she could barely make him out. Then she saw a glint of very white, even teeth and knew he was flashing her a smile.

"Uh—" When she leaned forward, jimmying a hand under his elbow, shivers raced up her arm that had zilch to do with the winter cold. Somehow, she found her voice. "Can I help you out of the—er—trunk?"

He merely grunted. "Sch-ried to get out. But I don't 'member this one."

This one? This one what? Sudden understanding seized her. He thought her trunk was a lock box of the sort from which he escaped during his shows. As her eyes adjusted to the dark, Holly decided he didn't look particularly perturbed about being trapped in the cramped space, either. She guessed he was used to it.

But why wasn't he furious? Was he toying with her, or truly not angry? Had she knocked the sense clear out of him? One thing was certain, he wasn't quite himself.

"Who...are you?" he said.

His voice sounded gravelly—less bass and more gruff. "Holly," she said cautiously, against her better judgment. "My name is Holly."

"You're a Holly berry?" His voice dropped, becoming barely audible. "Right damn time of the year for 'em."

Was he trying to flirt with her? She inhaled a breath so quick and sharp that it burned her lungs. What exactly was happening here? The guy didn't look ill, except for the nasty gash on his forehead. And he wasn't livid, even if he did curse more than she would have expected. Well, maybe he wouldn't call the police.

"Oh, thank you," she whispered at the realization.

"You're sh-sure welcome."

Any relief she'd felt faded. His accent was gone. That's what was wrong with his voice. The British cadences had disappeared as surely as coins from beneath his scarves. Not having a clue as to what to make of that, Holly edged closer.

Sighing, he grasped the ledge of the open trunk and with a quick grunt, pulled himself up, so he was sitting cross-legged.

She stared at him in stupefaction. His muscular body had actually seemed to collapse, to accommodate the compact space. "You really do seem fine," she whispered giddily, thinking she hadn't felt this light-headed since he'd kissed her. Joe Ray might not be in mint-perfect condition, but he was alive.

She pressed a hand to her heart. Deep down, she'd been convinced the damage would be far worse. A flood of apologies poured from between her lips. "I'm sorry it took me so long to come back out here. I had to walk Irma to her door. She broke her hip this year, you know...."

What was she saying? Joe Ray Stardust didn't know a thing about Irma. Nevertheless, feeling flooded with relief, Holly couldn't curb her words. "And Stella wanted me to bring her dinner. Then the kids put on their own pajamas and Benji got his wrong side out. Anyway, I knew if I didn't go ahead and put the casserole in the oven—"

Holly realized Joe Ray was squinting at her through watchful, guarded eyes. Her heart sank, and she bit her lower lip. *What have you done to this man, Holly?*

She glanced toward her cottage. Somehow, she had to get him inside and evaluate him. "Look," she forced herself to say, "are you all right?"

In response, he swung a leg over the trunk, then slowly lifted a finger to the gash on his forehead. The air he drew through his clenched teeth made a sizzling sound. He shrugged. "I doubt it. But I could...sch—" He winced. "Sure use some casserole."

"Here, maybe I could help you out of there," she suggested gently.

Looking none too happy about needing female assistance, he draped a long, sinuous arm across her shoulder. As harmless as the gesture was, the way his fingers curled around her upper arm gave her pause. He was so close— too close. Dangerous and forbidden. She almost wished she was a meaner person so she could flee, simply leaving him to fend for himself. He might be a tad disoriented, but he was still powerfully male—and married.

Just get him out of your trunk, Holly. That's step one. Sighing, she wedged herself hard against him for leverage, then slipped an arm beneath his cashmere coat and snaked it around his back. Her fingers wound up curving around his waist. In spite of her bulky gloves and his thick sweater, she could feel his flat, hard belly. Ridges of corrugated muscle made it feel like an old-fashioned wooden washboard.

"Thanks, sweetheart."

Something in his tone made her head jerk upward. Too late she realized his face wasn't but inches away. His eyes were truly as midnight blue as a deep, dark winter's night lit by a full moon. He winked at her.

Obviously, she'd done him serious harm tonight. But it couldn't touch the damage he was inflicting on her now. Oh, she knew very well he was a married man. Everyone in America knew it. But just looking at him was wreaking havoc with her usual good morals. She'd nearly forgotten she hated him, that he was involved in a chain of events that had all but ruined her life.

"God, you're gorgeous," he commented huskily.

She steeled herself against him, lacing her voice with venom. "I don't think you ought to say that."

"Why not?"

"I just don't." She tried to place his accent. He used various voices during his shows. Was this one she hadn't heard before? "C'mon." She mustered her most businesslike tone. "Get out of the trunk."

Once his feet were solidly on the ground, he leaned heavily against her. At first, she thought it was simply because he felt unbalanced, but then his head slowly angled downward. Snowflakes were catching in his hair again, dusting the dark strands. All at once, with a violent movement, Holly veered back. Her voice was nearly a growl. "Don't you dare kiss me!"

He merely shrugged. "Can't blame a guy for trying."

"Holly?"

When Irma's voice sounded from the enveloping darkness, Holly's heart hammered against her ribs. Her eyes cut toward the nearby pines, as if seeking escape. She was half tempted to push Joe Ray inside the trunk again. How could she explain his presence here?

"Holly?" Irma shouted, her voice nearing. "That's you out there, isn't it?"

Holly realized her eyes had riveted on Joe Ray's forehead. The gash left by the mallet had been bleeding and the surrounding skin was turning black and blue. What was she going to do?

"You'd better watch out for your hip, Irma," she yelled, hating the pleading urgency in her tone. "You'd better stay right where you are."

Lowering her voice, Holly said to Joe Ray, "Can you stay right here for a minute?"

"Sure."

But the second Holly let go, he staggered a pace. Her cheek wound up pressed hard against his broad chest, and when his muscular thigh wedged against hers, heat infused her limbs. She didn't know which was worse—his bothersome proximity or the fact that she was stuck here. Caught in the act. Finished.

"I'm bringing you and the kids fresh-baked cookies," Irma yelled.

"And I'm right behind Irma," Stella called out in a thin voice. "I'm bringing down your plate and bowl from last night."

Then Holly heard the engine. Her heart seemed to drop to her feet, and her head turned slowly toward the road. *Oh no, not Zeke, too.* But sure enough, Zeke Harden, the man who managed Mr. Berry's property, was chugging up the hill in his old red VW bug.

The world was closing in on her—and fast. As Irma's and Stella's silhouettes bobbed toward her, Zeke merrily laid on the fancy horn he'd bought for the holidays. It played the opening bars of "Auld Lang Syne."

Nearer, Joe Ray's body heat seeped through his clothes, warming Holly's side. When he rested his head on top of hers, an electric jolt shot straight down to her toes. Was it her imagination or were the man's lips grazing the top of her cap?

There's one saving grace, she thought. *It's pitch dark out here. Maybe I can pass Joe Ray off as a family friend.* She doubted it, though. After all, he was famous.

It was a real long shot. Or no shot at all, she thought glumly as the front door flew open and the kids bounded onto the porch. "Please get back in the house, kids," Holly called out.

"But we're gonna have a snowball fight!" Treasure shouted.

"No, you're—"

It was too late. Holly watched in resignation as the kids raced into the yard, coats and boots hiding their pajamas. At least when they started tossing snowballs at each other, it slowed their approach.

Holly drew in a deep calming breath—only to choke on it. Joe Ray's wallet was lying open on her spare tire. It didn't look as if there were any bills inside, but she could see a number of credit cards.

Just as Holly slammed the trunk shut, Zeke braked his car in the road, leaving the engine idling. As he cranked down his window, Holly watched Stella and Irma slow their steps. Then the two seniors stopped dead in their tracks and gawked.

Reflexively, Holly's anxious grip tightened on the first thing she could find, which happened to be Joe Ray. Misunderstanding, he snuggled closer. His pine scent mingled with the surrounding trees and wafted to her nostrils, making her want to swoon.

"Stella and I didn't mean to interrupt anything," Irma said in a startled voice.

The kids bounded nearer, kicking up snow. Then they, too, stopped. Even in the dark, Holly could see their startled dark brown eyes. As if sensing the severity of the situation, Treasure reached down and grabbed Benji's hand.

"Everybody—" Where should she start? Holly wondered. And how much of the truth should she tell? No doubt, they all wanted to know how Joe Ray Stardust had landed at the Pine Cottage Estates. "Everybody, this is—"

"Your husband?" Zeke called in pleased surprise. The wiry man's head popped out of his car window, and sprigs of his red ringlets blew in the wind. "Well, I'll be hogtied."

Irma shoved the cookie tin she was carrying under her arm, then put her hands on her hips. "Holly, why didn't you let us know those kids were telling the truth?" She shot Benji and Treasure a long, level look. "I'm sorry, but when you two said your daddy was coming home for Christmas, I really thought you were pulling my leg."

Benji and Treasure nodded numbly, their eyes still fixed on Joe Ray.

Holly felt faint. The kids obviously recognized him. But why didn't Stella and Irma? They'd been to his show this afternoon. Of course, Irma kept saying she needed new bifocals, and Stella was so depressed about the holidays that she didn't notice much.

But why didn't Joe Ray say something? There was a hint of wariness in his heavily lidded eyes, but otherwise his expression remained unreadable. After all she'd done to him, was the man trying to help her out of a jam? He merely watched as Zeke got out of the VW and slammed the door. When Zeke reached them, he casually shook Joe Ray's hand.

"Those kids have given us an earful about you," Zeke said. "Pleased to see you finally made it home."

"Good to meet you," Joe Ray returned with effort. "Ho-ho-Holly's told me so much about you."

Zeke's deep belly laugh caught on the night winds. "Sounds like you've had a few cups of Christmas cheer, buddy."

"I guess we can forgive him," said Stella who despised drinking. "Seeing as it's the holidays and all."

Heavens, Holly thought, feeling faint again. Not only did her neighbors think Joe Ray was her husband, but they also thought he was drunk. Even worse, she was still trapped in the man's embrace. When she caught Irma's delighted expression, she mustered a wan smile and glanced at Joe Ray. His expression hadn't changed. He seemed to be taking his cue from the people around him. But why?

Zeke clapped Joe Ray's shoulder. "Judging by that gash on your head, it looks like you took a tumble. Well, I'll let you sober up before I come around about the rent."

Joe Ray arched an eyebrow. "Rent?"

Zeke nodded and named the figure.

Hearing the sum, Joe Ray chuckled, and Holly's temper flared. That kind of money might mean nothing to him, but it was a lot to her—especially now that she'd lost her job.

"Mommy..." Treasure began uncertainly.

Holly's eyes zeroed in on her daughter. For the next minute they carried on a wordless conversation. Holly's gaze narrowed, warning Treasure not to speak. Treasure's eyes widened as if her mother had lost her mind.

"Well, thank you!" Zeke said jovially.

Holly turned to Joe Ray again just in time to catch the flash of a gold money clip and to see Zeke pocketing a wad of bills. "Oh no," Holly protested.

"We've got to pay the rent, Holly," Joe Ray said. Leaning heavily against her, he replaced his still-bulging money clip in his slacks pocket.

"Well, that makes you two good for the next six months," Zeke said, sounding impressed.

Six months.

The words reverberated in Holly's brain. Joe Ray Stardust had just paid six months worth of her rent! Somehow she had to put an end to this. "Well, I guess we'd all better get inside," she ventured.

Stella nodded in quick agreement, clutching her old-fashioned swing coat to herself, her teeth chattering. "I'm cold anyway!"

"Cole," Joe Ray repeated. "*I'm* Cole."

Holly's eyes shot to his sculpted face. Did he mean that his name was Cole? Of course Joe Ray Stardust wasn't his real name, she thought, feeling slow-witted. It was far too stagey to be genuine. But had he lost his memory or something?

Irma's eyes narrowed. "I thought his name was Bobby."

"Bobby Cole..." Holly found herself explaining, steadfastly avoiding the eyes of her children.

"Just Cole," Joe Ray said.

Shadows danced over the planes and angles of his face. His jaw was turning dark with a hint of stubble that made him look rakish and cavalier. *Cole.* Holly thought the name suited him. His hair and eyes, after all, were the blue-black of the coal that had long been mined from these West Virginia hills.

Cole. Yes, it would be easy enough to call him that.

Stella shivered. "Well, I think he looks just like that fellow we saw down in Charleston tonight."

Holly tensed. "Oh, I don't think—"

"Why, Stella, he sure does," Irma interjected.

"You must mean that magician," Zeke said. "Joe Ray Stardust. I watch him all the time on TV."

Joe Ray or Cole or whoever he was suddenly shook his head as if to clear it of confusion. "There was..." he began in a slow contemplative voice "...a show tonight."

"There sure was," Irma said. "We all went."

Fighting panic, Holly continued burning the name Cole into her mind. If she thought of him as Cole, she wouldn't slip and call him Joe Ray. But who was he? With a start, she realized she didn't need to know—she needed to get rid of him!

"Well, I'd better get the kids inside," she said.

"You need to attend to that bump on Cole's head, too," Irma added.

Within moments, the kids and Cole were inside and Holly had led Cole into her tiny upstairs bathroom. On the way, she couldn't help but notice how his eyes drank in the well-worn but clean interior of her cottage: the combination living room-dining room downstairs, the small eat-in kitchen.

He'd peered into the partitioned room the kids were sharing, too, his eyes drifting over Benji's large collection of bird's nests, pine cones and rocks. Treasure collected anything with hearts—pens, pencils, decorative boxes. Seeing that, a faint smile had curled Cole's lips.

Holly wasn't sure, but she thought he expected to recognize the place. Did he really think he was her husband? *Impossible.* "Have a seat." She mustered a brisk, nurse-like tone and pointed toward the closed lid of the toilet.

"First, I want to clean that gash." *Then I'll determine what's going on inside your noggin.*

While she riffled through the medicine cabinet, she could feel Cole's eyes studying her. And when she glanced at him, she had the sudden impression that her bathroom had shrunk. She drew in a deep breath as if sucking air from the room would actually make more space. Then she grabbed a packet of bandages and tape.

"Mommy," Benji and Treasure said from the hallway.

Holly glanced past Cole, toward the kids. They were clad in pajamas and socks, and their cheeks were still flushed from the outdoor air. Their dark brown eyes were wide, their lips pursed into small red dots. Treasure's long, wavy hair was a mess of tangles and Benji's was flattened from wearing his hat. They were still holding hands—and staring at her as if she'd changed into a stranger before their very eyes. She would lay down her life for them. But right about now, she could barely meet their gaze.

"Wait here for a sec." Holly inched around Cole and strode into the hallway. "I think the rubbing alcohol's downstairs."

The kids scampered after her, and just as she reached the kitchen cabinets, Benji grabbed a handful of her sweater hem and yanked.

"Mommy," he whispered, "that's Joe Ray Stardust!"

"I think that might be a stage name, honey," Holly managed to say, as if having such a person in their home was the most natural thing in the world. She grabbed the alcohol from a top shelf, then realized Treasure was eyeing her suspiciously.

"What's a stage name?" she asked.

"When people become famous stars," Holly explained, "they sometimes make up a name that's fancier than their real name. So it's probably better if you call him Cole."

"But what's he doin' here?" Treasure said.

At least Holly could answer that honestly. "Getting ready to leave, honey."

"But how'd he get here?" Benji asked.

Holly bit back a sigh. Why did her kids have to be at ages where everything was a question? "It's a long story, you guys."

Treasure stared at her. "Everybody thinks he's our daddy."

Holly smiled wanly, trying not to think of all those lectures about lying. "Well, he won't be here very long, so—"

"Can he eat dinner with us?" Benji asked.

"We'll see. Meantime, why don't you two go ahead and set him a place at the table?"

That made Treasure beam. She loved domestic tasks, though heaven only knew what the table would look like. Holly headed out of the room again, dropping a quick kiss onto each small head. In the bathroom, she squeezed past Cole's knees. "I'm back."

He nodded. "Felt like forever."

Without warning, his large palms settled on her waist. As she doused the gauze with alcohol, she assured herself that she needed to be this close to him to treat his head wound, and that the soft pressure of his knees was nothing more than a mild irritant. "This'll sting a little."

He shrugged.

When she dabbed his head, his fingers tightened slightly on her waist, sending an unwanted shock of awareness straight through her.

She quickly bandaged the gash, but she still felt worried. In the harsh light of the bathroom, his eyes looked cloudy and unfocused. No doubt, he'd suffered a concussion, if not worse. And he probably wasn't playing games. No, his thoughts were genuinely scrambled, either from the blow to the head or the impact when he'd fallen on the ice. The cut was still bleeding periodically, which probably meant he needed stitches.

A guilty lump formed in Holly's throat. "I better take you down the hill to Dr. Kester's...."

He tilted his head and surveyed her as if from a great distance. "We...had a fight."

He said it cautiously, as if unsure whether it was true. Holly stepped away and stored the antiseptic and gauze in the cabinet. "Well, I wouldn't worry myself about that."

"C'mon, Holly, why are you mad at me?"

Her mind raced. Whatever she'd done to him, it had affected his memory. And, as much as she didn't want to admit it, that was dangerous stuff. He didn't seem to remember her accidentally hitting him with the mallet and, while that meant she couldn't get into trouble, he could be in medical danger.

Cole winced. "Can't we just talk about it?"

Benji and Treasure's pounding footsteps saved Holly from responding. The kids skidded to a halt at the bathroom door.

Benji gasped. "Mr. Star—"

Treasure elbowed him. "Cole's coat is moving, Mommy."

Looking perplexed, Cole followed Holly downstairs, where she'd left the navy garment over the newel post. Trying not to notice that a grease stain shaped like her lug wrench now marred the shoulder of the cashmere coat, Holly grasped a soft lapel and whisked back the fabric. As she did so, she realized the silk lining was full of pockets.

Just as she found the wiggling hidey-hole, one of Cole's hands reached inside it. The next thing Holly knew, a little white bunny with a huge red bow around its neck was hopping across her living room toward Benji and Treasure.

"Merry Christmas, kids," Cole said.

"He's for us?" Benji dropped to the knees of his race-car print pajamas. "Can we call him Fuzzy?"

"We can keep 'im and everything, Mommy?" Treasure begged breathlessly.

The kids looked so happy that Holly's heart stretched almost to breaking and she nodded. Instantly Cole seated himself on the sofa and started showing the kids how to properly handle the rabbit.

Shooting him a surreptitious glance, Holly continued snooping through his pockets. She found playing cards, coins and a tightly packed plastic bouquet of mistletoe, poinsettias, and holly. She even found a collapsed top hat and what looked like a folded cape. *So much for believing in magic,* she thought dryly.

And then she found his plane ticket.

In place of a name, the first-class ticket merely said "Staff." The flight was leaving from the Chuck Yeager Airport in Charleston in just three hours.

Someone's watching over you. Now she could end this crazy fiasco in such a way that the Samuels would never get wind of it.

She'd quickly cordon off an area for the bunny. She'd feed everybody. Then she'd bundle up the kids again. It was getting late, but she simply couldn't put Cole on a plane without taking him to Dr. Kester. After that, she'd drop Cole at the bus stop at the bottom of the hill, or else take him to the airport.

The time frame was tight.

But she could make it.

Glancing at Cole again, emotion twisted inside her—a twinge of loss, a touch of regret. Wouldn't she ever have a good man in her life? He didn't really *look* like the cheating sort, and he seemed so at home with the kids. She should have guessed he would. After all, he performed for kids, and he had two of his own.

But it wasn't just that. It had been so long since she'd been this attracted to a man. Or so mystified. After all, with his various accents and names, Joe Ray Stardust—or Cole—just didn't add up.

Tonight, she could swear she'd seen startled, heartfelt recognition in his magical midnight eyes. Was it because he'd seen her last year—in a whole world away from here, when she'd hidden in the shadows in her red velvet gown, her heart crushed because Bobby Samuels had played her for a fool?

Maybe, she thought. And yet she was just as sure there was more to that look. Because tonight something had sparked between her and Cole, and it had culminated in a sinful, fleeting kiss. Right before his lips touched hers, she could swear his eyes said he'd found a soul mate. It was as if she were someone he'd lost long ago and suddenly found again.

Why shouldn't she think it? she wondered defensively, as her throat tightened. She was a lone woman. And it was only a harmless fantasy.

In reality, she well knew, the man had to go.

Chapter Three

"Bye-bye."

When Benji and Treasure crooned the words from the back seat, Cole's emotions suddenly felt as fragmented as his thoughts. He could swear his heart was breaking into a thousand tiny pieces.

Holly leaned through her open car window. "You just go on now, Cole." She shooed him away with such a dismissive backhanded wave that he could have been a pesky gnat.

"You're not even wearing your wedding ring," he muttered in disgust. He tried to center his hazy mind, but the only thing he could recall was their kiss tonight, how she'd arched toward him, clearly longing for him, even as she'd pushed him away. Self-righteously twisting the gold band on his own finger, Cole glanced over his shoulder, through a set of double doors hung with holiday wreaths. The airport was deserted. So were the roads. He glared at Holly again.

She merely stared back.

And Cole wished his wife didn't look so damn independent, as if she didn't want or need him. Because no matter how much physical pain he was in, he still knew she was all he'd ever want in a woman.

Beneath the arch of her eyebrows, her changeable brown eyes sparkled like stars winking under crescent moons. Her healthy scrubbed skin glowed in the darkness, suggesting honesty and decent living, and her long wavy chestnut hair smelled of clean winds in winter.

Her mouth was her most arresting feature—wide and full. He just wanted to see those shapely lips curl into a smile. Or to feel them pressed hard against his mouth again. He found himself imagining her breathlessness and the fragrant scent of her soap. Cole wasn't sure, but he figured his wife had always reminded him of the things he loved most, like hiking in crisp air through pine forests. Or fixing knotty mechanical problems until everything else in the world was utterly forgotten.

But she was sure one tricky woman. Which was why he was standing here in the blowing snow. Why had he let her fool him into getting out of the car? Sure, she'd fed him dinner tonight, the best tuna-noodle casserole he'd ever eaten. But immediately afterward, the woman had actually tried to ditch him at the bus stop near their home.

Not that he'd let her. Fortunately, his well-honed body was reacting faster than his mixed-up mind. And now, in one sudden, nimble move, he stepped from the curb, reached right through Holly's window and grasped her door handle. With the speed of greased lightning, his thigh wedged into the partially open driver's side door.

Reflexively, Holly tried to slam the door shut again.

Pain shot through Cole's knee to his toes. "Thanks," he growled. Wasn't it enough that his head was killing him?

"Please, Cole, just leave!" With a quick push, Holly shoved his aching knee. In a single gesture, she slammed her door, punched down the lock with a fisted hand, then quickly cranked up her window. She left a scant inch at the top.

"Go!" she repeated, her breath clouding the air.

A long string of expletives threatened to spew from between Cole's lips, but he glanced toward Benji and Treasure and somehow refrained. The kids had unfastened their seat belts and scooted over to gape at him through the side window. Noticing his son's black eye, Cole's temper rose. At dinner, he'd asked how Benji had gotten the shiner, but both Benji and Holly were evasive. It was as if Cole wasn't even a real part of the family anymore. He'd almost felt like a guest.

"Holly," Cole reminded in a vaguely murderous tone, "I'm your husband." The kids were within hearing distance, yet Cole couldn't help but add, "And as foggy as I feel, I'm beginning to get a real clear idea about why I haven't bothered coming home lately."

"Please," she begged through the tiny crack in the window. "Please, you don't understand...."

"I sure don't," he shot back. "That pill Doc Kester gave me when he stitched up my head is wearing off. And your response is to throw me out of the car, into the freezing cold while I'm fighting nausea and dizziness. Not to mention pain."

God, was she heartless. He'd slipped on a patch of ice in a parking lot—that much Cole remembered. Still, if he didn't know better, he'd think somebody had clubbed him over the head. Otherwise, *strange* was the only way to describe the sensations. Or stunned, maybe...blocked. It was as if some crazy dentist had numbed an important part of his brain with Novocaine.

But sometimes, Cole felt nearly lucid. His mind was like a thousand-piece picture puzzle. The whole landscape was there—houses and waterfalls and gardens—except for one little missing piece. Cole just wished there was someone he could turn to, someone who could find that puzzle piece, snap it into place and complete the picture.

That person obviously wasn't his wife. His eyes narrowed. Hadn't she pledged to love him in sickness and in health? And darn it, at the moment, he felt sick.

Sure, the kids had looked surprised to see him. From the way the neighbors talked, he realized he hadn't been around for a while. *Or never, damn it. I remember the snow, the hills, the smell of pines... but not the house. Did Holly rent it since I last came home?* "I have to know things, Holly," he found himself saying. "Don't you understand? I need you to help me remember."

"I can't," she whispered mournfully.

Cole sighed and glanced in the back seat. Lately, he must have been an awful husband and father. And he felt sure that apologizing didn't come naturally to him. "I'm sorry about all of this, kids," he forced himself to say.

Treasure shot him a pitiful expression, her eyes narrowing until she winced, her lips pursing as if she were in as much pain as he. The fact that the two heart-shaped barrettes in her long dark hair were lopsided only made her look even more adorable. Gripping her mother's headrest, she craned her neck forward. "Don't worry, Cole." She cooed his name as if it rhymed with *Noel.* "Me 'n Benji aren't too, *too* mad, Co-el. Cross my heart 'n everything."

The speech made him feel like a real heel. Just hearing his daughter's sweet, squeaky voice say his name made his chest feel tight. How long had she and Benji been calling him Cole instead of Daddy?

He frowned, wondering just how thoughtless he'd really been. Somehow, he had to get well. He had to remember. And then he could decide whether or not he wanted to redeem himself and start over with Holly.

"Your plane's leaving," Holly said insistently.

Cole realized he'd shut his eyes and opened them again. How long had he simply been standing here? *Cole, you've got to think. What happened? What were you and Holly fighting about in that parking lot? Were you ready to leave her and the kids for good? Was that why you have a plane ticket?*

Mustering his suddenly failing strength, he said, "I won't calmly back away, Holly. Not now, not ever. I'm not leaving you or our kids."

Holly's eyes slid guiltily from his. Staring straight through the windshield, she swallowed hard. "Your plane ticket is in your pocket. I wrote down the address for the studio at Rockefeller Center. That and the directions for how to deal with your head injury are safety-pinned to your lapel."

What studio? Glancing down in mortification, Cole felt too angry to ask. Sure enough, a piece of lined notebook paper was pinned to his coat. Funny, he didn't remember Holly putting it there. How could his own wife let him walk around like this? He looked like an idiot. Reaching up, he snatched off the paper. As it caught the brisk wind and blew away, he decided he'd about had it. "Dr. Kester said you're supposed to take care of me."

"Dr. Kester says it's better for you to try to remember on your own," she countered.

Was that why she wouldn't tell him what they were fighting about? "Dr. Kester said a lot of things—that my memory could come back in patches, or all at once." *He also said you might have traumatic amnesia, Cole, where you're using the head injury as a convenient excuse to mentally check out. Try to remember. Are you running away from Holly?* Cole sighed. "Just let me in the car."

"I—I can't."

She was weakening. He could see it in her eyes. As furious as he was, he had no choice but to soften his voice persuasively. "I promised you that I'd be home for Christmas." He couldn't remember, but he must have. Irma mentioned it. "And Holly...now I'm here."

Holly's jaw set with determination. "Quit torturing me!"

"*I'm* torturing *you?*" Raising his voice made his head ache all over again. "I might not remember our first kiss right now," he continued with forced calm, "but I definitely recognize this old routine. You're feeling guilty for throwing me out, but you expect me to make it easy for you."

She groaned. "That's not true!"

"You *told* Dr. Kester you'd be with me all night!"

With a sharp intake of breath, Holly rolled up the window the rest of the way. Cole could merely gape at her—and clutch the roof of her car as another wave of nausea passed over him. Trying to fight it, he staggered back a pace.

And then Holly stepped on the gas!

How could his wife abandon him? She was driving off, leaving him alone and injured on a deserted road! And with Christmas just days away! Already, the freezing cold was seeping into his bones. And he realized he had no gloves. The darn car might need some work, but at least it had been warm. He glanced toward the uninviting doors of the airport, then at the departing car.

"Holly, come back!" As he shouted the words, a hot searing bullet seemed to shoot through his head. So did the realization that whatever he'd done to his wife, it had been so bad that she wasn't likely to forgive him.

In spite of the pain, he stared at Holly's slowly receding taillights. She was inching along, with her foot barely pressing the gas pedal, and he was sure she was watching him in the rearview mirror. Lifting his arm, he whistled. He'd just follow her in a taxi.

A taxi? Frowning, he squinted down at the pavement and concentrated hard. For a second, the missing piece hovered over the puzzle of his mind. The gate to a shut-down channel of his brain opened and jumbled images crowded in, filling the landscape. Way in the distance, he saw a friendly little beer joint decorated for Christmas, with paper stars taped to a jukebox and a cardboard Santa attached to a cash register.

Nearer were noisy streets, teeming with bright yellow taxis of the sort he'd just tried to hail. There was a huge estate with a stone mansion that had pine wreaths on all the windows, too. And a tall, sophisticated woman whose blond hair was drawn into a French twist, but whose face remained a blur.

Cole's heart skipped a beat. Had he been two-timing Holly with that woman? With a start, he felt positive the blonde was supposed to meet his plane tonight. But he had a great-looking wife and kids. How could he do such a thing?

"Damn," he muttered. He'd almost had it.

And then it was gone.

Well, Dr. Kester had sworn it was only a matter of time until his memory returned. Cole would just have to wait it out. He stared at Holly's car again. Benji and Treasure were standing on the back seat—no doubt against their mother's wishes. They'd turned around to face him, their palms pressed against the back windshield, their faces so close that their breaths fogged the glass. As much as Cole didn't want to admit it, the kids were utter strangers to him. But somehow, it all *felt* right. As if he were *supposed* to have two kids.

Cole sighed. Even from this distance and in the dark, he could see Benji's mouth move. "Bye-bye," his son said.

Then poor little Treasure tried her best to smile.

Flowers. A Christmas bouquet would help. Cole forced himself to wave cheerfully at Treasure, then he snapped his fingers.

But nothing happened.

Sheer terror made his body freeze. Then it grabbed Cole's very soul and shook it hard. Had whatever happened tonight totally destroyed him? Losing his mind was one thing, but losing his magic was another. Where were the poinsettias and mistletoe and holly that were supposed to pop forth from beneath his sleeve? *Damn it, Holly, come back,* he thought illogically. *The magic's not working. And, sweetheart, if you leave me, it'll be gone forever.*

He snapped his fingers again.

Nothing.

Then all at once, red and green confetti began to fall. Mixing with the snow, the bits of festive paper stuck to Cole's coat, blew into his hair and were whisked away by the wind. It wasn't what was supposed to happen, yet he hoped it would make Treasure smile a real smile.

But Cole never knew.

Because the taillights suddenly dipped over the crest of a hill and vanished. And his wife and kids were swallowed up by darkness.

DETERMINED TO RESTORE some normalcy to her life, Holly took a mug of steaming cocoa to the living room once the kids were in bed. Following her time-honored nightly ritual, she seated herself on the comfortable two-seat settee she used in lieu of a larger couch, tugged on her

favorite pair of warm woolly socks, then curled her feet
snugly beneath herself, draping an afghan across her lap.

Then—and only then—did she draw a deep breath and
allow herself to exhale. As she did, she shut her eyes, feeling aches and pains she'd ignored for hours. She felt a
strange sense of communion, too, with every other unmarried mom who probably did this exact same thing each
night.

Then she remembered that she was the only one of them
who'd nearly killed Joe Ray Stardust. Or discovered the
probable fact that his real first name was Cole. *Or kissed
him.* Holly's eyes popped open.

Centuries could have passed since she'd sat in Judge
Selsa's courtroom. Or lost her job. Or felt the hard heat of
Cole's body pressed against hers.

Now the sensations rushed in on her again. She felt
Cole's relentless lips capture hers, flooding her with desire, overwhelming her with longing. That firm expressive
mouth had demanded—and gotten—her softest, most
pliant response. She'd felt so powerless and so helpless,
except to yield and arch against him in need. Only now,
long after the heat of that kiss in the cold of the night had
made her shiver in confusion, did she dare recall how one
of his long nimble fingers had traced the column of her
throat and how the darting flame of his tongue had ig-
nited her blood.

She'd never felt anything like it. Years ago, Bobby
Samuels had awakened her body, but tonight, the unexpected passion she'd found in Cole's hungry mouth had
promised there was more. Yes, with Cole's kiss, the door
to another world of love and desire had opened a tiny
crack.

It had happened so quickly, too, like a flawlessly exe-
cuted sleight of hand . . . and mouth and heart. As if with

one puff of smoke, or wave of a wand, it was done. In a flash, his magic lips threatened morals Holly had spent a lifetime preserving.

She'd almost given in and forgotten every last one of her deeply held convictions; she'd almost forgotten Cole's wife as he seemed to have forgotten her. Holly had simply wanted to follow his lead wherever their dangerous dance might take them. Cole had contributed to Bobby's demise and to her own comedown in the world. But whatever payback she'd once sought, tonight she'd only wanted to take it from the sweet vengeance of his lips.

Oh, she supposed there was no real danger in admitting that now. Cole was gone. And she was safe. Besides, what woman wouldn't be attracted to him? He was reliable, a dedicated family man who loved kids and gave to charities. Beyond that, he possessed an almost eerie magnetism to which crowds were drawn.

Well, she was glad she'd driven him to the airport, rather than letting him take the bus, which had been her first inclination. She'd been so anxious to send him on his way...and then, of course, she hadn't been. She raked her fingers through her long dark hair, massaging her scalp. "This has been one long day," she murmured shakily.

Glancing around her living room at the familiar objects, she tried to convince herself that this evening had all been a dream. *A nightmare, Holly,* she corrected. And yet, the man had left so many reminders of his brief presence in her life.

A pair of Bobby's old gloves were still folded on a stair step, for instance; she'd pulled them from a drawer, but had forgotten to give them to Cole. Cole's large footprints were still visible, too, trailing through the snow and to her front door. And when she'd tucked in the kids, they'd asked for countless reassurances that Cole would be fine.

With baby gates, she'd fashioned a makeshift pen for Fuzzy, and now she watched the bunny lope across his newspapers toward a pile of plastic grass left over from last Easter. Curling on top of the bright green grass, the bunny settled down to sleep.

Tomorrow, when she bought rabbit food at the pet store, she'd ask Mr. Warring again if he'd hold on to the dachshund for Benji. Any belief her son still had in the magic of Christmas would be destroyed if Santa didn't bring that puppy.

Outside, snow had started to fall. This time, it was real snow, not wet flakes or blowing flurries. It was the kind of steady snow that could fall all night long, blanketing the earth by morning. Tomorrow, for a sleepy minute, she'd probably gaze at the untouched snow and wonder if she was the only person left on earth. Tonight though, she thought only of Cole's footprints. Already, as the pine boughs began to bend beneath the weight of new snowfall, his once well-defined prints were fading. By tomorrow, her strange encounter with Cole would be truly nothing more than a dream.

She sighed, forcing her mind onto practical matters. She *had* to get a tree tomorrow and look for another job. With Christmas a mere week away, she had no choice but to ask her folks for a loan, too.

"The wallet," Holly said flatly.

How could she have forgotten to give Cole his wallet? It was still in her trunk!

She pressed her fingers to her temples. Well, she'd simply mail the wallet to the Joe Ray Stardust studio anonymously. No one needed to know where it came from.

But Cole's going to remember everything, Holly. She'd ignored that for hours, the same way she'd ignored her ex-husband's bad behavior for years. Yes, denial was something with which she had a fair acquaintance. And she didn't even dare contemplate that Cole currently thought he *was* her husband.

And how was she going to pay his medical bill? she worried. Not that seeing Dr. Kester had done much good. He'd used so many oversize words to explain Cole's condition that Holly had written them down, but then Cole had unceremoniously thrown the fool paper to the four winds.

Cole hadn't suffered permanent damage, though. That much she knew. His memory could—and would—return. It was only a question of when. She imagined Joe Ray Stardust—otherwise known as Cole—remembering everything and plotting his revenge. What was she going to do? Should she research the things about Cole that didn't add up? If he threatened to take legal action, should she try to blackmail him?

"Now, there's the spirit of Christmas in action, Holly," she whispered dryly.

And then she remembered Cole's eyes. Arresting and magical, those beautiful, dark blue eyes had held many things, maybe even danger. And yet they'd held a capacity for love and a wealth of kindness. No, she wouldn't have to stoop to blackmail. At least she hoped not. *When I send the wallet to New York, I'll include a nice explanatory note,* she decided.

"If he even gets there." She'd secretly watched him, making sure he'd entered the airport. No doubt, since he was so famous, someone would meet him in New York. But what if they didn't?

Feeling panicked, she stood.

Then she sat back down.

Oh Lord, should I drive to the airport again? If only a rule book existed for situations such as this. Emily Post may have played croquet, but Holly doubted Emily had ever clubbed a man with a mallet. *Please,* Holly prayed with sudden, heartfelt fervor. *Please make sure he gets home safely.*

Then her lips parted in astonishment.

As if in answer, she heard far-off singing so heavenly that the voices had to be of angels. Soft and melodious, the music undulated on the waves of the night winds. Chills rose on her arms.

Lifting her chin, Holly stared through the window. In the distance, lights flickered in the darkness. A candlelit procession was making its way up the hill—one long ribbon of white lights winding through the snow-dusted pines.

"Carolers," she whispered.

It was probably Reverend Starkey from the nearby church where she'd started taking Benji and Treasure. Many members of the congregation had volunteered to join the choir for this night of caroling, and donations were being collected for a children's hospital. Straining her ears, Holly made out the words to "Hark the Herald Angels Sing."

Yes, hearing those voices did seem like an answer to her prayer. Heaven knew she'd acted on instinct tonight, fearing that her altercation with Cole would be made public and that Judge Selsa would give her kids to the Samuels. Calm washed over her. As the carolers reached her door, a rustling sounded on the stairs.

Benji squinted against the living room lights. "That sounds pretty, Mommy."

"Can we come down there?" Treasure crooned. "Please?"

Holly smiled. "You sure can."

Once the kids were settled on the settee, wrapped in the afghan, Holly reached into her pocketbook. Her wallet was nearly empty, but she withdrew four quarters, then she opened the door. "C'mon in," she urged with a wave of her arm. "It's too cold to stand out there. Can I offer you some cocoa?"

Reverend Starkey, a large man with thick gray hair and friendly gray eyes, stamped his feet on the welcome mat. "Thanks for the offer, Holly," he said as he came inside, "but you're our last stop."

"Really, Holly," said a woman Holly recognized from coffee hour. "It's later than any of us realized. We're going to sing a last carol, then head home."

It was a tight fit, but the group of fifteen or so people, who were carrying candles and small donation boxes, squeezed into the living room.

Reverend Starkey glanced at the children. "What about 'Silent Night'?" he suggested.

Opening hymnals, the group began to sing and the room swelled with music that filled Holly's heart. As joined voices spiraled upward, stretching for ever higher notes, they lifted Holly's spirits. Come what may, she knew she had the strength to face it. And the knowledge she was never really alone. Someone up there was watching out for her—and for Cole.

She found herself softly singing, "Sleep in heavenly peace."

And with those words, she pressed the quarters into Benji's and Treasure's palms and gave the kids a soft pat. They kissed her, then went shyly toward the visitors and carefully dropped their coins into donation boxes. As the singing continued, they headed upstairs again. Soon, she would tuck them in a final time, but by then, they would be fast asleep.

"Thank you all for coming," Holly said moments later. "I'm sure we'll see you on Sunday."

"Good night, Holly."

"'Night." In spite of the cold, Holly stayed in the crack of the open door for a moment and waved.

The burden on her shoulders had lifted. Returning inside, she locked the door, then went upstairs knowing everything was fine. Cole had gotten on his plane. By now his flight was being met by someone who'd recognize him. That person would realize something was amiss and take Cole to another doctor. When Cole's memory returned, he'd understand and forgive her.

Yawning, Holly entered her room. She opened her tiny closet, gently tugged her sweater over her head, then casually looped both it and her bra over a hook on the back of the closet door. Just as she lifted her favorite flannel gown from a second hook, she heard a noise behind her and froze.

Shivers raced up her bare back, making each vertebrae tingle. She could swear someone—a very *male* someone— had cleared his throat. Was an intruder in her house? *Get ahold of yourself. Think of the kids and don't panic.* Clutching her nightgown to her exposed breasts, Holly pivoted.

"Oh no," she murmured in panic. "Not you."

But it was Cole.

He was lounging on the quilt and he'd clearly been on her bed long enough to get good and comfortable. Pillows were scrunched between the headboard and his broad shoulders and he'd stripped down to his white T-shirt, slacks and thick wool socks, leaving his coat and sweater draped over a nearby ladder-back chair. The rounded toes of his black boots peeked from beneath her bed.

"What are you doing here?" she asked in a near whisper.

Cole merely surveyed her from beneath swollen-looking eyelids, his emotions hard to read. His eyes held hints of challenge, but they were lazy and dreamy, too, as though he'd just awakened.

Holly guessed he'd removed his own bandage, probably giving in to that timeless male urge to pridefully parade nasty wounds and battle scars. But now the fool man's five neat stitches were exposed, and the area around his gash was turning a ghastly blue.

Strangely, relief flooded her. She'd imagined so many nightmare scenarios: Cole wandering away from the airport and freezing on the runway, or Cole deplaning at JFK only to be lost in New York's teeming crowds.

But he was safe.

And in my bed! Holly groaned aloud. Sure, she'd prayed for a sign that Cole had made it home safely, but not to *her* home. Yes, heaven very definitely worked in mysterious ways. Cole's eyes narrowed as if training his gaze on her required effort. Or was he getting a better look at her breasts? A rush of hysteria made Holly's throat close tight. Her cottage was tiny, but when her eyes darted toward the hallway and bathroom, both seemed miles away.

If she could only take time out to think—and dress. Mustering her coolest, most dignified tone, she managed to say, "Now, if you'll please excuse me."

But where was she going?

Clutching her gown to her breasts more tightly and squaring her shoulders, she stepped inside her closet as if that were the most natural thing in the world. Then she slammed the door. In the darkness, she madly wrestled her nightgown over her head.

As she unzipped her skirt and let it fall to the floor, she imagined flinging open the closet door and simply running away. Not that it would work. Cole—or Joe Ray Stardust, anyway—was billed as the man who could defy any lock, rope or chain. How could she escape him?

Lord, the man thought they were married, and she couldn't get rid of him! He kept coming back like a bad penny. Or like something more threatening. A boomerang.

Taking a deep breath, Holly pushed open the closet door. As rubbery as her legs felt, she somehow crossed the room and shut the door to the hallway, so the kids wouldn't awaken. Turning, she fixed her gaze on Cole as if his daunting masculinity didn't worry her in the least.

"How did you get in here?" she demanded.

He shot her a lazy smile. "Huffed and puffed and blew the house down?"

Feeling glad he was no longer slurring his words, Holly steeled herself against that deep bass voice, which still held no trace of a British accent. "Ah," she couldn't help but return, "so I guess you're supposed to be the big bad wolf."

"Sure." A faint smile flickered over his lips. "And now you know the answer to the question of who's been sleeping in your bed."

"Aren't you confusing the Three Little Pigs with Mama and Papa Bear?"

He arched an eyebrow. "Am I?"

She took a hard look at him, thinking that if he had kids Benji and Treasure's ages, he'd know that. But then, all his recollections were jumbled. *And you're letting the man's crazy banter sidetrack you, Holly.*

"How did you get in here?" she demanded.

Cole's wry, seductive chuckle floated to her ears. "Called a taxi, then came in with the carolers."

She should have known. "Look, Cole..." As she started toward the bed, her eyes inadvertently took in how his T-shirt clung to his biceps and stretched over his broad chest. Through the cotton, she could see hints of his nipples, strong pectorals and dark chest hair. Thinking the better of getting any closer, she stopped a few paces from the bed.

The movement brought another smile to his lips. His voice carried a soft taunt. "You were saying?"

Her mouth went as mealy as dry oatmeal, and her voice carried a faint pleading note. "Cole, you can't stay here. C'mon, please get out of my bed."

Cole's eyes turned steely. "I've got every right to be here."

The embarrassed heat that flooded her cheeks spread to her limbs. If Cole started demanding that she perform wifely duties, she'd be in dire straits. If only she could use this opportunity to probe him, to find out exactly what he remembered. But how could she explain the severity of the situation without admitting she'd accidentally assaulted him?

"No matter how much you deny it—" Cole's voice turned gruffly husky "—the way you kissed me tonight tells me you've missed having me in your bed."

"You couldn't be more wrong!" Holly's eyes anxiously panned the small room: the clean but worn beige carpet, the pictures of her kids on her bedside table, the neat arrangement of knickknacks on her dresser. *I may not be well-to-do,* she thought. *But I'm normal. How can this be happening to me?*

She groaned. "You didn't use your ticket! It wasn't refundable and I can't afford to buy you another one!"

Cole grinned like the Cheshire Cat. She watched in horror as he ran the flat of his palm over the quilt. Patting the bed, he indicated that she should sit next to him. His slow, winning smile, so obviously calculated to charm her, couldn't have been more annoying. And Holly didn't move a muscle.

"I've got plenty of money." He stretched an arm behind him, draping it along the low-slung headboard, as if to call her attention to the limber elegance of his body. "But somehow I don't think I'll be spending it on plane fare."

His tone struck a nerve. "Pretty sure of yourself, aren't you?"

"Absolutely."

"There's more to this than meets the eye," she assured.

"All I know about eyes," he retorted, "is that you're the apple of mine." His grin tempered to a bemused smile. "Besides, there's always more to a situation than meets the eye. Years of tinkering with magic taught me that."

"Tinkering?" she urged, feeling desperate to know what he recalled.

He merely nodded. "Since you're stuck with me, want to tell me what I'm missing in this particular situation?"

Yes. No. She was so confused she could scream. Even worse, when her eyes landed on his again, they stayed there as if transfixed. The gash on his head and stubble on his jaw only lent him a rakish air, adding to his already overbearing sensuality. Why did he have to turn up at Christmastime, when she was feeling so lonely?

"Maybe you just need a bouquet, Holly..." His voice had turned as soft as the snap of his fingers. As he waved his fingers in the air with a whimsical flourish, something popped into them. Unable to fight her curiosity, Holly crept forward a few more cautious paces.

"A hard-boiled egg?" she said.

"Shoot." He placed the egg on her bedside table. "It was supposed to be mistletoe."

Mistletoe was the last thing she needed around this man. Her knees buckled, and she reached out and groped the table for support. Whatever she'd done to Cole must have scrambled his magic, too. And he was a famous magician. Surely, he'd sue for loss of livelihood.

"Please—" She leaned forward, as if her physical proximity alone could move him from her bed. "Please, let's go downstairs."

"I'll get the trick right next time," Cole murmured, sounding tired. "Besides, there *is* something to be said for good intentions."

"Yeah." She ran her hands distractedly through her waving hair. "They say the road to hell is paved with them."

He sighed. "Look, I'm sorry for whatever I've done."

"You haven't done anything!" she burst out, her guilt becoming unbearable.

He glanced at her. Lightly touching the gash on his head, he didn't speak for a moment. Then his voice became a persuasive whisper. "So, then what's the problem between us, Holly?"

There were so many she wouldn't know where to begin. And maybe, the worst was that he was married. Surely his wife was looking for him by now. And there was no choice left but to tell him the truth. *You've got to help me remember, Holly.* That's what he'd said at the airport. Now she decided she would. She had to. Even if Dr. Kester had said he should remember on his own.

As she edged nearer, her eyes pleaded with his, already begging his forgiveness. Reaching out, he lightly pinched a sliver of her flannel gown between his thumb and fingers.

"Cole," she ventured, leaning over him, "I've got something to tell you, and you're not going to like it."

His quick smile didn't meet his eyes. "As long as it's not that you don't love me anymore."

The words caught her off guard. Lord knew, she didn't want to break a deluded man's heart—and yet she had to. "I've never loved you."

With gentleness that belied his strength, his hold on her tightened. His voice softened, but it was laced with threads of steel. "Mind repeating that?"

Gazing deeply into his eyes, Holly was sorely tempted to lie, to say they were really married, that she'd pledged her heart to him even if he couldn't remember it. She'd say she'd always loved him, fall onto the bed, and spend one blessed night in the man's arms. "I don't—" Feeling him so close, a shiver caught her unaware. "I don't love you."

With a start, she realized he was furious, but reining in his temper. Not that she blamed him. Tonight she'd tried to ditch him at both a bus kiosk and an airport. "Cole," she continued, her voice gaining resolve, "we're not married."

She waited to see the light of dawning comprehension. Instead, Cole glared at her. Feeling helpless, she stomped her foot. "We never were married. And you're not the father of my kids."

The man's face became a mask of sculpted granite. A faint tick was discernible in his cheek.

"I clobbered you over the head—" She rushed on, suddenly heedless of the consequences, feeling relieved to be rid of her guilt. "It was me who hurt you, Cole. It was an accident...."

"I don't remember that." His voice was deceptively even.

She heaved an exasperated sigh. "Of course you don't!" How could her pent-up confession free her from guilt if he refused to listen? "Please believe me, we're not married!"

Something—a glimmer of recognition perhaps—ghosted over his features. "You're saying Benji and Treasure aren't my kids?"

For a fleeting second Holly thought she saw pain in his eyes—a raw, bone deep hurt that had nothing to do with his physical injuries. "We're not a family," she assured softly.

Cole let go of her nightgown. Relief coursed through her until he caught her hand. With a quick yank, he pulled her onto the bed and on top of him. When she scrambled away, one of his corded arms wrapped around her back. The other circled her waist in a viselike grip, locking her inside his embrace. No matter how hard she tried, she couldn't catch her breath.

He was staring down at her. "What did you just say?"

"Benji and Treasure aren't your kids."

One of his strong hands released her, just long enough to brush a stray tendril of hair from her eyes. "You must be furious."

"I'm not making this up."

He merely shrugged.

She'd about had it. Without warning, she wrenched away, but she didn't get far. Somehow, in the quick melee, his hard-muscled thigh wedged between her legs, her hem rose on her calves and her face wound up pressed even harder against the enticing wall of his chest.

She was winded, but Cole barely seemed affected by the tussle. "Holly," he said calmly. "I've got a real problem here. The last thing I need is you playing mind games with me."

He sounded tired again. Dr. Kester had said he might fade in and out. "You have to believe me," she pleaded.

His eyes nearly closed. "No offense, but I'm bigger than you. If you tried to hit me, I would have stopped you."

He had a point. Not only was Cole bigger, he was quicker on his feet. On stage, he'd moved so swiftly that Holly barely saw him get from one place to another.

"Besides," he continued, "you're the gentlest person I've ever met."

Where was he getting his information? she wondered as his eyes suddenly drifted shut. Guiltily, she remembered the doctor saying Cole needed his sleep. Taking advantage of the situation, she edged away. She was almost free when his iron grip found her upper arm.

"Where are you going?" he whispered.

"I . . . thought I'd check on the kids."

"Don't go," he said simply, pulling her so close.

She couldn't escape his strong grasp, only try to fight the heavenly sensations caused by having his hard body so close to hers. Without their coats and sweaters, she could feel every irritating inch of him. How his thigh was wedged between her legs, how her breasts were crushed against his chest.

"Please, Cole . . ."

His voice lowered. "If anything tells me you're my wife, it's this."

"What?" she croaked.

"Aw, honey," he whispered. "You're on fire. Your skin's boiling hot. No matter how mad you are, there's no use denying you still want me."

It was true. She wanted him. But she couldn't have him. "You just don't understand—"

"I understand just fine. No matter what's gone wrong between us, we've still got a chemistry. As long as we have that, there's a chance."

"You can't do this."

"But I can."

Without warning, his lips covered hers for the second time that night. She evaded them, but not before their firm persuasive pressure begged her to forget who he really was and urged her to enter into this deluded world where he was her husband and the father of her children. With that quick kiss, Cole meant to conquer her. And to win his right to get back into her bed.

"You *can't* do this." She wrenched away, her racing mind seeking an avenue of escape. "And—and I'll tell you why."

Leaning back, Cole gazed at her. "Why?"

The only way to win this game was to play on his terms. Before she entirely thought it through, she said, "You've made your bed and now you've got to lie in it."

That caught his attention.

"You—" Her ex-husband's face swam before her eyes and a dam broke. Things she'd wanted to say for a year tumbled forth. "You don't even have a job."

Cole's grip relaxed. "I don't?"

"You keep refusing to look for one, too." Having tapped into her problems with Bobby, the words wouldn't come fast enough. "You never come home, then you call from wild parties in the middle of the night and wake up the kids. I'm sick of hearing all your pie-in-the-sky dreams about show business. And..." She could barely say it. "And I know you had an affair!"

Cole looked so guilty that she wondered if he really was having an affair. But he released her. That was the important thing. Her temperature was still hovering high above normal. The tips of her breasts ached from wanting to feel his touch. But she had to forget all that, and to concentrate on keeping him away from her while she figured out what to do next.

Cole sighed. "You... know I had an affair?"

Somehow, she doubted he had, especially since the mere idea of it seemed so distasteful to him. Nevertheless, realizing she had the upper hand, she waved her finger in his face. "Indeed I do. And if you think I'll so much as kiss you now, you've got another think coming."

Cole looked as if the pain of his head injury had caught up with him again. Holly told herself to not feel sorry for him. But of course she did.

"I'm sorry, Holly. I swear, I'll make it up to you."

As guilty as she felt about her lies, she was relieved. The man wouldn't kiss her again. His eyes drifted shut. When his jaw flinched, she instinctively reached forward and finger-combed the silken strands of his hair. "You okay, Cole?" she asked with worry.

"Sweetheart, I'm just so sorry about how I've treated you. I don't know which hurts more right now, my head or my heart."

Holly's own heart squeezed tight. In her lifetime, the only man she'd found had been Bobby. Bobby... who didn't even have a heart, much less talk about how it felt.

Would the stars ever shine on her, and bring her a guy like Cole... or Joe Ray Stardust?

Chapter Four

"Hmm..." A man trained his gaze through binoculars a final time, trying to glimpse Holly and the stranger between flakes of falling snow. "Well, Stella and Irma are wrong about that being Holly's ex-husband." He'd known that much the second he'd laid eyes on the mysterious visitor.

As Holly's bedroom light was extinguished, he replaced the binoculars on the windowsill and gazed at the blanket of snow that lay between Holly's house and his. Pure and untouched, the snow shimmered under the moonlight, making him think of a clean slate...and a clear conscience.

Which he sorely lacked, he thought. At least since he'd agreed to spy on Holly and help Jessica Samuels get custody of her grandchildren.

Are you really going to steal Holly Hawkes's Christmas? he wondered, lifting his eyes guiltily from the pristine snow to Holly's darkened cottage. Could he go through with it?

It would be easier if Holly wasn't so nice. But she'd been taking Stella dinner every night. And when Irma broke her hip, Holly had done all Irma's errands. Just today Joyce and Mac Ryan, the newlyweds in number four, were saying how wonderful she was. Linda in number eleven swore that Holly's special chili recipe had single-handedly gotten Linda engaged to her marriage-shy trucker boyfriend, Jumbo Stirling. Apparently, Jumbo was on his second helping when he proposed, saying he *had* to marry a lady who cooked like Linda.

Yes, Holly was the salt of the earth. A little down on her luck, maybe. But only because Bobby Samuels had taken her for a ride.

Bobby Samuels.

He remembered how the girls had chased the wild, rich, overly indulged boy like bees after pollen. In high school, Bobby had flaunted dark-haired, dark-eyed good looks and lured all the girls with pipe dreams about wanting to break into the entertainment business. Holly had fallen hard—and deserved better.

Well, she's not going to get it now. He hadn't watched all the goings-on at her cottage tonight, of course. As soon as he'd seen the two lovebirds fall into bed through a slit in the curtain, he'd set aside his binoculars and taken the opportunity to make a few phone calls. Between Stella and Irma, he'd pieced together a detailed account of this evening's events, right down to which Christmas carols the kids had sung in the car.

But why hadn't he seen the stranger arrive the first time this evening? And why was Holly claiming he was her husband? The fellow didn't have a car, and the buses were few and far between after five o'clock. Once, Holly and the kids had driven away with the man then returned alone. Later, a taxi had puttered up the hill. The mystery man had come back and followed a candlelit caroling procession inside Holly's house. It was all very curious.

Well, even though he was spying on Holly, he couldn't help but hope that the man would brighten her holiday. *Before you destroy it.*

His eyes narrowed. Most folks at the Pine Cottage Estates were single, so they didn't do much for Christmas. But why hadn't Holly put up decorations? Maybe she couldn't afford them, he thought with a sinking heart.

Not that he could help her. Heaven knew, he was even broker than Holly. That's why he'd agreed to spy on her and to report his findings to Jessica, who was willing to pay for any information that might help her and Robert Senior win the case against Holly next week.

On Christmas Eve.

The thought of Holly losing custody of her kids on Christmas Eve was just too much to bear. Oh, that witch Jessica Samuels had him caught between a rock and hard place. There was no way out. And in this sad Christmas pageant, Holly and the kids were just going to have to play sacrificial lambs.

He sighed. He'd hoped, even prayed, that he'd find nothing untoward in Holly's behavior. But after tonight, he had an earful to tell.

Jessica Samuels was going to be very interested in the stranger at the Pine Cottage Estates, the man who was taking liberties with Holly and apparently sharing her bedroom. It wasn't Holly's husband, as she was claiming...or her ex-husband, Bobby.

But who was he?

JOE RAY STARDUST.

A fuming Glennis Gaynes stared at the name emblazoned across the coffee mug in her hand. Damn Joe Ray, she thought with passion. He'd sworn they could talk last night, but he hadn't even bothered to get on his plane.

"How insulting," she muttered. "As if I had nothing better to do than to hang around Kennedy Airport waiting for a man."

Well, did you, Glennis?

Ignoring that chiding inner voice, Glennis quickly spun on her heel. As she charged down a hallway, the hem of her tailored emerald green suit skirt swished against her silk stockings while her coffee sloshed dangerously close to the lip of her mug. She had no idea when her feelings toward Joe Ray changed. Maybe it was on her recent thirty-fifth birthday when she'd decided there must be more to life than her career. Or maybe when she'd redecorated that darn empty Connecticut mansion for Christmas again this season.

Whatever the case, she'd become obsessed with the man, and her emotions were out of control. She pushed through a set of swinging double doors so forcefully that they continued flapping in her wake. Just being in the busy taping studio made her feel better. As the producer and director of this show, she was in control of everything. Except, of course, for Joe Ray himself.

Glennis headed down the steep steps, her high heels clicking past rows of seats used by Joe Ray's live audiences. Her resident troubleshooter, Derek, was marking the positions of the cameras. Overhead, technicians were double checking equipment—stage lights and sound speakers, feedback monitors and the flashing sign that reminded audiences to applaud.

In the orchestra pit, the music director and pianist, Larry, was having the Joe Ray Stardust band tune up for rehearsal. Glennis ignored a trumpeter's hackneyed rendition of "Jingle Bells," and glared at the stage, her critical green eyes roving over every detail.

The backdrop was the Manhattan skyline. Bright gold stars shot over the tops of the painted buildings and left trails of glitter in their wake that spelled out Joe Ray Stardust. Potted poinsettias were positioned on either side of a brick chimney from which Joe Ray would make Santa appear, and plastic wreaths that the bunnies would hop through littered the stage. Glennis's set designer, Charmaine, was seated precariously on the highest rung of a ladder, hanging a large gold star at the top of a freshly cut pine tree.

Glennis stopped on the bottom step and very slowly turned toward the only occupied theater seat, vaguely wondering if steam was coming out of her ears. What was Fred James doing here again? "Fred," she said.

"Glennis," he returned just as simply.

She shot him a purse-lipped stare. Years ago, she'd attended media courses at New York University with Fred who was now a talking head for one of the tabloid TV shows. "Why aren't you down the hall in studio four?"

Fred smiled. "Because *you* happen to be in studio two, Glennis."

"Where I have a show to run," she returned coolly. Lifting her chin, she stared at the band. "Larry, can you *please* do something about these tired orchestrations!"

The band director raised his eyebrows. "Excuse me?"

"'Rudolph'?" Glennis nearly shrieked. "'Deck the Halls'? I mean, aren't there any *new* Christmas carols?"

"No." Larry gawked at her. "Glennis, these songs are traditional. That's why they're called Christmas carols and—"

Glennis cut Larry off. "Charmaine?"

The set decorator nervously fiddled with her hair weave and glanced warily at Glennis from the top of the ladder. "Yeah?"

"Keep Joe Ray's rabbits away from those damn poinsettias. Those plants are poisonous, you know. And I want to see Hanukkah and Kwanza represented on that stage." Glennis's voice rose. "Why, this is the most un-politically correct holiday set I've seen in my ten years with this program!"

Charmaine sent Larry and Derek an uneasy glance. "But, Glennis, you're the one who decided we'd call this a *Christmas* show...."

If Joe Ray didn't turn up before tonight's live taping, Glennis thought dryly, there wasn't going to be a show at all, Christmas or otherwise.

"Hey, Ms. Scrooge," Fred said softly as he came up next to her. "Where's your holiday spirit?"

"On some other planet," Glennis promptly growled. "Now, has anyone seen Joe Ray?" It was the question she'd been dying to ask all morning.

Unfortunately, everyone shook their heads.

"He wasn't on his plane last night." Glennis threw up her coffee-free hand. "Derek, you're my troubleshooter, so find him."

"Maybe he's with his wife," Fred remarked pointedly.

From the orchestra pit, Larry played a few bars of the wedding march.

Charmaine had the nerve to chuckle. "Or have you forgotten the man's married, Glennis?"

"My memory's quite intact, Charmaine." But how could all these people believe Joe Ray was married? Glennis wondered in disgust. *Because you've spent ten long years making sure everyone in America believes it.*

"Oh, I forgot." The trumpeter who'd been playing "Jingle Bells" leaned toward Larry's microphone. "Earlier, some lady left a message saying Joe Ray came down with a cold and couldn't make it today. I guess the caller was his wife...."

Glennis's manicured fingers lifted to her cheek reflexively, as if she'd just been slapped. Musicians—why did they have to be so scatterbrained? This was impossible. Of course Joe Ray had to make it to work today. "A woman who said she was his *wife* called?"

The man frowned. "Just some woman...she had a real sweet voice."

Glennis could have done without that last detail. Joe Ray was hers. She'd discovered him all those years ago. She'd been the first to recognize his powerful star quality, the first to be drawn to his overwhelming magical magnetism.

"Well, I have good reason to believe that Joe Ray isn't with his wife," Glennis snapped. "Now, what exactly did you say to this woman?"

The trumpeter winced. "I...guess I got things all wrong. I told her I thought he was off all this week, anyway. I thought the live taping was next week, after Christmas."

Some days, Glennis truly hated artistic types. "Why would we tape a Christmas show *after* Christmas?" she snarled. "The show is *tonight*. And in order to tape the show, we need the star. So, Derek, could you *please* check this morning's inbound flights from Charleston? If Joe Ray didn't take a plane, check trains, buses and car rentals. I want to know the exact mode of transportation by which he left that Civic Center last night." *And the exact person with whom he left.*

Derek sighed and reached for his cell phone. "We'll find him, Glennis."

Her voice rose to a fever pitch. "Need I remind you that millions of viewers will be watching this show, people? Have you forgotten?"

"I could go through my Rolodex," Fred offered. "I do have a few contacts, you know."

Slowly, Glennis turned. Like many men in the visual entertainment industry, Fred possessed skin-deep good looks—in this case, gorgeous slate eyes, golden blond hair and a winning smile. But Fred couldn't be more dangerous. He had a crush on her—and the best contacts in the business. For him, discovering Joe Ray Stardust's dual identity would be the story of the decade. And if such a story broke during the holidays, it would get the ultimate in media play.

"The last thing I need is your help, Fred," she said succinctly.

Fred shrugged. "Too bad. I always enjoy a good challenge, Glennis."

"So do I, Fred." Their eyes met and held. "So do I."

Fred might be thinking of her as the challenge, but Glennis was thinking of Joe Ray's friend. Not that Glennis was worried. She'd long vanquished competitors who stood between her and what she wanted. And right now, what she wanted was Joe Ray. She'd have him, too.

But she had to find him first.

SNUGGLING UNDER THE WARM quilt and pressing his cheek against the cold pillow case, Cole let his dreaming mind drift. He was dressed in a fine wool suit and seated behind a black lacquer desk; one hand was on the phone, the other riffled through pink slips. Which call should he return first, the movie star's or the agent for the rock band?

"Larry," a woman shouted, "would you *please* play me the opening score for Thursday night's show?"

As if by magic, Cole's desk vanished and he was inside a theater. Onstage, a woman in a suit was turned away from him, one hand smoothing her blonde French twist, the other gesturing toward the glittering Manhattan sky-line that formed the backdrop for the stage. Was he having an affair with her? *She's not a dream person, Cole. She's real. You've got to remember her.*

Cole concentrated hard as the woman turned around. He'd expected warmth and radiance, but this woman turned out to be the proverbial ice princess—pretty but cold. "I want Larry to open with a loud, crashing score," she called with a wave. "What do you think, Joe Ray?"

Joe Ray... That's me.

But what was her name? Gloria...Gladys. No, it was Glennis. Cole was sure of it.

He opened his eyes—only to wince in pain. Last night, his whole head had hurt, but this morning, a dull, localized ache had settled in the area of his forehead.

Not that he cared. His arm was gently curled around a woman's waist. Squinting downward, his eyes roved over the top of the head that was neatly tucked into the crook of his shoulder. Long, wavy, sexily disheveled chestnut hair cascaded over his biceps and the rumpled quilt barely covered her. Even though he was still dressed, she wore a blue plaid flannel gown that had twisted around her body, the hem rising on her shapely calves. One of her hands rested on his chest and her relaxed fingers splayed on his T-shirt.

Holly, he realized. *My wife.* For a moment, he lay very still. The mattress was even with the windowsill, and he gazed through a tiny crack in the curtains, feeling Holly's steady breaths warm the skin of his chest. Then he rested his chin on her head, so her hair teased his stubbly jaw-line. As he brushed his lips slowly over the silken strands, he inhaled the sweet, clean scent of apple shampoo.

Was he in Weller's Falls...or in New York City? *No, you're in Belle, West Virginia. It's right outside Charleston.*

But what had he been dreaming? Moments ago, it had been so vivid...more like reality than a dream. Cole shut his eyes again, his mind stretching for the images, but they stayed just beyond his reach. His lost memories were right behind a door that was now creaking open on protesting hinges—

Suddenly, it slammed shut again. Cole opened his eyes, not really caring if he remembered the secret past that had been behind that door. There was only one place on earth he wanted to be today—in the here and now. Living in the present with this heavenly woman in his arms. Well, he thought, who really understood the mysterious magic of the mind?

"Holly?"

"Hmm?"

Her throaty, sleepy hum seemed to reverberate deep inside his own chest. She wasn't awake yet. Had she left the bed earlier? He thought she might have made a phone call, but he wasn't sure. *Who cares? She's here now.* She felt so wonderful that it could have been years since he'd held a sleeping woman. He only wished he could remember their past together.

As she cuddled closer, her body's soft curves molded to his leaner, firmer frame, making him undeniably aware of how her full breasts pressed against his chest and how her belly dipped against his waist. Her legs twined around the long lengths of his for warmth, her toes occasionally wiggling, sweetly burrowing in the folds of his slacks, under his calves.

No woman had ever filled him with need the way she was now. The thick, fiery, molten lead of his desire for her poured ever so slowly through his veins...until it quickened, livening and dancing in his blood. As her heat suffused his limbs and the flamelike tongues of longing licked into the far corners of his body, he grew hard with wanting her, and yet so heavy with sleep and desire that he merely reveled in the sensations and didn't bother to move.

Soon, he *would* love her...lift her soft gown, shift and settle her weight on top of him, wrap her legs ever so tightly around him, and moan as he buried himself deep inside this sweet woman. Now, he imagined searing hot skin gliding silkily over still more skin—and how he'd hold Holly so close that she wouldn't know where she ended and he began.

Ah, this was all so perfect. Uncomplicated and simple. If he never remembered a thing beyond this blessed moment, Cole decided he couldn't give a damn less.

He glanced over the top of Holly's head at the window. Careful not to disturb her, he gingerly lifted a finger and tugged at the curtain until he could really see outside.

Just looking at the winter wonderland stole away Cole's breath. What could be more beautiful than that fresh blanket of virgin snow—except Holly? Overnight, a whole new world had appeared. Not a soul had ventured across the landscape, leaving the ground as blankly empty as the mental space where Cole's memories used to be. Yes, the freshly fallen snow made the ground look like a clean slate. And Cole had the strangest, eeriest feeling that he'd been given one last chance.

You'd better not blow it.

Far off, a Texaco sign rose above the slanted snowy rooftops. Guessing it was a garage, Cole decided he'd look for a job there this morning. He had no idea what he'd been doing. He had some cash in his pocket and somehow he kept thinking he had a hefty bank account somewhere, but Holly said he was unemployed. Well, he may have sold Rayburn and Son, but he still knew how to work on cars. He'd hike up the mountain and cut down a Christmas tree, too. Then he'd find out why no one at the Pine Cottage Estates had put up holiday decorations.

Maybe fixing up the house would make Holly happy. She was mad at him. And he couldn't stand it. Especially not if she continued to mold herself around his body as if he were the gift and she was the wrapper. His mind might be missing a puzzle piece, but his body knew she was a perfect fit.

Yeah, even if he couldn't remember it, they'd shared a past, all right. And he'd been a fool to treat her badly. Lazily, his eyes took in her luscious, sleep-tousled hair while his long, nimble fingers threaded through the strands.

Feeling suddenly unsettled, his eyes darted from Holly to the window, scanning the gray snowy sky and the other houses. With the force of sudden awareness, he could swear someone was watching him, but it was Thursday and a workday and not a soul was in sight.

Thursday.

That niggled at his mind, too. Somehow, he was sure Thursday was a particularly important day of the week for him. Thoughtfully, he tugged the curtain fully shut. His movement roused Holly, and she hummed sleepily, snuggling against him again.

Ever so gently, Cole turned toward her, his mouth seeking a kiss, nuzzling apart her lips. He trailed his splayed hands from her shoulders, down over her flannel-covered back, until his palms cupped the soft cushion of her behind. Gently, with a moan of longing, his palms squeezed her flesh, drawing her hard against him, then he pulled her fully on top. Against his chest, he felt the tips of her breasts constrict as her arms circled his neck.

"Wake up, sweetheart," he whispered.

Just inches away, her lovely brown eyes opened in sleepy slits, then widened in surprise. Instantly she scooted off him, burning him everywhere she touched, leaving him in agony.

But he let her go. As much as he hated her rejection, he was hardly going to beg. As she edged away, taking the quilt with her, his hand slid over her a final time in an intimate caress he was sure she'd remember long after the actual touch was gone.

As she sat up, pulling the quilt around her shoulders, hot color rose in her pale cheeks, making Cole think of old damask fabrics and roses in the snow. God, she looked gorgeous. And he'd wager she was every bit as aroused as he was.

She blew out a confused sigh. "I must have fallen asleep."

Raspy and sensuous, her voice alone made him want to demand that she lie down again and make love with him. Hell, maybe he *would* beg if he thought it would work. It wouldn't, so he forced himself to smile. "You can sleep on top of me anytime."

"I was supposed to go down to the settee." Her voice carried a note of censure.

"It's too small to sleep on. Besides, who said you were supposed to do that? It definitely wasn't me."

"My sense of good morals," she returned.

So, she hadn't forgiven him his transgressions. *But she will.* Lithely, Cole rose from the bed. As he crossed to the closet, he felt her eyes roving over his back, betraying her desire. Opening the closet door, he looked through the clothes.

He hadn't left much. But when he saw the fine fabrics of his few sports coats, shirts and ties, he tensed. Still feeling Holly's eyes roving over his back, he slowly turned his collars and read the labels. These clothes were more expensive than he'd imagined they could afford. While somehow it did seem as if he owned fine garments, the few ties looped over a wire hanger were of such tightly woven silk that the sale of one could feed his family for a week.

He vaguely remembered paying the rent last night, so he must have worked sometime. Holly's few fancier dresses possessed designer labels, too. Thoughtfully, his hand trailed over a red velvet gown and cape encased in plastic. It seemed special.

So did the navy leather jacket behind it—one with white sleeves and a gold collar and cuffs. As he touched it, images from his dreams shot through his mind—a stage and a fancy office with large windows. Then he felt vaguely angry with himself. After all, Holly said she was tired of him entertaining pie-in-the-sky dreams about show business. Just as he pulled the jacket from the closet, to check the back for a logo, Holly cleared her throat, distracting him.

"There are jeans and shirts in that bottom drawer," she said.

Cole looked over his shoulder.

She pointed. With a final glance at the jacket, Cole replaced it, noticing it smelled musty, as if he hadn't worn it for years. In the bottom drawer, he discovered an electric razor kit that appeared unused. His jeans had been folded for so long they remained creased even after he shook them out.

As he stacked an outfit on top of the dresser, he started to ask Holly exactly how long it had been since he'd come home, but her rejection was making him feel edgy. He didn't particularly want her help right now. He'd rather pretend everything was normal, at least until he remembered more.

Besides, what did he need to know? Last night Irma said he'd promised to come home for the holidays. Holly had given him an earful, ending with the fact that he'd had an affair.

"Cole?"

He sighed. His body ached for Holly, but he was going to have to take it slow. He glanced over his shoulder again. "Hmm?"

Holly squinted inquisitively. "You okay?"

He flashed her a quick smile. "Sure, why?"

"Well . . . you were just standing there."

His jaw set. The fact that his brain was seriously scrambled was starting to bother him. Not that he'd admit it. He pulled off his T-shirt and stripped down to his briefs. Holding his dirty clothes in a fist, he turned around.

"Where do these go, sweetheart?" With a start, he realized she looked positively stricken. Her eyes looked everywhere but at him, and she repeatedly cleared her throat as if something had lodged there.

"Fold the pants because they'll need dry cleaning," she said in a strangled voice. "And I guess you can put your shirt in the bathroom hamper."

He raised an eyebrow. "You guess?"

She nodded. "I think there's a robe in the drawer . . ."

Cole didn't know whether to be amused or offended. "Don't tell me it's been so long that my body makes you nervous."

Holly inhaled sharply. "Well . . . yeah."

"I figure you can get used to it again."

"I wouldn't count on it."

The woman was definitely awake now. He grabbed the terry robe and put it on. Mustard yellow, his worst color.

Cole was about to ask Holly what possessed him to buy the robe when the door opened. Benji and Treasure shot across the room like a streak of light. Benji lunged onto the bed while Treasure, playing the little lady, daintily climbed aboard. She was the spitting image of her mother, with long waving hair and dark eyes, and she was wearing a white flannel pajama set, printed with tiny red hearts.

Benji gasped. Treasure whirled around and stared at Cole in shock. Her eyes shot to her mother's. "What's *he* doing here?"

Cole's temper flared. Treasure was talking about him as if he weren't even in the room. Wasn't he accustomed to getting just a little more respect? He could swear there'd been a time when people tiptoed around him, flattering and fawning over him.

"Treasure, if you've got a question about me, you can ask me directly." Cole got into bed again, with the rest of the family. Casually, he leaned his back against the headboard and put his hands in the pockets of his robe. No doubt, he was going to have to assert more authority here. He glanced between Treasure and Benji, and when he saw his son's black eye, he winced. "Kids," he continued levelly, "I want you to know I'm here to stay."

They stared at him as if he'd lost his mind.

Which you have, he thought. He looked at Holly, who stared warily at the floor. Cole sighed. "I asked you last night, and now I'm going to ask you one more time, Benji. What happened to your eye?"

"Nicky Chamberlain." Benji shifted uncomfortably on the mattress. "He beat me up."

"He's from day care," Treasure supplied.

Cole leaned closer to Benji. "Why did he hit you?"

Benji looked at his mother. When Holly said nothing, he continued, "'cause of I don't have a dad."

It was a low blow. No wonder no one wanted to tell him this last night at dinner. "Benji, you *do* have a dad."

Benji's dark eyes turned watchful. "I do?"

Cole nodded.

"Who?"

Didn't Benji think Cole cared at all? "Me." Cole forced himself to continue. "And I don't want you two calling me Cole anymore. You'll call me Daddy."

At that, Treasure's eyes nearly popped out of her head. When the phone rang, she jumped off the bed and fled as if the hounds of hell were on her heels.

"Mommy!" Treasure shrieked a second later.

Looking as white as the pillowcases, Holly rose. "C'mon, Benji." Still staring at Cole, the boy took her hand and let himself be led toward the door. "Er...Cole," Holly continued, "why don't you go ahead and hop in the shower?"

Why are you so determined to exclude me from everything that goes on around here? "I'll take a shower," he said tersely, "but you know what, Holly?" Their gazes met and held. He wasn't sure, but he thought he saw guilt in the depths of her eyes.

"Hmm?"

He shook his head. "This is sure one strange family."

Right before Holly vanished with his son, she merely said, "Stranger than you've guessed."

"HELLO?" Holly wedged the phone receiver between her cheek and shoulder, then pointed to the kitchen chairs. As the kids dutifully sat, Holly opened the newspaper, which she'd grabbed from the mail slot in the front door.

"Hello?" she repeated. Since Treasure's phone skills still left much to be desired, callers often remained stunned for full minutes. Holly continued riffling through the paper until she found the job ads.

Finally, a voice said, "Uh...this is Mr. Warring, from over at Pretty Pets."

Oh, no. Not this, too. "Well, hello."

Mr. Warring cleared his throat. "How are you this morning, Ms. Hawkes?"

In big trouble. Her kids were staring at her with expressions of extreme mistrust, and her skin was still on fire, burning with the warm pressure of Cole's body. Sudden panic made her heart pound harder. She'd meant to nurse Cole last night—not fall asleep with him. "I'm fine. How about you?"

Hearing Mr. Warring's heavy sigh, Holly's heart sank. She twined her fingers around the phone cord, and her eyes darted to Benji's.

"You know the puppy you wanted for your son?"

Holly turned away from the kids. "Yes?"

"Well, someone wanted to buy it yesterday...."

Relief washed over her. Mr. Warring hadn't sold the dachshund. But how was she going to pay for it? She needed to reserve what money she had for groceries and emergencies. She thought of Cole's money clip, then cut off the thought. If she used his money, she'd truly be taking advantage of him. Already, she had to figure out how to repay the rent he'd given Zeke.

Guiltily, she thought of the call she'd made to the Joe Ray Stardust studio this morning. Somehow, she'd wanted to let people know he hadn't vanished, and it was clear that no one was looking for him. The man who'd answered the phone said he was sure Joe Ray wasn't due back until af-

ter the holidays. *I just hope no one discovers he's gone
until after court next Tuesday. That's all I'm asking.*

Holly snapped to attention. "Hmm?"

"I said I can't keep holding on to this dog, Ms.
Hawkes..."

"Could you give me just a couple more days?" she
murmured, her eyes roving over the classifieds. If she
could find a new job today, maybe she could get an advance on her first check.

"Sure, but I can't wait much longer."

"Just three or four more days," she said again. She
didn't want to further involve Cole in her life, but maybe
he could baby-sit while she went job hunting. Last night
had been such a late night for the kids that she hadn't
awakened them for day care this morning.

"I can give you until next Monday," Mr. Warring said.

Today was only Thursday. "Thanks...oh, thank you."

She hung up the phone and turned around, only to realize that Benji and Treasure were still staring at her expectantly. She pulled out a chair and sat down opposite
them at the kitchen table, wondering what to say about
Cole. From upstairs, she heard the shower running and
forced herself not to imagine the fine-looking, totally nude
man who was now standing beneath those water jets.

"Kids," she began softly, "we're in a bit of a bind and
I need your help."

Benji repeated words she'd said many times. "So, we
gotta pull together as a fam'bly?"

Holly nodded. "That's right, honey bunch."

Treasure's elbows settled on the table. "If Gran'mama
finds out we got Joe Ray, do we gotta go live with her 'an
Gran'pa?"

Holly drew in a sharp breath. *No one ever gives kids
enough credit for understanding the adult world.* She'd

tried so hard to keep her calls with Danice private. As angry as Holly was, she still wanted Benji and Treasure to have relationships with their grandparents—provided the kids were still living under her roof. Somehow, she kept her voice calm. "How did you know Grandmama and Grandpa are hoping you might want to come live with them?"

"We've got ears," Treasure said.

Benji sniffed miserably. "I'm not gonna go, Mommy."

"No one's going anywhere," Holly assured them, wishing she knew it was true. "Meantime, I know it may be hard to understand, but Joe Ray is sick. I think he might get better even faster if we go along with him and make him feel at home here."

Benji toyed with the edge of a place mat. "Is he gonna stay forever?"

"Just a few days."

Treasure looked relieved. "For Christmas?"

At the small, excited leap in her daughter's voice, Holly felt her own spirits rise. "Well . . . maybe."

Benji looked confused. "He's gonna visit just for Christmas like Santa Claus?"

At that, Holly's lips quirked. "Exactly."

Benji's light brows furrowed. "He's like our own Santa Claus in our house?"

Smiling, Holly reached across the table and clasped her son's small hand. "Yeah, Benji, we'll just think of him as our own private Santa Claus." *And if he helps me out by watching you guys today, then he really might be our Saint Nick.*

"But, Mommy—" Treasure shot her a level look "—what if there's no such thing as Santa?"

Benji said, "Is too!"

Treasure stared skeptically at her brother. "How do you know?"

"'Cause he's bringin' me my hot dog puppy. Right, Mommy?"

Hell could freeze over and I'd get that puppy. "That's right."

For the moment, both kids looked satisfied.

And now Holly could concentrate on her next hurdles: fixing breakfast, finding a job... and fighting her undeniable desire for the family's new resident Santa.

Chapter Five

Holly curbed her car and stared through her snow-spotted windshield at the Pine Cottage Estates' sign. Standing on a stepladder in front of it, a man was bundled in a red down jacket and black knit hat. He had a paint can in one hand and a red-coated paintbrush in the other. On the snowy ground was a paint-splattered cardboard box full of supplies.

Judging by the jet black waves peeking from beneath the hat, Holly ventured a guess as to the man's identity. "Cole?"

"Just a sec," he called over his shoulder.

She glanced around, her heart skipping a beat. "Where are Benji and Treasure?"

"Over at Mr. Berry's with Irma."

"Oh, good," she said. Shamefaced, she slid her hand inside her jacket pocket, checking the contents. She'd taken Cole's wallet from the trunk, thinking she ought to at least bring it into the house. Now, she felt sure Cole would discover it in her possession. For all she knew, X-ray vision was in his repertoire of tricks.

Taking in his broad back and shoulders, she suddenly recognized the red jacket. It was one Bobby hadn't worn for years. Cole had found the gloves she'd left on the stair step last night, too. He was larger than her ex, but Bobby had worn his clothes baggy, so they fit Cole perfectly. While Holly's mother had chastised her for keeping so many of Bobby's things, Holly had kept hoping she'd meet just the right person to whom to give them.

Well, I guess you have now. Her throat went dry. From the back, Cole looked absolutely gorgeous. And the freshly painted sign looked as good as he did. Its background was as white as today's fresh snowfall, and inside a square border of glistening green holly leaves, the words Pine Cottage Estates were written in bright red cursive.

Beneath the sign, the two missing floodlights had been replaced and flurries spiraled in front of them. While the early afternoon sky was gray-white with snow, the sign was so festive that Holly felt it warm her soul.

She leaned her head through the open car window, the cold air stinging her cheeks. "The sign looks great," she called, even though she knew she should be fighting the easy familiarity between her and Cole. *Holly, just because no one's looking for him doesn't mean you can afford to get friendly.*

"You don't think it's too Christmassy for year-round?" he asked.

"Not at all." The sign was red and green, but it would be inviting at any time. She watched Cole lift his brush and dexterously dab red dots for berries into the centers of the holly leaf clusters.

Holly berry. He'd called her that last night as he'd drifted to sleep. Was he painting holly leaves on the sign because of her? *No...he's painting berries because Mr. Berry's the owner.* Thinking that, she continued, "What are Benji and Treasure doing down at Mr. Berry's?"

"You'll see," Cole said cryptically.

"Did they get lunch?"

"Sure." Cole glanced at her over his shoulder. "Candy bars, hot cocoa and some ice cream."

Holly's lips parted in protest. "You didn't."

Cole's eyes crinkled with laughter and his lips curled into an irresistibly sexy smile. "What do you think?"

She surveyed him skeptically. "What did you feed my children?"

"Our children," he corrected.

Feeling completely unsettled, Holly managed to nod.

Cole nimbly stepped off the small ladder and gathered his paint supplies. Carrying them, he headed for the car. As he passed her open window, he leaned in and kissed her cheek. Before Holly could react the man was already gone, leaving mere impressions behind: his feathery lips, the ghostlike passing of a stray lock of hair that had brushed her cheek, a whiff of pine trees and apple shampoo.

Cole stored the supplies in her back seat, next to the rabbit food she'd just bought, and then got in the front seat. Instantly the car seemed to shrink.

"Peanut butter and jelly on whole wheat," Cole said.

Holly had no idea what he was talking about. All she knew was that his cheeks were ruddy from the cold and his dark eyes were twinkling with devilment. She realized her gaze had settled on his lips. "What?" she croaked.

Seemingly oblivious to how his kiss had affected her— or to how forbidden it was—Cole merely chuckled. "Okay, I admit it. I gave the kids a candy bar for dessert, but I made them share."

"Fine," she said shakily. Cole looked so awake and alive and full of good humor that surely some part of his memory had returned. Wincing, she reached up and pushed his hat away from the stitched gash on his forehead.

"How's it look today?" he asked.

"Better," she said, feeling relieved. She watched him tug off his hat and gloves, then rake his long fingers through his hair. Her eyes roved over the few silver strands in the jet waves. With a sudden laugh, she found herself adding, "But it looks as though you've got tinsel threaded through your hair."

"Time for the Grecian Formula?"

"I love your hair."

He shot her a playful smile. "You do?"

What was she saying? She nodded curtly, then quickly averted her gaze. Realizing that wet flurries were melting on her windshield, she turned on the wipers, then stared at the sign again. "And you paint really well."

"Zeke did the background, and Irma stenciled the leaves and letters. All I had to do was stay inside the lines."

Holly's eyes trailed over him again. He made her whole car smell so fresh and clean that it could have been parked in the woods. But Cole was married, even if he couldn't remember it now. And even though she doubted he really was a cheater, it was a possibility. She mustered a cool tone. "You don't look like a guy who's inclined to stay within the lines."

His midnight eyes softened with apology. "I won't go out of bounds again, Holly."

But I'm so afraid I could. "Maybe not."

Their eyes met. The car remained quiet, except for the steady hum of the motor and the hypnotic pass of the windshield wipers. Holly fought it, but she couldn't stop comparing Cole to Bobby. Years ago, Bobby's wealth had made him seem so desirable and unattainable. Now, Cole was so much further from her grasp. And infinitely more dangerous. Lord, she should be shot for even fantasizing about him. *Is there something wrong with me? Am I destined to be attracted to unavailable men?*

She sighed. *Or injured men who bring out the nurse in me?* After all, Bobby's many weaknesses had played one long, sad song on her heartstrings. And now, so was that damnable gash on Cole's forehead.

She cleared her throat. "Irma stenciled in the letters?"

"What were you thinking, Holly?" Cole said gently.

Feeling suddenly breathless, Holly shoved the gear in Drive. "That we ought to get home."

Cole shrugged. "Irma used to be an art teacher, you know."

Holly told herself to take her foot off the brake and start driving. Instead, she merely sat there, gripping the steering wheel, feeling Cole's inquisitive eyes on her face. "How did Irma manage to do the stenciling? Her hip's still bothering her."

Cole leaned so close that his cheek almost grazed hers, and he pointed to the side of the road. "I upturned that barrel and sat her on top of it."

Holly chuckled. "Bet she loved that."

Cole smiled. "Actually, I think she did."

"Well the sign looks great."

"Wait until you see the rest."

"The rest?"

Cole nodded through the windshield, then his eyes returned to hers. "Of course, I could sit here all day."

And I could sit here forever, she thought dreamily. At the realization, she stomped on the gas pedal with such force that her car fishtailed on ice.

"Careful," Cole said, "or we'll spend the rest of the afternoon pushing you out of a ditch." He pointed at the pavement. "I called the city today. Turns out, this road's on their property, so they came and salted it. If you take it slow, you'll get over the few patches of ice that are left."

He'd called the city? Somehow—maybe because Bobby had never been of any help—that touched her. Holly hazarded another glance at Cole. Even though nothing more could ever happen between them, he was teaching her a few things about what she wanted in a man. *But don't forget he's spoken for,* she reminded herself as she drove up the hill. He might paint signs and make sure her roads were salted, but there was only one person she could rely on—herself. With a sigh, she swung the car into the driveway.

"I got a job," she said.

Cole stared at her in surprise. "Why didn't you tell me?"

She shrugged. "It's only retail."

"Only retail?" He squinted at her as if she were crazy. "But that's great, Holly."

She exhaled slowly, realizing that Joe Ray Stardust probably wasn't a snob. "It's at a dress shop called Country Casuals in the Express Mall," she continued. *The Samuelses' mall.* She could only hope Judge Selsa decided in her favor and that she didn't run into her ex-in-laws when she went to work next Monday.

"Country Casuals." Cole nodded as if he liked the sound of it, then he frowned. "But I was hoping we could all go to day care together tomorrow. And Saturday, I was going to tune the car and take a look at the clutch."

Did Joe Ray Stardust—or Cole—really know how to fix a sticking clutch? That he was inserting himself into her life so easily was disturbing, but she managed a shrug. "Monday's the only day I need to work between now and Christmas. Country Casuals hired kids on school break to help during the holiday rush, but business picked up so much that they need a full-time person now."

Holly sighed. Her life had gone so out of control in the past twenty-four hours that she'd forgotten about parents' day at day care tomorrow. Santa was coming and the kids were making ornaments. She moaned. "I need to bake cookies to take."

"Already baked them," Cole said. "And I told Benji we'd help him make the star for the top of our tree."

She was still processing that Cole had baked cookies, so the reference to a tree made no sense at all. She'd promised herself she'd buy one today, but she couldn't bear to stop and ask her parents for money. "Tree?"

"We'll hike up the hill and cut one down just as soon as you change into jeans." Cole caught her gaze. "Not that you don't look great in that skirt, Holly berry."

She tried to ignore the pet name. "You're going to cut me a tree?"

He nodded. "While you change, I'll finish up down there."

Down there? Her eyes darted to the windshield. "My word," she whispered in shock.

Cole had a way of commanding her full attention, so she hadn't noticed much else. But all the tenants of the Pine Cottage Estates were gathered around the tall blue spruce in front of Mr. Berry's house. Cardboard boxes were strewn across the snow, and Zeke was moving up and down a tall ladder, taking ornaments from Benji and Treasure and hanging them on the tree. Jumbo Stirling was untangling lengths of black electrical cords, and his new fiancée Linda was coming down a hill opposite, carrying a thermos. Even Mr. Berry, who rarely ventured outside, had rolled onto his wide front porch in his wheelchair. Seeing Holly's car, Irma and Stella waved.

Holly and Cole waved back. Then he squinted. "What happened to Mr. Berry's legs?" he asked, as if wondering whether or not he should already know.

"A car accident some years back." Holly glanced at Cole. "He lost his wife, too. The medical bills nearly broke him, I think."

"Medical bills..." Cole murmured the words as if they meant something. Shaking his head, he continued, "Well, what do you think of the ornaments?"

Holly smiled. *I think Christmas came to the Pine Cottage Estates today.* Magically, wreaths had appeared on all the doorways. A lit-up Santa shined in a window. Everyone, her children included, was helping Zeke hang ornaments. On the car radio, "The Little Drummer Boy" had begun to play. Now, Holly heard the line, "I have no gift to bring." And yet, looking at the scene below, she knew everyone had some special gift to give.

"The kids and I did a door-to-door this morning," Cole said. "Turned out, most everybody had boxes of ornaments. They quit putting them out since they were spending Christmas alone. Stella had tons of stuff, and Mr. Berry keeps lights in his basement. He gave us a string of them and some small, decorative birds, too—cardinals and blue jays and sparrows. He said his wife used to use them in flower arrangements, but that they'd probably look good in a tree."

Holly couldn't quite keep up. "I can't believe Stella's decorating her house. She's been so upset ever since that fight with her son."

"What's that about, anyway?"

"Her only son, Jonathan, recently married and moved away. Since he's well into his forties, I guess Stella just assumed he'd always be around. Anyway, she says he left because he doesn't love her anymore. But of course it's not true. He had a job offer elsewhere." Holly shrugged. "I just can't believe she got out her holiday decorations."

Cole chuckled softly. "Well, Benji twisted her arm."

Holly smiled, still amazed by how Cole had rallied the tenants. "Stella always was a sucker for male persuasion."

"Wish you were."

Oh, but I am. Holly's eyes slid guiltily toward Cole's.

"Look." Cole pointed.

Just as Holly glanced through the windshield, a thousand lights sparked on all around them. From far below, a great loud cheer sounded from the tenants of the Pine Cottage Estates. In the foggy gray afternoon, the dusky hills had come alive with bright white lights that now twinkled from all the pine trees and from the decorated big blue spruce. In each window of Mr. Berry's old stately manor house, an electric candle shone.

Holly held her breath, biting back a rush of emotion and wishing she could give Cole a warm hug. Everything looked beautiful. For the first time, the Pine Cottage Estates looked like somewhere she truly wanted to live.

"Thanks, Cole." Watching her kids run merrily through the snow, she felt as if Cole really might be their Santa Claus.

"And guess what, sweetheart?"

She didn't know how much more of this she could take. "What?"

"I got a job, too."

She gasped in protest. "You can't." Who had employed him? There wasn't much call for magicians around here. Or maybe there was, she realized as her eyes flitted over the lit-up trees on the hillside. All day, Cole had been practicing his wonderful magic. "You're working?"

Cole's voice turned edgy. "Of course I intend to work. I'm staying, Holly, so you might as well get used to it. Now, as soon as you change, we'll go get that tree."

The next thing she knew, he'd gotten out of the car and slammed the door. For long moments, she simply watched him walk down the hill. His long, lean legs moved with such nimble agility that his feet barely seemed to touch the ground. She stared at the blanket of snow, half expecting him not to leave footprints.

But of course he did. He was no angel. He was a flesh-and-blood man. And he wasn't about to let her forget it.

"C'MON," HOLLY SAID. "Tell me who hired you."

Any pique Cole felt earlier seemed to have vanished. He laughed and readjusted an ax in his gloved hand; with his other, he grabbed an edge of her coat pocket. At least his wallet was now hidden safely under her mattress. She knew the name Joe Ray Stardust was on everything, too, she thought, feeling a twinge of conscience about her spying.

And worry, as well. Maybe it was no use fighting him. Especially not after what he'd done today. Because of her experience with Bobby, she never would have guessed that a man with wealth, position and power could possess the soul of a saint. But it seemed as if Cole did.

Far ahead of her and Cole, the kids pranced up the hill, powdery snow dusting the air near their feet. As if he meant to catch her unawares, Cole edged closer. "Now stop that," she warned.

He laughed. "The job's near home...."

Holly came to a standstill. "And I refuse to budge until you tell me where."

His grin tempered to a smile. "Isn't it beautiful up here?"

She nodded. Below, lights sparkled in the green pines, and the snow-covered roofs made the cottages look like gingerbread houses. Years ago, when the Pine Cottage Estates were well maintained, they were probably adorable. They were logically laid out, all surrounding Mr. Berry's house, and right now Zeke's little red car puttered up the inviting circular road. As she surveyed the scene, she tried to ignore how Cole's eyes were roving over her face. Finally, she gave in and looked at him.

He glanced quickly toward the kids. "Keep looking for that tree, you guys," he shouted. "We want the best one on the hill."

With a start, Holly realized she'd better keep moving. She shrugged off Cole's grasp, tucked her hands firmly into her jacket pockets, then headed toward the kids. "C'mon Cole."

Cole made a point of passing her. "I like it better when you're following me," he teased over his shoulder.

She didn't exactly mind it either, she admitted. Her eyes trailed from where the thick down-filled jacket accentuated the breadth of his shoulders, all the way down to where the old faded jeans hugged his perfectly shaped behind, and where the ax swung at his side, making him look like the world's sexiest lumberjack.

"We got it!" Treasure shrieked. "Me 'an Benji got it!"

Up ahead, Benji and Treasure were chasing each other through the snow, running in weaving figure eights through a thick copse of pines. Slowing her approach, Holly watched Cole lean, drop the ax and catch a handful of snow in his palm. He packed a snowball and gently tossed it at Treasure. It broke against the back of her navy coat, leaving a white, powdery dot. Treasure whirled around, giggling.

"Daddy!" she exclaimed in shrill censure.

Daddy? Holly's heart hammered in her chest. She was still reeling from shock when Treasure and Benji fell to their knees and started packing their own snowballs. Working as a team, with Benji replenishing the supply and Treasure using her stronger throwing arm, they attempted to pummel Cole. Most of the snowballs missed, but when one hit, the kids screamed with laughter.

And Holly felt more worried than ever. She should have known the kids would take to the man in the few hours she'd been gone. Everyone at the Pine Cottage Estates had. Besides, when she'd gone inside her cottage to change, it was clear they'd been having fun.

Cookies shaped like stockings and angels and bells were cooling in the kitchen. The decorations Mr. Berry had given them were laid out in the living room near Fuzzy's pen. And Cole had cut strips of construction paper, helping the kids begin a long paper chain for the tree.

Holly had found letters to Santa, too. Cole had taken dictation from the kids in his neat tidy print. Both kids had said they wanted Stella's appetite to return and for her son to come home.

"We're gonna get you, Daddy!" Treasure squealed. "C'mon, Benji, get 'im!"

Cole ducked—but only to ensure that Benji's snowball would hit him right in the chest.

"I got 'im!" Benji shrieked with pride.

"Time out," Holly called. When a snowball broke against her shoulder, she put her hands on her hips.

Cole laughed. "Gotcha, sweetheart."

Theirs was a truly sticky situation, Holly thought. And as much as she'd like to wish otherwise, it would probably end badly. After all, how could something like this possibly turn out right? Another snowball broke against her back. This time, it was the kids. With her mind still on

Cole, who was now coming toward her, she had to force herself not to crack a smile.

"My, don't you look serious," Cole said.

As the children began to play in the snow again, Holly sighed. Doctor Kester had said it was important for Cole to remember on his own, but maybe if she prodded just a little, she could find out more about him. She was sure there were secrets in his past...secrets she could use against him if it came to that. Knowing where he'd gotten a job would be a start.

"C'mon," she urged softly. "Where's your job?"

His hand slipped beneath her elbow. "Down at the Texaco station."

She gasped. "Working for Jack Deegan? Pumping gas?"

Cole's eyes darted toward the kids, checking on their safety. "Jack needs someone in the garage."

"You're working on cars?"

Cole's only response was to lean forward and nibble her earlobe. Veering back with lightning speed, Holly tried to ignore how his warm breath sent tingles of awareness to her freezing toes. "Please stop that."

He chuckled. "Jack needs someone who knows motors inside and out," he continued, his lips twitching. "Someone who can start them up and keep them running."

There was no mystery as to whose motor Cole was talking about. Holly's mouth went dry and she licked at her lips. Somehow, this seemed like a replay of the conversation they'd had in the Civic Center parking lot, right before he'd first kissed her. "Cole, my motor's just fine."

"I've definitely heard it purr on occasion..." Cole glanced pointedly at the kids again. "But right now, I'm afraid my timing's off."

Holly's gaze followed his. She couldn't have felt more relieved that the kids were here. "Guess so."

Cole's expressive mouth curved into such a wicked grin that Holly felt weak-kneed. "Well, I'll be sure not to lose the key," he said with a ribald chuckle, his midnight eyes piercing hers.

She squinted at him. "The key?"

He nodded. "Later, maybe I'll put it in the ignition and—"

Holly gasped, realizing he wasn't talking about cars. "Drive away?" she quickly suggested, hating the shrill, excited edge in her voice.

"Sweetheart—" He was clearly enjoying unbalancing her. "I mean to drive you right into oblivion. But I do promise to be a gentleman." He lifted his finger and playfully traced her cheek. "And a gentleman always warms up the car first."

She tried to look angry. "You're incorrigible."

His eyes made no apology. "Yep."

"One, two, three," Benji and Treasure suddenly screamed. "We got our tree."

"C'mon." Cole reached right into her pocket, grabbed her hand and tugged her forward. As they passed the ax he'd dropped in the snow, Cole's long arm swept down and retrieved it.

"So, where's the tree?" Holly asked the kids.

When Benji and Treasure merely giggled, Holly's eyes shot heavenward, then she glanced at Cole. He was trying to keep a straight face, but kind amusement was in his eyes.

"The tree behind you, kids?" he asked gently.

Benji and Treasure nodded, their wind-flushed faces set in prideful expressions.

The tree was at least twenty feet tall and nearly as wide. "It's...a little big," Holly finally offered apologetically.

Benji and Treasure's eyes darted toward Cole for confirmation. Holly didn't know which she felt more—surprised or offended. Since this morning, the kids had completely fallen under the man's spell. *And so have you.* In spite of her suspicions that Cole was hiding something, he was still winning her trust.

Cole pointed at another tree. "That's about the size we need."

Treasure groaned. "That's got big old holes in its branches!"

"Yuck!" Benji exclaimed in disgust.

"Well, that's why you two are so important to this mission." Cole planted the ax in the snow and leaned on it. "I only know about size. When it comes to getting a pretty tree, you all have to decide."

"I know what pretty looks like," Treasure said helpfully.

Cole smiled. "So, get going."

As Benji and Treasure started surveying the surrounding trees, Holly felt Cole's hard body nestle next to hers. He playfully pulled her backward, then seated himself on a fallen log, leaning the ax by his side.

"My behind'll get wet," she protested.

Wordlessly, Cole reached inside his jacket, pulled a folded sheet of newspaper from somewhere, then laid it across the log. Was there anything he didn't think of?

Holly sat down. "Did you really get a job at the Texaco station?"

His eyes captured hers. Everything in the depths of those midnight irises asked if she'd ever forgive him for the affair she'd said he had. He shrugged. "I've missed work-

g on cars. I wish I never had to sell the old station, but
ith Dad's medical bills, there was just no choice.''

Holly peered at him. Apparently, his father had be-
›me ill and Cole had sold a gas station he'd owned. No
›nder his memory seemed jarred by the mention of Mr.
:rry's medical situation. "The station..." she echoed,
ntly prodding.

Cole nodded. As he shut his eyes and drew in a deep
eath, Holly's heart skipped a beat. Was he fighting to
gain a memory or merely enjoying the crisp outside air?
›r excruciating seconds he remained silent. Would his
emory return like this—all at once, without any warn-
g? "Cole?"

He opened his eyes.

She stared at him, sure he'd just remembered every-
ing.

"Someday," he said with another shrug, "I guess we
ght to drive up to Weller's Falls. Just to look around, see
hatever became of the place."

Holly's mind raced. She'd never heard of Weller's Falls,
t Cole had mentioned a garage and upstate New York.
id his accent indicate a northern New York upbringing?
But what about the information in *One Magic Christ-
as*? Inside the back cover flap, right above his bio was a
apshot of the Joe Ray Stardust estate in Connecticut.
hind tall wrought-iron gates was the imposing house, all
corated for Christmas with wreaths in every window.

Holly's blood quickened. *What if every last word of the
e Ray Stardust biography is a lie?* she wondered in
ock. What if Joe Ray Stardust was just some guy from
›state New York? Stage names were common enough,
t what if he'd given himself a new accent and a whole
w identity? Now, maybe he was remembering his life as
was before he became Joe Ray Stardust.

It wasn't that far-fetched. Irma read magazines that featured celebrities. Their lives were full of such fabrications. For instance, married sex symbols who didn't want to lose their images often pretended to be single.

Holly's eyes leaped to Cole's gorgeously sculpted face. He was staring out over the mountaintop as if he were Paul Bunyon...not a New York City celebrity. Lord, what if he had no wife or children?

Stop it! That's crazy!

She averted her gaze. Of course, Cole was married. But he didn't *seem* married. No man in love would pursue another woman the way he'd been pursuing her. And no decent man would forget his own kids.

She glanced up. Heavens, he was staring at her as if he really was in love with her. But who in the world *was* he? For long moments, she returned his gaze. Deep and mysterious, those eyes were as enigmatic as he was. Was anything about his life the truth?

She had to know.

And she'd start with finding Weller's Falls. She had to be ready for anything when his memory returned. Especially since there was a chance he'd lost his ability to perform magic. No, she assured herself, researching his marital status was the least of her motives.

"Holly?"

"Hmm?"

"What are you thinking?"

She sighed. At least she could answer that honestly. "You."

"Good." Cole's fingers edged beneath her hat, his eyebrows furrowing in a mock frown as his fingers caressed her ear. "Hmm. What's that I feel?"

"Surprise me."

He snapped his fingers, then drew a gold-wrapped piece of chocolate from behind her ear.

Smiling, Holly unwrapped it and popped it into her mouth. "Thanks."

Cole sighed. "I keep trying for mistletoe."

The last thing she needed was another of his enticing kisses. She shrugged. "I was starved."

Cole looped an arm casually around her shoulder. "I may lack talent but at least Zeke keeps telling me I look like Joe Ray Stardust. You know. That magician on TV."

Somehow, Holly managed not to choke on her chocolate. Fortunately, the kids bounded into view.

"We got 'im picked out," Benji said breathlessly, coming to a halt right in front of them.

Treasure pointed over her shoulder. "It's over there."

"It already fell down," Benji supplied, "so we don't have to cut it."

"Guess that saves me some work." Cole extended his hands. "Well, kids, you'll have to pull me off this log."

When the kids grabbed Cole's wrists and tugged, he made a show of staggering to his feet. Then he reached down and grasped Holly's hand. "Coming?"

"Do I have a choice?"

He smiled, pulling her to her feet and right against his chest. "Nope."

"Then I guess I'm coming," she said. She just wished she knew where, precisely, they were all heading.

Chapter Six

"Holly?" Cole's voice was as melodic as the music float-
ing to the kitchen from the living room. "Can you come
here when you get a chance?"

"Be right there." She continued humming along with
"Joy to the World," thinking Cole truly was magical with
mechanics. In addition to reassembling her tape player,
he'd fixed two loose door knobs, the leaky upstairs sink
and an old toaster oven.

As Holly took off her apron she gave the kitchen a last
satisfied glance. The stew wouldn't be done for another
forty-five minutes, but she and Cole had helped the kids
ice the cookies. Now they were packed in tins to take to day
care tomorrow, and Holly headed for the living room, only
to stop and lean in the archway between the rooms, her
eyes roving over the homey scene.

Christmas had come today—and not only to the outside of the Pine Cottage Estates. No, Christmas had swept
inside her cottage as well, whirling through like a great
wind. Imaginary dust and cobwebs were whisked away,
and now a warm, cozy fire was crackling in the fireplace.

Next to the hearth, Cole had placed a small stool, so the
kids could leave milk and cookies for Santa, and four
stockings hung from the mantel. He'd arranged pine-

cones and candles on her end tables, and tied green bows around the bases of her lamps. Yes, her cottage had come so alive that she half expected the chairs and pictures to start dancing, the way they did in Disney movies. Every nook and cranny of the place smelled of pine... and of Cole who was lying on his back under the tree.

Benji and Treasure were seated at the table in the living room, looking like angels, with their small dark heads bowed over their construction paper chain and their eyebrows furrowed in concentration.

Cole was certainly a magician. He'd found Fuzzy a real cage, which was now in the kids' room. And from Mr. Berry's, he'd brought a sweet-smelling length of rope pine that seemed as endless as the ropes he lengthened on television. He'd twisted the pine all the way down the bannister, then fashioned a perfect red velvet bow around the newel post. Even though Benji and Treasure had settled on a tree that was only marginally smaller than the one they'd first picked, Cole had somehow fit it inside the living room.

"Holly, honey?"

Holly's eyes drifted to the kids, who had stopped working. "I'm right here."

"Turn on the lights!" Treasure urged.

Cole snapped on the strand of tiny white lights that ringed the tree, but Holly, who couldn't take her eyes from her children, only saw them from the periphery of her vision. She'd never seen the kids look happier. Their full cheeks were rosy, their eyes bright and alive with the excitement of Christmas.

Her heart swelled with feeling, wistful and bittersweet. By the day, her babies grew beyond her. Time kept slipping into the future while their childhoods receded into the past. One day she'd wake up and they'd be grown. Not a

thing would remain of their childhoods—or of this night—
but her memory. She shut her eyes.

*Remember this moment, Holly. Remember it forever.
Keep this picture of the kids next to your heart.* She opened
her eyes. *And please,* she prayed fervently. *Oh, please,
don't let the Samuelses take them.*

Cole shifted under the tree. "Are all the lights on?"

Holly blew out a shaky breath and forced herself to look
away from the children, at the tree. "Yeah."

Leaves rustled as Cole scooted from beneath the
branches. Just looking at him lightened Holly's mood.
Tiny twigs clung to his shirt and luscious hair. The muscles of his flat abdomen clenched as he sat, then he rolled
to his feet. The tree was a foot taller than Cole, but he
seemed to tower over it.

"Gorgeous," Holly said.

"Me or the tree?"

Both. "The tree."

"It doesn't have no holes," Treasure assured.

Cole's eyes didn't leave Holly's. "Any," he said, absently correcting Treasure. Flashing Holly a smile, he began circling the tree, double-checking the lights.

Holly's own smile froze. *You keep forgetting this man
doesn't belong here.* All evening, she'd caught herself in-
dulging the wishful thought that he wasn't really married,
and that he'd stay, so she could get to know him.

Cole turned from the tree to the kids. "How are you two
doing?"

Treasure giggled and glanced at her mother. "He's
Santa," she explained, "so we gotta be the elves."

Benji said, "My chain's pretty good."

Cole's eyes caught Holly's, then he glanced at the kids.
"Our own chain gang."

Her lips twitched. "That's the worst play on words I ever heard."

"Give me time."

"I'm an elf, not a chain gang," Treasure reminded, scooting from her chair. She bounded across the room, turning off the tape player. Holly started to protest, but Treasure flicked on the TV—and Christmas music filled the room again. There was probably a special on every channel tonight. Treasure skipped to Holly's side.

"Hmm?" Realizing her daughter intended to impart one of her many secrets, Holly bent down, while Treasure stretched on her tiptoes and cupped her hand over her mouth. Treasure's voice was barely audible.

"It wasn't like this before, Mommy."

No, Bobby had never helped make their house a home.

Treasure raced on. "Is Daddy—I mean Daddy Bobby gonna come home?"

Holly guessed Treasure was contemplating the possibility of having two daddies—Daddy Bobby and Daddy Cole. But how could she fault her daughter for having fantasies that she herself was having? Holly whispered, "I don't know if he'll visit for Christmas."

Treasure fell off her tiptoes, then looked at Holly, her expression uncertain. Leaning close again, she whispered, "If he comes, can Daddy Cole stay, too?"

Somehow, Holly doubted "Daddy Bobby" would be anywhere near the kids this Christmas. Last she heard—during an argument with Jessica, no less—her ex-husband was partying at some ski resort in Colorado. She forced herself to smile. "Sure," she whispered.

Cole shot her and Treasure a curious glance. "What's going on over there, ladies?"

Holly gave Treasure a playful pinch. "Never tell a man your secrets."

Treasure giggled, grabbed Holly's hand and led her toward the table. "Mommy's got some real big secrets," she said, teasing Cole.

Glad she was next to a chair, Holly sank into it. For the first time, it occurred to her that the kids might tell Cole the truth about who he was. Not that they knew how he got here.

"Daddy's gonna help me finish my letter to the real Santa," Benji said. "'Cause we gotta mail it tomorrow."

Holly shook her head as if to clear it of confusion. Was she really going to show up at parents' day tomorrow with Cole posing as her husband? *You can't. Someone will recognize him.* But so far, no one had. And Cole seemed determined to go.

He surveyed the table. "After we do the Santa letters, we'll take Stella a hot bowl of stew. I can get my coat, too."

Holly raised her eyebrows. "Your coat?"

Cole nodded absently. "This morning Stella took it to the dry cleaners where she works. She said she could get that grease stain off the back, and there was a cape in one of the pockets that she promised to press." Cole squinted at Holly. "Where *did* that stain come from?" Before she could respond, he shook his head as if it didn't matter. "Well, I guess we should finish decorating our tree tonight, too."

When Cole sat next to Holly, the light touch of his palm whisked around her waist like a magic wand, stirring her blood and making butterflies in her tummy take flight. She was still feeling those fluttering wings when she realized Cole's touch had vanished every bit as mysteriously as it had appeared.

He'd picked up the living room phone extension and was punching in a long-distance number. Holly's heart dropped to her feet. Was he calling New York? Had he been fooling her about his memory loss all along?

Catching her expression, Benji said, "We're calling Mrs. Lewis's son, and we're gonna tell him he's gotta come home for Chris'mis."

"He's in California, you know," Treasure added importantly.

Feeling stunned, Holly listened wordlessly to what ensued. Cole spoke with Jonathan about Stella's holiday depression and lack of appetite. It turned out that Jonathan and his wife, Maggie, desperately wanted to visit, but they'd just spent their savings on a house and now didn't have the money to travel. Before Holly realized what was happening, Cole had tossed his money clip to the table and he and the kids were counting the money.

"We'll phone you back," Cole said.

While he called the airlines about fares, Holly tried to protest, but the kids didn't understand.

"I thought you said Chris'mis was about being nice to people, Mommy," Treasure said in censure.

Within moments, Holly relented, and Cole made plans for them to pay for the tickets later in the evening. Then he called Stella's son again. With a little arm twisting, Jonathan and Maggie agreed to use the tickets with the proviso that they could repay Cole after the holidays. They couldn't wait to surprise Stella.

"Now," Cole said as he hung up the phone, "do you want me to finish your Santa letter, Benji?"

"Yep." Benji handed the letter to Cole.

Holding it between a muscular thumb and forefinger, Cole read the letter with care. "Okay, so have you seen the red pen?"

Benji frowned in concern and started shuffling the supplies on the table, peering beneath paper strips and glue, tape and ribbons. Treasure slid off her chair and searched the floor. Both kids came up empty.

"Ah—" Cole grinned. "Vatch carefully."

Hearing the German accent, Holly froze. So far, Cole hadn't been using his various accents. But he'd begun talking about his past today. He'd mentioned Weller's Falls and medical bills. No doubt, his memory was returning in bits and pieces.

The thought didn't bring her much comfort. Nor did his hands. In amazement, she watched their swift, deliberate movements that were so calculated to engage the eyes of watchers. His hands were so fast that her eyes saw nothing more than traces. His wrists were fluid, like flowing liquid. And those fingers mesmerized.

In a heartbeat, the hands stilled, poised above the table, so gracefully they could have belonged to a dancer.

Benji gasped.

"Vatch," Cole whispered again. "Vatch carefully now." He snapped his fingers—and a marker appeared in his hand.

Holly's eyes widened. It had come from nowhere, right from the thin air. Her gaze skated from Cole's fingertips, over his corded forearms, to his well-delineated biceps. The man was wearing nothing more than a tight white T-shirt. He had no sleeves, no watchband behind which he could have tucked the marker. "How did you do that?"

His midnight eyes dropped over her, their movements as seductively secretive as those of his hands. As his full mouth curved into a smile, she found herself leaning toward him as if he'd put her in a trance. "How?"

He came so close that his warm, minty breath fanned her cheek. And then he whispered one word. "Magic."

Benji sighed. "But Cole—er—Daddy..."

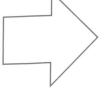

NO COST! NO OBLIGATION TO BUY!
NO PURCHASE NECESSARY!

PLAY "LUCKY 7" AND GET FIVE FREE GIFTS

HOW TO PLAY:

1. With a coin, carefully scratch off the silver box at the right. Then check the claim chart to see what we have for you—FREE BOOKS and a gift—ALL YOURS! ALL FREE!

2. Send back this card and you'll receive brand-new Harlequin American Romance® novels. These books have a cover price of $3.75 each, but they are yours to keep absolutely free.

3. There's no catch. You're under no obligation to buy anything. We charge nothing—ZERO—for your first shipment. And you don't have to make any minimum number of purchases—not even one!

4. The fact is thousands of readers enjoy receiving books by mail from the Harlequin Reader Service®. They like the convenience of home delivery...they like getting the best new novels months before they're available in stores...and they love our discount prices!

5. We hope that after receiving your free books you'll want to remain a subscriber. But the choice is yours—to continue or cancel, anytime at all! So why not take us up on our invitation, with no risk of any kind. You'll be glad you did!

Holly glanced at her son, only to find that he looked positively stricken.

"It's blue," Benji ventured apologetically.

Holly's eyes shot to the marker just as Cole placed it on the table. Sure enough, it was blue.

Cole frowned. Placing his elbows on the table, he stared into his own open palms for a long moment as if mystified. Holly watched in fascination as his hands began to move again. They made flourishes in the air that made him look like a master pianist playing an invisible piano.

"C'mon," he whispered. Then he snapped his fingers and another marker appeared. "Green," he muttered. With another loud snap, a third marker appeared. "Orange," he pronounced.

And then, with ever more rapid snaps of his fingers, Cole grabbed markers from the thin air and tossed them to the table, calling out their colors. "Yellow... brown... purple... pink...."

he stopped and stared down.

the markers was red.

"Ready for a Joe Ray Stardust Christmas?" an announcer boomed. "We sure hope so, boys and girls. Because here's your host. Joe . . . Ray . . . Starduuust!"

No doubt, this would make the man's memories come flooding back. Holly couldn't bear to look at him. Nor could she quite process the fact that the man sitting next to her was also on television. Her pulse accelerated as Joe Ray Stardust strolled onto the stage dressed in a simple black sweater and slacks. Stopping in front of a decorated tree, he glanced behind himself at the glittering backdrop of the Manhattan skyline.

Then, quicker than the eye could see, two red scarves appeared. He twirled them in the air and they became real live red cardinals that perched on his hands. Lithely, he placed the birds in nests in the Christmas tree onstage. Snapping his fingers again, the live cardinals instantly became decorative, papier-mâché birds. The real birds magically appeared in Joe Ray's hands again and then f

Holly glanced at her son, only to find that he looked positively stricken.

"It's blue," Benji ventured apologetically.

Holly's eyes shot to the marker just as Cole placed it on the table. Sure enough, it was blue.

Cole frowned. Placing his elbows on the table, he stared into his own open palms for a long moment as if mystified. Holly watched in fascination as his hands began to move again. They made flourishes in the air that made him look like a master pianist playing an invisible piano.

"C'mon," he whispered. Then he snapped his fingers and another marker appeared. "Green," he muttered. With another loud snap, a third marker appeared. "Orange," he pronounced.

And then, with ever more rapid snaps of his fingers, Cole grabbed markers from the thin air and tossed them to the table, calling out their colors. "Yellow... brown... purple... pink...."

Finally he stopped and stared down.

But not one of the markers was red. For a long moment, no one dared say a word.

Holly finally found her voice. "I—I think I might have a red pen in my pocketbook."

Cole's eyes met hers in silent thanks. She started to get up when she realized Benji looked even more upset than before. Now he was staring in horror at the TV.

The loud crashing theme music for the Joe Ray Stardust show blared into the room. Holly watched in mortification as a rapid montage of photographs played on the screen: the Christmas tree at Rockefeller Center, a hansom cab on Central Park, the decorated mansion at the Joe Ray Stardust Estate.

"Ready for a Joe Ray Stardust Christmas?" an announcer boomed. "We sure hope so, boys and girls. Because here's your host. Joe...Ray...Starduuust!"

No doubt, this would make the man's memories come flooding back. Holly couldn't bear to look at him. Nor could she quite process the fact that the man sitting next to her was also on television. Her pulse accelerated as Joe Ray Stardust strolled onto the stage dressed in a simple black sweater and slacks. Stopping in front of a decorated tree, he glanced behind himself at the glittering backdrop of the Manhattan skyline.

Then, quicker than the eye could see, two red scarves appeared. He twirled them in the air and they became real live red cardinals that perched on his hands. Lithely, he placed the birds in nests in the Christmas tree onstage. Snapping his fingers again, the live cardinals instantly became decorative, papier-mâché birds. The real birds magically appeared in Joe Ray's hands again and then flew offstage.

All at once, Holly's heart pounded hard against her ribs. She'd kidnapped a national treasure. Worse, she'd screwed up his ability to perform magic. Very slowly, she forced herself to look at him. He was staring so intently at the screen that she wished the floor would simply open and swallow her. She inhaled sharply, and at the sound he turned.

His memory was back. She was sure of it. And she was history.

"I can't believe how good that guy is." Cole frowned, jealousy twinging his voice. "Do you really think I look like him?"

Weakly, Holly whispered, "Well, maybe just a little."

IT HAD BEEN ONE LONG DAY. And the kids had probably stayed up too late again. But it was Christmastime, and Cole had needed to help them finish their Santa letters. He glanced around. He'd straightened the living room enough for the time being.

He just wished the neighbors had talked more when he'd asked about his relationship with Holly. But Holly apparently didn't kiss and tell. Cole couldn't help but admire that. Or the independent way she'd been living without him, raising the kids on her own. Still, he wanted her to want him, to need him.

Ambling toward the stairs, he made a point of colliding with her. Before she could utter another of her damnably annoying protests, he spun her around and right into his arms.

"Lord, you're fast," she murmured.

"Only when it comes to getting you in my clutches. After that, I always slow down."

She attempted to wiggle from his embrace. "I bet."

Holding her tight, he glanced up the stairs. Eyes twinkling, he cocked his head. "Not a creature is stirring," he whispered. "Not even a mouse."

"Guess again." She nodded upstairs. "The kids want you to say good-night."

When she gently disengaged herself, his whole body missed the warmth of her. He wanted to feel the gentle curve of her belly against his midsection again and the trace of her breasts against his chest. She turned and headed upstairs, and he followed on the narrow staircase, contenting himself by staring at the delectable twitch of her backside.

Upstairs, she leaned in the doorway of the kids' room, watching him. He could feel her eyes trailing over his shoulders, his back, his behind. All day, he'd felt those bothersome eyes, their touch so intense that they could have been her fingertips.

As he circled around the partition separating the kids' beds, he decided he'd have to start working harder. The kids needed their own rooms. And if he ever got his and Holly's love life back on track, he wanted a room where the two of them could make noise. Share a good laugh if they wanted to.

When he reached Treasure's bedside table, he noticed the glowing face of a heart-shaped clock and wondered if his daughter could tell time. That he wasn't sure disturbed him. So did the fact that he'd ever left her and Benji. He knew what it was like to be a parentless child, so how could he have deserted his own children? It seemed impossible. Tugging up Treasure's covers, his heart went out to her and he made a show of tucking her in and kissing her good-night.

Kids had great powers of regeneration, Cole thought as he circled around to Benji. It was Holly who wasn't forgiving him. Benji was healing physically, too. "That eye looks better, kid."

Benji grinned. Even though he'd lost the fight with Nicky, he was proud of the shiner. "Your stitches look great, too," Benji said.

Cole chuckled. "Thanks." He tousled Benji's hair, kissed his forehead, then switched off the light. "'Night, kids."

"'Night, Daddy."

Daddy? The word seemed to bounce in the dark room, echoing off the walls. Suddenly, the light from the hallway looked strange and overly bright.

Something's wrong.

Cole left the bedroom door ajar, allowing a crack of light for the kids, then he leaned against the wall in the hallway, shut his eyes and pressed a finger to his temple.

"Cole," Holly whispered in alarm. "Are you all right?"

He tried to ask Holly to stay still, but the quick wave of his hand came out as a bold, practiced flourish. *A magician's movements.*

But of course he was a magician. He'd been a hobbyist for years.

"Cole?" she whispered again.

"Just wait a minute," he whispered back.

He felt her palms on his chest, resting against his pectorals, her fingers stretching toward his shoulders. He wanted to hold her, but he had to concentrate. All day he'd wrestled with the strangest sensations. Small things had niggled at his mind. Like the grease stain on his good navy coat. It was shaped like a lug wrench, but he knew he'd never wear such a good coat to work on a car. Usually, he had the common sense not to lie down on his wrenches, too.

And then there were the memories of his parents. No doubt, he'd thought of them over the years. But today the memories had flooded back. Maybe it was because he was with Holly and the kids. Safe in the bosom of his family, it hurt less to think about a family he'd lost, or about that Christmas in Weller's Falls years ago, after his father had died.

But what had happened then?

He kept remembering some beer joint, which was strange since he didn't drink much. Booze made his fingers move too slowly; sleights of hand became impossible. But he kept seeing the glare of a neon sign, the yellow paper stars taped to a jukebox. Every time the cash drawer opened, a cardboard Santa waved.

He remembered the mysterious blond woman, too. Just a tall figure wrapped in fog and an elegant camel hair steamer coat, her face unclear.

Cole sighed and opened his eyes. Holly was staring at him with such an expression of concern that he smiled. Catching her hand, he curled it on his chest, next to his heart.

"I'm okay," he whispered.

She frowned. "I don't think you are."

She looked so upset that she could have been personally responsible for his injured state. His eyes drifted over her face. Every time he looked at her, he discovered something new. It was almost as if he'd never even seen her before yesterday.

She licked her lips, moistening her wide, naturally red mouth and making it glisten. He'd never seen brown eyes so soft and warm and inviting. Lifting his free hand, he brushed tendrils of hair from her forehead. Very softly, he said, "I guess I'd better lie down."

When alarm crept into her eyes, his temper flared. Not that he'd let her see it. But how could a woman who wanted him as much as she did keep denying herself? There was nothing to stop them, nothing to keep them apart.

"C'mon," he said gently. He pushed off the wall and pulled her down the hallway with him.

"I'd better finish cleaning," she said.

"I already did. And the fire's out. At least the one downstairs." The one inside *him* was burning strong.

As they entered their bedroom, he twirled her around in a lithe movement that landed her right where he wanted her—in the bed.

"Cole," she said sharply.

He fought to keep the raggedness from his voice. "What?"

"Don't."

He rolled away, but he kept hold of her wrist. Placing a pillow behind his head, he settled her into the crook of his shoulder, so she had no choice but to curl her head against his chest. Because her closeness had kept fire in his blood all day—alive and hot—his voice turned harder, terser than he'd meant it to be. "Let me make love to you."

"I . . . I'm just not ready."

"But I am." He drew her closer still, willing her to feel the hard pressure of his thighs against her legs, the tense muscles of his arms as they circled her back more tightly.

"I know you are," she said, her voice strained.

"You can't punish me forever." But even as he said it, he knew she wasn't punishing him at all. She might not be making love to him, but her pliant body was melting in his arms. She was made for him. She was magic itself.

Against her will she molded to each inch of him. "I'll only punish you a few days longer," she promised.

"Really?" he asked huskily.

"Yeah," she whispered.

Then they merely lay there, with him wishing she'd let him love her. The heat of her wasn't enough. It burned down the length of him, but he wanted so much more. He wanted her lips against his cheeks, her arms around his neck, her thighs around his hips. But it was almost as if he were forbidden.

"I'm proud of the kids," she finally ventured, her voice strangled.

"Hmm?"

She shrugged. "The way they put everybody on their Christmas lists, not just themselves."

"I can't believe Jonathan and Maggie are actually flying out here on Saturday." When Holly said nothing, he glanced down and realized she was gazing at him tenderly.

"That's all your doing," she said.

"Why did you put up such a fight when I gave the money to the kids?"

She sighed. "I just didn't want you spending the money."

"It's more than that."

Her eyes flitted around, as if she weren't quite sure what to say. "Well...Benji wanted a puppy and...I don't have the money for it."

Cole's chest constricted. He'd had no idea he was depriving Benji of something. The whole family had gone to the airport tonight and nearly spent Cole's last dollar. Until now the pleasure on Treasure's and Benji's faces as they'd purchased the tickets had been worth every cent. "Why didn't you tell me?"

There was a long pause. "I just didn't."

There was no excuse for the lack of communication between him and Holly. Still, she sounded so miserable that he decided not to mention it. "It'll work out."

"How so?"

Her eyes were so earnest that his heart wrenched. "Because it's Christmas, sweetheart. Now c'mere."

"I'm already here," she whispered. Even though her body had warmed against his, she very definitely sounded as if she wished she were elsewhere.

He stared at her with all the intensity he could muster. "C'mon."

She watched him warily. "Why?"

He took in how the mussed tendrils of her hair curled on her cheeks. "Because I need to remember everything about us. Starting with our first kiss."

She swallowed hard. "But I really don't think—"

"If you don't want to talk about the past," he warned with a lazy smile, "we could always start on the future."

Holly's eyes widened. "What do you want to know?"

"Everything." He chuckled softly. "And if you tell me everything, I'll promise not to kiss you."

She became a little less tense. "Everything?"

He nodded. "Where we met, what you wore, how our first kiss tasted."

Holly hesitated for a moment. And then as he began to angle his lips toward hers she quickly said, "I'll start with the Christmas party where I first saw you...."

Chapter Seven

"Oh, c'mon," Holly whispered. Drawing aside a kitchen curtain, she peered anxiously into the snowy, early morning sky, then toward Stella's cottage. Holly had sent Cole and the kids to retrieve last night's dinner dishes, and the second they'd left, she'd riffled through the Triple-A atlas until she found Weller's Falls. Now she was calling the town's library.

It's early, but someone has to be there. After the many things that had transpired last night, Holly was more desperate than ever to discover Cole's origins.

"Library and Archives," a man suddenly snapped breathlessly. "This here's Mackey."

An image of the speaker leaped to Holly's mind: bearish, bespectacled and as ancient as the hills. "Uh, sir, I'm calling from West Virginia. My name's Holly."

"Well, Holly, hang on. It's snowin' up a storm and Louann—that's my wife—well, she couldn't find my rubbers. So, she said I had to take off my boots and put 'em by the heater first thing. She doesn't want me sick on Christmas."

In Weller's Falls, the phone receiver clunked on a hard surface. Holly tugged open her kitchen curtain another inch. *Good. Still no Cole.*

But there would be.

He was showing no signs of vanishing. And every moment he stayed, things became more complicated. For both her and the kids, the presence of such a strong, good-humored man was simply impossible to resist. She could only hope her suspicions were right and that he wasn't married.

This morning she'd glanced outside only to have Cole wave at her from the backyard. He wore jeans, a top hat and his freshly pressed black cape. While Holly doubted many men could get away with such an outfit, Cole had cut an arresting figure. Tall and stark in all that snow, he'd looked more like a shadow than a man. Only when she waved back at him had she sensed something was amiss.

Finally Cole had laughed. "No footprints."

Sure enough, he'd been surrounded by untouched snow. She was nearly convinced he'd floated to where he was standing—until she saw a nearby pine branch. Apparently, he'd swept away his prints, then flung the makeshift broom aside.

She'd smirked. "Oldest trick in the book."

His laughter filled the early morning air. "Ah, sweetheart, I could show you a few tricks that are far older."

She knew he could. Even worse, she wanted him to. Last night her mind had run wild as she'd spun their romantic past. She'd never thought of herself as creative, but with Cole so close, the kind of love story she'd dreamed about since she was a girl rolled right off her tongue. It was the love story she'd thought she was going to live with Bobby Samuels but never did. And it was the love story she'd begun to hope she could somehow live with Cole.

She'd told him that they'd met at a Christmas party near a vat of hot apple cider spiced with cinnamon. They'd danced to soft carols, her white-gloved hands skating over the lapels of his dark suit, the full skirt of her long red velvet gown swirling around his calves. Long after the music ended, they'd kept dancing. And later, inside an open sleigh with snowflakes glistening in their hair, Cole had held her close and they'd kissed for the very first time.

"Right then," she'd said, "we knew we belonged together, Cole." She'd explained that it was as if they'd met somewhere before. Because when they kissed, it felt like a memory. And with that one kiss, they remembered they'd loved each other forever.

Of course, it was all a lie.

But it *felt* true. And maybe that was the important thing. Her first date with Cole might never have happened, but it was perfect. And it would always remain the most magical night of Holly's life.

"Holly?"

Mackey's voice interrupted her reverie. Before the man could disappear again, Holly rushed on. "I need to locate an old acquaintance from Weller's Falls. His dad owned a gas station, so I'm hoping I can get a list of those in the area."

Mackey chuckled. "Well, there's only been two in all of Weller's Falls history. Nat Gringer's place and Rayburn and Son, which got sold to the current owner…oh, 'round about ten years ago."

Holly couldn't quite believe it. "Thank you."

"They don't call me an archivist for nothing. Lived here all my life, and I'm eighty-four come March."

Holly's lips twitched into a smile. "Do you know what happened to the Rayburn family?"

"Well, Nancy Rayburn died years ago and after Tim passed on, their son sold the garage to take care of the bills. He wasn't but about twenty. Later I heard he got a logging job up near Watertown."

Holly's heart was racing. "Was his name Cole?"

"Why, yes..." Mackey's voice grew slow with memory. "Why, I do believe it was."

"Thanks so much," Holly said. Cole Rayburn had to be the man in her home. But how and when had he become Joe Ray Stardust? Her mouth went dry. "Did Cole ever marry?"

"Dorry Connery over at the high school would have to help you with that. She organizes the reunions. Want the number?"

"Please." Holly scribbled as Mackey dictated.

"Well, you have a fine Christmas." Mackey chuckled. "And if you're ever in town, drop by for coffee. Mine's a heck of a lot better than what Joe makes over at the bar."

Half wondering about Joe's bar, Holly smiled at the offer. *We ought to visit Weller's Falls.* That's what Cole had said. She imagined meeting the colorful Mackey, and decided having coffee with the archivist would probably be fun.

Within moments, she had Dorry Connery on the line. "So you see," Holly said wrapping things up, "I'm a...friend of Cole's and I thought I'd replace his lost high school year book as a Christmas gift."

"I've been looking for Cole Rayburn for years!" Dorry exclaimed. "He missed his five- and ten-year reunions, and I've always said I'd find him before the fifteenth. Well, if I send the yearbook by express, it'll arrive in plenty of time for Christmas. I'll include the information on the next reunion, too, and you can just drop me a check."

"Could you use my name and address on the return? Cole visits frequently, and I'd hate to have him suspect..."

"Of course!"

Holly glanced through the window. The kids and Cole were heading down the hill! Quickly rattling off her address, she watched Cole lift the kids, letting them hang from his arms like monkeys. They laughed as he swung them in circles.

"Do you know if Cole ever married?" Holly asked.

"I heard a rumor he didn't from one of his tenth-grade classmates," Dorry said. "But it could just be a rumor. Like I said, I've never tracked him down."

Just as Holly replaced the receiver, Cole and the kids breezed through the kitchen door. Cole's lazy smile reminded her of what she most wanted to forget—that she'd accidentally fallen asleep in his arms again last night. At least she'd kept her clothes on, she thought defensively, and she hadn't kissed him. Her settee was too small, and her only other alternative was to sleep on the floor, since Cole refused to leave the bed. Besides, with every breath, she became more convinced he wasn't really married.

He glanced at the phone. "Who was that?"

Holly's eyes darted from his kissable lips to his sparkling eyes. Her mind raced. "Uh..."

Cole grinned. "Was it about my Christmas present?"

She nodded. After all, in a way it was. If his picture matched the one in the yearbook, then this man really was Cole Rayburn, son of a car mechanic from upstate New York. And if everything about his life was a lie, then it stood to reason he wasn't married, either.

And if he wasn't married, Cole might well get what he seemed to want most for Christmas—her.

COLE HAD INSISTED on driving to the day care party, and Holly could only hope no one would recognize him. Next to him, she readjusted her festive red scarf over her cream dress. When she reached into her shoulder bag to make sure she hadn't forgotten the Santa letters her fingers touched an unexpected object. She pulled it out.

"That red marker!" Treasure exclaimed from the back seat.

Cole shot the pen a peeved glance. With a wan, apologetic smile, Holly dropped the marker inside her pocketbook again. Cole had changed from his cape into his navy coat, but his top hat was between them in the front seat. And now, as if she'd had enough magic for one day, Holly squashed the hat so that it collapsed, becoming as round and flat as a pancake.

Benji pointed over the seat at a mailbox. "Stop!"

Treasure groaned. "We're gonna see Santa, so why do we gotta *mail* our letters?"

She had a point. "Maybe we should just take the letters to Santa," Holly said.

Cole shrugged. Parking beside the mailbox, he glanced into the rearview mirror. "Benji wants to drop them in the mail."

"Yeah." Benji sighed. "Just in case Santa forgets."

"I might forget," Cole said softly, as if reading Benji's mind, "but Santa never does."

"Then, Mommy, you gotta get out of the car," Treasure said, "but Daddy Cole can't."

Holly glanced at Treasure. "Why can't Cole come?"

Treasure sighed as if adults were the most slow-witted people she'd ever encountered. "Just 'cause."

Holly exchanged a curious glance with Cole, then helped the kids out of the car. Once they were on the sidewalk, she automatically leaned in front of them. With practiced maternal gestures, she tugged their mittens up, their hats down, and double checked their coat buttons.

Then she half walked, half lifted the kids the few snowy steps to the mailbox. Smiling downward, Holly's eyes roved over the unsealed envelope Treasure handed to her. In red ballpoint, in Cole's tidy print, the envelope simply said, "To Santa Claus, North Pole."

"Take out my letter," Treasure said with a smile, "'cause you gotta write sump'in."

Holly did as she was asked. With her glove, she rubbed a dry spot on top of the mailbox, so she could use it as a desk. Drawing the red marker from her bag, she said, "What do you want me to write?"

Treasure glanced toward the car and lowered her voice. "Tell Santa I want Daddy Cole's magic to come back."

Holly dutifully wrote the words, her heart swelling with pride. So many of the kids' Christmas wishes were for others. "There," she murmured, starting to refold the letter.

"And me 'n Benji want Daddy Cole to be our real Daddy," Treasure rushed on.

"But, Treasure," Holly began in protest. Over the top of her daughter's head, she could see Cole patiently waiting in the car. No doubt, this crazy charade would end the second they reached the day care center.

Someone was bound to identify him. Especially if he started practicing magic tricks, the way he had been all morning. On one pretense or another, Holly had tried to talk him out of coming, but the man was determined and obviously used to getting his way. At least he'd changed clothes, she thought dryly. After all, a top hat and cape were awfully unusual outerwear in Belle, West Virginia.

Suddenly she gulped. In the car, Cole shifted his weight in the seat, then he remained very still, with his fingertips pressed to his temples. Even from here, she was sure his eyebrows were furrowed in concentration, as if his missing memories were a mere hair's breadth away.

"Mommy," Treasure crooned. "I'm 'lowed to ask Santa Claus for whatever I want. Daddy Cole says so."

"Okay," Holly murmured. At the bottom of Treasure's letter, Holly carefully wrote, "I want Daddy Cole to be my real Daddy."

Then she sealed the envelope. One by one she lifted the kids, letting them deposit their letters in the mailbox, then she took them back to the car.

Benji refused to get inside. "Can't I see my puppy?" he said.

Cole got out of the car. "Do we have time?"

Holly glanced down the sidewalk. Pretty Pets was only a few doors away. The shop wouldn't be open, but the puppy would be in the window. Unless, of course, Mr. Warring had sold it. She glanced at her watch.

"Please?" Benji begged.

"Sure," she said with a smile. "C'mon."

The kids were on either side of her, and their mittened hands tightened around hers as if they were preparing for a long journey. Benji stretched his free hand upward and snuggled it into Cole's much larger palm. As the four of them walked hand in hand down the street, Holly caught a glimpse of their reflection in a store window.

They looked like a family. Her kids, with their dark hair and eyes, really could be Cole's. In fact, Benji's strong, square jaw was more like Cole's than Bobby's. And one day Treasure would probably have Cole's sculpted cheekbones, thick eyebrows and high forehead.

Just as they stopped in front of Pretty Pets, Holly shot Cole a long, veiled glance. *You keep forgetting your goal is to somehow cure this man without getting into trouble—not to find out whether or not he's married. Besides, once he remembers what you did to him, he's hardly going to be forgiving.*

"Isn't he great!" Benji exclaimed. "He's gonna make friends with Fuzzy. And he's named Hot Dog."

Above Holly, painted in canned snowflakes on the store window, were the words *Happy Holidays!* Below her, Benji was peering inside the window with rapt, reverent attention, his breath fogging the glass. The sleeping long-haired dachshund puppy was curled in a ball on a red-and-green plaid pillow inside a basket-style doggy bed. He wore a bright red collar, and his long, pointy nose was resting on his paws.

In the window on the opposite side of Pretty Pet's doorway was a little red electric train that Benji loved nearly as much as the puppy. Mr. Warring had kept the train running around the clock, so window shoppers could enjoy it during the off-hours.

Now, the train puttered on its looping track, weaving figure eights above a miniature town. Glitter-dusted, snow-white felt served as the ground, and Holly's eyes traced over the homey landscape: the tiny, steepled church, the neat rows of small plastic houses, the evergreens and box-woods. She realized Cole was watching the train, too, with such a thoughtful expression that her heart raced. Was he thinking of Weller's Falls, that small town from his past?

"Look, Mommy!" Benji pressed his palms against the window. "Hot Dog just woked up and smiled at me!"

She found herself grinning down at Hot Dog, who really did seem to be smiling. The puppy wrinkled his wet nose, yawned and thumped his tail.

"Don't worry," Benji crooned. "Santa's gonna come and get you outta that window for Chris'mis. And the reindeers'll drive you over to my house."

Holly's eyes traveled from the top of Benji's head to Cole. "What am I going to do?" she mouthed.

"We'll think of something," he mouthed back.

And she was sure they would. She'd erected so many emotional barriers during her marriage to Bobby; they'd closed around her like a steel cage. But Cole was like a superman. He'd grabbed those bars in tight fists and stretched them open. Married or not, he was setting her free again.

That seemed so good and true that Holly felt sure it was all right to care for Cole. Besides, she wasn't reacting to his sex appeal alone. She was reacting to the kindness she sensed in his heart.

"CUTE DECORATIONS," Cole commented.

"They really are," Holly murmured with relief, still unable to believe that none of the parents had recognized Cole. The female contingent had cast a few frankly appraising glances his way—and looks of envy in hers. Otherwise, nobody paid Cole much mind.

They'd arrived late, so the only chairs left were kid-size. Although Cole's lithe body had collapsed as easily as his top hat and folded right into the tiny seat next to Holly, it did draw attention to the fact that he was very much a man. Harshly, Holly reminded herself that this wasn't a date, then she glanced around.

Striped stockings, cardboard Santas and greeting messages hung from all the walls, and wrapped gifts were strewn beneath an artificial tree, which the kids were now decorating. Long, low-slung tables were littered with glue and childproof scissors, and at either end of the room, extra art supplies—ribbons, glitter and pipe cleaners—were up high on the shelves, out of the reach of tiny prying fingers.

For the past hour, while waiting for Santa to arrive, the children had been busy making ornaments. As soon as they were done, they'd hang them on the tree and start another. Because Benji had been so intent on making a bright yellow star for the top of their tree at home, his teacher had elected him to make an identical star for the tree here.

"Daddy Cole," said Benji, "after I talk to Santa, I'm gonna make you a star, too. Okay?"

Cole chuckled. "I'd rather be a regular guy than a star any day."

The word play went over Benji's head, but Holly quickly averted her gaze. It landed on Santa, who was now seated at a gold throne on a raised platform in front of the room.

"He's passable," Cole whispered.

Holly nodded. Santa was suitably heavy around the middle, with a genuine white beard and bushy eyebrows. A cameraman stood to the side, ready to snap pictures of the kids when they sat on Santa's knee.

"Go on, honey." Holly lightly tapped Benji's behind. "Go with Treasure."

"Santa Claus won't bite," Cole assured.

As Benji followed his sister toward the throne, Cole leaned close. The scent of mints and coffee, soap and fresh winter air wafted over Holly, and Cole's warm, enticing breath feathered against her ear, making her heart feel too big for her chest. It was horrible, probably even a sin, but she was starting to wish that Cole would never recover. She wished they could go on like this, living this absolutely wonderful lie.

Heaven knew, it was sweeter than any truth she'd ever known. And even though Cole's magic was scrambled, he still possessed more than most men. *Stop thinking like this, Holly. At least until you find proof that he's not married. If he is married, you're committing adultery in your heart.*

"Who's that woman in the red sweater?" he asked.

"Which one?"

"The one who keeps shooting you apologetic glances."

Holly followed Cole's gaze, and her eyes landed on a short-haired, thirty-something woman. "Nicky's mom."

Cole frowned. "That kid punched Benji's arm when we came in."

Holly sighed, forcing herself to be fair. "Benji was fine. And Nicky's mother reprimanded Nicky. She's actually very nice." Holly sent Cole a wicked glance. "Can the poor woman help it if she gave birth to a monster?"

"Guess not."

Cole slid an arm over the back of Holly's tiny seat, letting his fingers trail over her dress sleeve. Then he tilted his head and surveyed the red scarf around her neck. With a quick, practiced hand, he smoothed it so that it draped more attractively around her shoulders.

She shot him a wry smile. "You're definitely good with scarves."

"A scarf's only as good as the woman who's wearing it."

"Good?" She arched an eyebrow. "So, are you trying to determine whether I've been naughty or nice this year?"

"I already know you've been nice." Cole chuckled. "I just keep hoping you'll turn naughty."

She shook her head, wishing it wasn't so incredibly easy to flirt with this man. "But then Santa might take me off his gift list."

Cole's midnight eyes flickered over her. "Don't worry. I'd put you on mine."

Holly sighed. Cole just had to be single. She felt it deep down in her bones. But would she stake her emotional life on it? Or her good morals? She wanted him to hold her, caress her, make love to her. But what if she was wrong about his marital status?

She glanced at Cole again, just as his gaze flickered over her face, then slowly dropped down the column of her neck. "Your eyes are twinkling like Santa's," she couldn't help but murmur.

"Want me to guide your sleigh tonight?"

"That's Rudolph's job."

Cole clucked his tongue. "How could I win against competition like that?" He playfully leaned his shoulder against her.

"Get much closer and people will talk," she whispered.

He shrugged. "Let them."

"Look." She pointed, glad for the diversion.

The camera flashed as Treasure boldly walked across the raised platform and hopped onto Santa's knee. For long moments, Holly watched her daughter whisper to Santa. Benji was next. Holly's heart squeezed as she watched her son shyly approach the throne. *He needs a father figure, to help instill confidence.*

But soon enough, Benji was talking to Santa Claus with ease. When Holly looked at Cole again, her heart skipped a beat. Cole's face was full of pride—a father's pride.

Heavens, he really thinks he's Benji and Treasure's father. Oh, Holly, you've got to try to talk to him again. What was Cole going to do when he realized the truth? Worrying about it was put on hold when one of the fathers clapped Cole's shoulder.

"Cole?"

Cole glanced up. "Hmm?"

"Anyone ever tell you you look like Joe Ray Stardust?"

Holly inhaled sharply, but Cole simply said, "Every day of my life." As the parent continued past, Cole gave a soft grunt. "That Nicky kid just shoved Benji again."

Holly's gaze darted to Benji. He was fine but very quickly making his way back to her and Cole. "I'm going to have to talk to Nicky's mother again."

Cole shrugged. "It hasn't done any good so far."

"Nicky won't quit it!" Benji angrily seated himself next to Cole. "An he's bigger, so I can't hit him back."

Cole leaned next to Benji. "I've got a plan."

Holly strained, but she couldn't hear anything else. She did see hope spark in Benji's eyes, though. With her luck, Cole would suggest Benji learn fancy karate chops or something equally vile. She hardly wanted a five-year-old bully to mistreat her son, but she didn't want Benji to start fighting, either. Wishing she knew what was going on, she smiled down and smoothed Treasure's hair.

"Listen up, everybody." Mrs. Smithers, the day care teacher, waved from the front of the room, then beamed at Benji. "Benji's made the star for the top of our tree, and now, maybe his father will help him hang it."

His father. The words were still playing in Holly's mind when Cole rose. Benji tugged down the hem of his red sweater, carefully lifted his star ornament, then tucked his tiny hand into Cole's. Watching her son walk with Cole to the tree at the front of the room, Holly felt a vise tighten around her heart.

Then she frowned. Cole and Benji reached the tree—but then simply stood there. For Cole, the top branch was within easy reach. So, why didn't he take the star from Benji and hang it?

C'mon, Cole, she thought. The whole room fell so silent that you could hear a pin drop. Holly felt rather than saw Treasure crane her neck around. When she patted her daughter's shoulder in quick reassurance, Treasure turned toward the tree again.

Then Holly's heart dropped to her feet. It stopped beating only to pound back into action with such force that she felt faint.

I'm not really seeing this.

But she was.

Benji's feet—clad in their pint-size snow boots—were slowly but surely leaving the floor.

"That kid's levitating," one of the parents said in shock.

"Mommy..." Treasure whispered simply, her voice breathless.

Cole smiled as Benji magically floated toward the top of the tree, his small outstretched hand holding the large yellow star and his legs, clad in green corduroy pants, absently kicking the air as if to propel himself.

When Benji hung the star, Holly suddenly heard the soft sighs of children all around her. One or two of them quietly, reverently clapped their little hands.

Then, with all the confidence of a seasoned angel, Benji casually floated to the floor again. Cole took Benji's hand, and the two started toward their seats as if nothing out of the ordinary had occurred.

"Is that how reindeers do it, Benji?" one little girl cooed as he passed.

Benji winked his black eye. "It sure is, Janice."

Then Holly watched in surprise as her son's gaze swept down the long table and landed on Nicky. "Sometimes I make other people fly," Benji continued, "'specially if they're mean."

At the prospect of being sent heavenward like a balloon full of helium, Nicky looked more than a little worried. Holly realized Benji's troubles at day care were over. And that in Cole her son had found a hero.

Chapter Eight

Clutching the stick shift of her red Porsche, Glennis applied steady pressure to the gas pedal. The sports car shot through the tall, wrought-iron gates of the Joe Ray Stardust estate and along a straight avenue lined with evergreens. Iron lampposts tied with bright red ribbons whizzed past, until the Porsche burst through the trees and the stone mansion popped into view. Glennis zipped the car around a circular driveway and fountain, then screeched to a halt. Flicking off the ignition, she charged toward the front door, determined to find some clue as to Joe Ray's whereabouts. He'd missed a live taping and she'd had to rerun last year's Christmas show.

Midway to the door, she stopped and glanced over her shoulder, fighting the sensation that someone was following her. *No one's there.*

She proceeded to the porch, punching a security code into the numbered grid. In the black-and-white tiled entrance hall, she turned, her full-skirted red wool coat swirling around her. As she removed her black hat, scarf and gloves, an image of Fred James popped into her mind and she almost smiled. As usual, the man was lurking around the studio, flirting with her. Yesterday, under the pretense of possibly using Fred as a guest on the Joe Ray

Stardust show, she'd requisitioned some of his video-tapes. Fred was much cuter than Joe Ray, she'd decided. But then, of course, Fred lacked substance.

She sighed and glanced around. Then she set off, marching purposefully through guest rooms, sitting rooms, and walk-in closets. Her spirits flagged when she reached the master bedroom. *What are you doing here?* she wondered. *This place is just an elaborate theatrical set. No one lives here.*

Looking around, her heart thudded with panic. The Joe Ray Stardust mansion was nothing more than an oversize doll's house. Everything—the chairs and tables and fresh linens—were intricately made, but unused. In reality, Joe Ray lived quietly in a simple brownstone near the Rockefeller Center studio, coming and going through a very private back entrance. Although he'd only visited the estate a few times for photo ops, these closets were full of unworn clothes in his size. Each year, she decorated the place for the seasons and updated the wardrobes in the children's rooms.

The deception was necessary, of course. Everything was budgeted to the Joe Ray Stardust Show, and the place was ready to exhibit if nosy reporters ever questioned Joe Ray's cover story. But why had she bought Joe Ray's "wife's" clothes in her own size? It had been easier that way, but now it all seemed so crazy.

If this house belonged to anyone, it belonged to her, Glennis realized, not to Joe Ray. She'd chosen everything inside it, right down to the last light fixture. For years, she'd been building her career. And in the absence of a family life, she'd created this dream home.

Just the way you created a dream man in Joe Ray Stardust.

Maybe Joe Ray wasn't any more real than this house, she realized with dawning horror. She'd painstakingly compiled his background from research reports, so maybe the man she thought she loved really didn't exist at all.

Who was Joe Ray? Beyond the facade she'd created for the studio, what did she really know about the man who'd once called himself Cole Rayburn? Unsure of what exactly she'd hoped to find here, she suddenly pivoted, fleeing the master bedroom as if she'd seen a ghost.

At the bottom of the red-carpeted staircase, Fred James caught her in his arms. The strands of his golden hair were windblown, boyishly tousled above the collar of his gray, cashmere coat. "How did you get in here?" Glennis growled.

"Through the front door," Fred returned. "You left it open."

Her pulse raced. "How long have you been inside this house?" she demanded.

"Long enough to find out no one lives here."

Glennis gulped. "But Joe Ray—"

"I'm a tabloid reporter." Fred yanked her closer. "And it's my job to penetrate celebrity smoke screens."

"I don't know what you're talking about," she said in a strangled voice.

"I'll get to the bottom of this, Glennis," Fred assured. "And believe me, given your misguided feelings for Joe Ray, I'll take real pleasure in exposing him if he's some kind of fraud."

She gasped. "You can't—"

"Indeed I can." Fred scowled. "Why are you so attracted to him, anyway?"

Glennis's mind raced. "Joe Ray's so real . . ."

Fred rolled his eyes as he picked up the thread. "...So removed from the false world of entertaining stories and pretty illusions we live for in the television industry?"

She nodded, wondering if she could use her female wiles to throw Fred off Joe Ray's scent. "He has...substance."

"Or are you deluding yourself, fantasizing that Joe Ray has all the qualities you lack?"

Angry color flooded her cheeks. No man had ever talked to her this way. "Joe Ray's deep," she snapped.

"And I'm shallow?"

"No offense, Fred." She tried to wrench from his grasp. "But yes."

His slate eyes roved over her face. Lowering his voice, he said, "Hasn't it occurred to you that you're every bit as shallow as I am?"

"Unfortunately—" her eyes flashed fire "—yes."

Fred shot her a perfect smile. "So, don't you see..."

She stared at him warily. "What?"

Fred chuckled ever so softly. "That our mutual shallowness makes us the perfect couple?"

THROUGH THE OPEN DOOR of the Texaco station garage, Cole watched Holly's sedan putter along the snow-dusted road toward Jack Deegan and the island of pumps. She was probably getting gas so they could pick up Stella's son at the airport this evening.

I don't care how many good deeds Holly does, I'm definitely losing patience, Cole thought as he reached behind himself and closed the hood of Zeke's car. He wiped his hands and tossed the rag onto the car roof.

Yeah, everything about Holly was starting to annoy him. This morning, over breakfast, each of her tender smiles had made him want to kiss her and kill her—and he'd had no clue in which order.

Not that he'd done either. Instead, he'd merely studied her—how she bustled around the kitchen with the natural light from the windows dancing in her hair, her hips swaying to holiday music. She'd seemed to make a point of ignoring him, keeping her eyes fixed elsewhere and busily chattering with the kids.

But then Cole would catch her gaze. And her eyes would stroke him, stoking the fire within. Everything in her expression said she really wasn't avoiding him at all. She was merely engaging in that age-old, male-female dance of pursuit and escape, persuasion and avoidance. She wanted him, and the sexy way she bustled about her business was calculated to make him want her even more.

It was working, too. But he was getting sick and tired of being teased to distraction. Last night, when Holly had tried to sleep downstairs, he'd put his foot down again, demanding that she curl next to him in bed. Then he'd wished he hadn't. As usual, she'd insisted on wearing her clothes and on talking instead of making love. He'd told her what he could remember about his folks and Weller's Falls as she drifted. Then, once she'd fallen asleep, she tossed and turned against him, leaving him in agony, so he'd lain awake all night.

Today was no better. Holly parked beside the gas pumps and got out of the car, chatting with Jack. Bundled in her green down jacket, and wearing a long skirt and lace-up boots, she looked as cute as an elf. Her hair cascaded from beneath a white cap and the messy way it tumbled over her shoulders made Cole's fingers itch to touch the strands. When she waved at him, he felt so annoyed that he decided he wouldn't wave back.

But then he did.

Just as Holly started walking toward the garage, the kids tumbled out of the back seat. It looked as if they were begging Jack to give them their first lesson in how to pump gas. They really were great kids. The protective tenderness that welled inside Cole every time he looked at them was nothing less than a gift—and all he wanted this holiday season.

How could he have stayed away from them? Just looking at Benji and Treasure took Cole back through the years, to the time after he'd lost his mother. He'd been seven and he'd missed her so much. Now, it was inconceivable to Cole that he'd ever left his own kids. Why had he walked away from the one thing he was sure he wanted—a family? It made no sense. And for the life of him, Cole couldn't remember.

Leaning against the side of Zeke's car, he watched Holly approach. She carried a small brown paper bag in a mittened hand. The red umbrella in the other made Cole smile. Even though it was faded and had two exposed spokes, Holly was never without it when it snowed. Cole made a mental note to try to get her a new one for Christmas.

Then he wondered how he could have forgotten her. The closer he came to remembering things, the more he wanted her. Strangely, with every new glimpse into his past, he felt Holly slipping away as if regaining his memory would mean losing her. He didn't understand it.

She entered the garage, closing and shaking her umbrella. "Hey there," she said, sounding breathless from the thin, cold outside air.

"Hello." When Cole punched a button on the wall, bringing down the garage door, her eyebrows raised in surprise. He chuckled. "Just trapping you."

"Unfortunately, our timing's no better than the other day." Holly shot a quick smile over her shoulder. "The kids are right outside."

Cole wanted to take her in his arms, but he leaned against Zeke's car, refusing to beg for her affections. She was walking toward him with slow, measured steps, almost as if she knew he'd kiss her if she came too close. "Holly, I'm not sure a grown woman should rely on preschoolers to protect her."

She plunked her umbrella and brown paper bag on the hood of Zeke's car. "So, you admit I require protection?"

"From my clutches? Absolutely."

Her cheeks, already rosy from the winter air, deepened a shade. "Speaking of clutches, you said you'd look at mine, so I brought the car."

Nifty way to switch the subject. Didn't the woman know how much he wanted her? She'd stopped just within his arm's reach, close enough that he could smell her skin. His voice carried a hint of censure. "You sure know how to weasel out of certain conversations."

She simply smiled, nodding toward the bag on Zeke's hood. "The kids and I packed your lunch."

"Thanks." Unable to stop himself, Cole quickly slipped a hand around her slender waist and drew her against his body. He cupped her chin, then slid his palm around her neck and under her hat, until the dark strands of her hair spilled through his open fingers, teasing his fingertips.

The soft humming sound emanating from deep in her throat was pure music to his ears. As he widened his stance, letting her legs fall between his, Cole's eyes narrowed thoughtfully. Since he wanted her so much, why was he keeping some of his cards so close to the vest? "All day," he admitted slowly, "I've been having flashes of memory."

"You have?"

He gazed into her eyes—and into a maelstrom of warring emotions. Her irises held a dreamy quality. And panic. But she also looked like the cat who'd just swallowed the canary. With a sudden awareness, Cole felt sure she'd trapped him in a web of deceitful lies and secrets.

Yeah, there was definitely more to their relationship than met the eye. For an instant, he wondered if he'd been a tyrant in their marriage. Had he hurt her in some way... battered or abused her? But no, he couldn't imagine doing such a thing.

All Cole knew for certain was that increasingly haunting images ghosted through his consciousness: his hometown glimmering in the snowy twilight of a long-forgotten Christmas, the small house he'd once shared with his parents decorated for the holidays. He sighed. Needing to feel Holly's warmth, he tried to brush his lips across hers. Not that he succeeded.

She veered away. "You said you've had flashes..."

He nodded. "But I still have no memory of our relationship." *Or of the stories you told me about how we met. About our first kiss in the sleigh and what it meant to you.*

"Maybe you'll never remember," she ventured.

The wariness in her tone gave him pause. "You make it sound like you don't want me to."

"Maybe I don't."

Were things so bad between them that she wanted to start from scratch? But that didn't explain why she denied the physical aspect of their relationship. "I know you're not telling me everything, Holly," he said huskily. "But you've got to. I don't care what Dr. Kester said. Promise you won't hold anything back from me."

She sounded miserable. "I'm not."

"But you are," he returned softly. "Physically and emotionally. I can feel how you are in my arms...." She was trembling against him and it wasn't from the cold. In spite of the layers of their clothes, he could feel her leaning closer, longing to be held and loved and touched. Swiftly reaching between them, he unzipped her jacket and drew her nearer, so her breasts pressed hard against his chest.

God, if she only knew how badly he wanted to remember. All day he'd tried to concentrate, to force the past back into his consciousness. He wanted to remember everything they'd shared—each hot kiss and intimate caress. Each night they'd stripped, sleeping naked and twined in each others' arms.

He wanted to remember the kids, too. Was he at the hospital when they were born? Had he been around to see their first steps? Hell, he felt as if he'd go crazy if he didn't remember everything soon.

Holly leaned back in his embrace, seemingly intent on evading his lips, but he was so desperately starved for the taste of her that she hadn't a prayer. Cupping her chin and ignoring her resistance, his mouth descended, capturing hers with a surety only a husband could claim. Tender and moist and sweet, he drew out the kiss. And whenever she tried to move, he merely deepened it, tightening his hold on her.

He'd never forced a woman, but with this kiss, he wanted her to feel his emotion, his passion. So, time and time again, he parted her resistant lips. His tongue darted between them, then flickered inside her mouth like a flame. If she could feel that and still walk away, he thought, then so be it.

But she didn't go anywhere. Seemingly against her will, her arms, so tense before, relaxed and circled around his neck. Her thighs, so close to his, melted around his body. Or was that just his wishful thinking? When Cole felt her nipples constrict against his chest, one of his dexterous hands slid between their bodies to cup her breast. Against his back, the metal of Zeke's car was hard and cold, but against his front, Holly was so undeniably hot and yielding that a surge of awareness shot to his groin.

"How can you deny this?" he murmured raggedly against her mouth, hoping his searing lips would make her see reason. But even as he kissed her, tracing endless circles around her pebbled nipple with his thumb, the haunting images returned. The noisy city streets and taxis and the mysterious blond woman.

And then those annoying memories vanished again, and the kisses took Cole nowhere but deeper and deeper into Holly. With each touch of their lips, his short-term memories of the present seemed to be receding, too.

Everything disappeared—the garage, the kids, his boss. Cole didn't care where he made love to Holly. Right here and now was fine. He *had* to have her—and these kisses that lured him away from his senses, from reason, and from memories that he somehow knew were better left buried.

If you remember, you'll lose Holly.

It was a crazy thought. And when Cole heard it in the deepest recesses of his consciousness, he merely rolled his thumb over her hard taut nipple again and nipped at her lower lip, tasting the honeyed salt of her mouth that was tinged with coffee and peppermint. As he touched her, he willed himself to ignore those crazy voices in his head—and the now undeniable fact that Holly had turned into a wildcat, still fighting his loving ministrations every step of the way.

"Please stop," she gasped, batting at his shoulders. *"Stop!"*

He sighed and leaned back. "But you want me." He could read her desire plainly. Raw need was just under the surface of her skin, as visible as the vibrant ink of a tattoo. But she didn't intend to heed it.

"Please," she repeated breathlessly. "You're working."

Working you into a heated frenzy. "I sure am."

Her voice was husky. "And it's your first day on the job."

"No, Holly," he murmured, tightening his hold on her waist, "I've been working on making you want me for days." He'd wanted so much to feel her like this, warm and flush against him. Outside, one of the kids squealed and the sheer relief that flooded Holly's features made him furious all over again.

She inhaled sharply. "Like I said, I'm afraid our timing's no better than yesterday."

"Damn it." He tried to bite back his temper, but it was difficult when her lips were inches away and her legs were twined around his. "Holly, you're making it impossible for us to get any closer."

Her eyes widened. "But we've done so much together...."

"We've done a lot as a family, but I mean just you and me, Holly. And you know it."

Looking contrite, she cautiously splayed her hands on his chest. Heat spread from her fingertips, seeping through his clothes, shooting through his body. His skin quivered beneath her touch.

His voice turned gruff. "If you don't want sex from me, Holly, then what *do* you want?"

She flinched. Her face colored and she backed away a pace. "Why does everything have to be about sex?"

That was rich. "These past few days, sex hasn't even entered the picture," he said testily. "But I'm still a man."

"I know it," Holly burst out, sounding every bit as frustrated as he felt. "God, do I know it!"

"No," he shot back, "I think you've forgotten."

"You're the one who's forgotten!" she exclaimed hotly. And then, as if she'd said too much, she pivoted and stormed toward an interior door that led to the service counter. "Enjoy your lunch," she shouted over her shoulder.

"I will," he muttered. But he knew he wouldn't. As much as he didn't want to admit it, his fight with Holly would take every ounce of enjoyment right out of it.

"YOU'RE A BAD MAN, Silas Berry." Feeling miserable, he wheeled closer to the window and trained his binoculars toward Holly's living room again.

He just wished Holly and Cole hadn't invited him to the surprise party for Stella. He wanted to see Stella reunited with her son and daughter-in-law, of course. But watching an emotional homecoming scene when he was busy destroying Holly's family just wasn't right.

Throughout the day, he'd watched clean white snow fall, and in this evening's twilight, the blanket on the ground had turned a deep, dusky rose. It almost looked as if the snow were lit from beneath, by the fire at the earth's core.

Usually his thoughts weren't so poetic. But then, the cottages around him usually weren't so cozy and inviting, either. After his wife had passed on, there hadn't seemed to be much point in decorating. Now the sight warmed him. Every which way he looked, the Pine Cottage Estates had been transformed for Christmas.

Including Holly's place. When the mysterious man who called himself Cole had first come home this evening, he'd argued with Holly. But then the couple had reached a truce and begun readying the cottage for their guests.

Mostly, Holly stayed in the kitchen cooking. Cole built a roaring fire while the kids brought him mugs of warm beverages and cookies. Not a half hour ago, Cole had helped Benji hang a bright yellow star on the highest branch of their decorated tree.

Now, Holly appeared, her hand cupped beneath a long-handled wooden spoon. After sampling the concoction, Cole nodded his approval. Then Holly leaned past him and, with a perfunctory, maternal gesture, she straightened the stockings that hung along the mantel. As she vanished in the direction of the kitchen again, her wooden spoon waved in the air like a magic wand, and the kids clamored after her like helpful elves.

They sure looked like a family. But he knew they weren't. The man everyone thought was Holly's husband was an impostor. And now Jessica Samuels knew all about him, too.

No thanks to you, Silas.

Replacing the binoculars in the windowsill, he wished he'd never agreed to spy on Holly. The scene in her cottage was so homey that it was breaking his heart. Even worse, Irma and Zeke would be here at any minute. They said they'd help transport him to Holly's.

Yes, moments from now, he'd be right inside the same cozy little cottage he'd been spying on. No doubt, he'd be waited on hand and foot by the very people he was destroying, too. He could almost hear Holly. "Would you care for some of Linda's cider, Mr. Berry? Or what about Jumbo's spiked eggnog?"

Hearing footsteps on his porch, Mr. Berry tilted his head. Then the doorbell sounded, playing a few bars of "Greensleeves" in special holiday chimes.

He shook his head. When all was said and done and Jessica Samuels had Holly's kids, he could only hope his much-loved tenants at the Pine Cottage Estates would understand his motives and forgive him.

Chapter Nine

"Oh, I almost forgot—" Stella ran back inside her cottage, then returned to the porch and handed Holly an Express Mail package. "I signed for this while you were at the garage today."

Benji waved from the yard. "Hurry, Mrs. Lewis!"

"Yeah, hurry up!" urged Treasure.

Stella started down the porch stairs. "I'm coming, kids."

Holly avoided Cole's gaze and scanned the mail. Sure enough, the return address was her own, but the postmark was from New York. This had to be the yearbook. With a pang of conscience, she shoved it under her arm.

Cole stamped his snow-encrusted boots on Stella's porch. "Aren't you going to open it?"

Holly playfully arched an eyebrow. "Maybe there's a present inside."

Cole grinned. "Hope it's mine." As Holly descended the steps, he draped his arm casually across her shoulder and steered her around a patch of ice. "Still mad at me?"

Their tiff at the garage today had bothered her more than it should have. She'd stayed inside the station with the kids while Cole looked at her clutch, then without so much as a thank-you, she'd driven away—or tried. She was still shooting Cole her haughtiest glance when she'd slid into a ditch near the gas pumps.

Cole pushed her out, however sanctimoniously, but his every heave-ho was calculated to let her know she'd gotten just exactly what she deserved. By the time she got home, she'd been in such a huff that she'd promptly overcooked a batch of fudge and then lost her temper with the kids.

She cleared her throat. "I wasn't really mad."

It was a lie. But one look at Cole told her that she could never stay mad at him for long. Maybe that, more than anything, told her she was in love.

When exactly had it happened? And why? It wasn't just the arresting combination of Cole's rugged, down-home good looks and cultured, self-assured elegance, or how comfortable he was with the kids. All Holly knew was that this man had swept into her world and magically transformed it. And that she wanted him desperately and completely, body and soul. Wanted him in a way from which there'd be no turning back.

In Cole's long, tapered fingers, there was a true Midas touch. Every heart he touched turned to gold. While Holly's pockets were just as empty as they'd been the previous week, she felt richer in spirit. Cole might pull rabbits from hats and vanish in a swirl of scarves, but his true gift for magic went far deeper. Right to the heart—to *her* heart.

Holly glanced around the hills. Lights from all the cottages blazed brightly, even though not a soul was home. Looking at her own deceptively darkened house, Holly saw only the lights of the Christmas tree. Inside, the tenants were hiding with Jonathan and Maggie Lewis, waiting for Stella.

"Looks like no one's home," Cole commented softly.

His voice almost surprised Holly. Walking side by side, their bodies fit so snugly that she'd almost forgotten he was there. But of course he was. That fact made the air around her suddenly feel warmer than a summer's night, and she melted, her insides turning as warm and runny as syrup over hotcakes.

"I hope seeing Jonathan and Maggie makes Stella happy," Holly said, trying to fight her body's response to Cole.

"Me, too."

"If nothing else, maybe the visit will help increase her appetite. She's so thin."

Stella was carefully helping Benji and Treasure over the ice and snow. The kids were on either side of her, holding Stella's hands.

After a moment, Cole shot Holly a rueful smile. "You know, Holly, you've got to talk to me sometime. Our problems won't just go away."

They sure wouldn't. She glanced at Cole in the rosy, evening light, thinking he was definitely in his element in the twilight. Just looking at him made her think of those other magical times that were so right for fantasies—between waking and sleeping, dusk and dawn, day and night.

Yes, twilight was where Cole belonged. Because twilight was a between time and Cole was a man adrift in such a netherworld, lost between his two identities.

"It's so strange..." he said softly.

His tone had become almost dreamy, as if he'd read her shift in mood. She shoved her hands deep into the pockets of her down jacket for warmth. "What?"

He sighed. "Don't get upset, but...I swear, I don't feel like I've ever been married."

Even though adrenaline surged through Holly's blood, she stopped in her tracks. By sheer force of will, she clutched the yearbook more tightly, then put one foot in front of the other again. Her heart was racing, and she couldn't quite catch her breath. *I know he's not married. He can't be. But I just wish I could find out exactly what he remembers.*

"You don't remember . . ." her voice trailed off and she cleared her throat ". . . having a wife?"

Cole shook his head. "No matter how hard I try." His voice dropped an octave. "You'll think this sounds crazy, but . . . I remember bits and pieces of this whole other life. One without you and the kids. It's . . . it's like I had no family at all." He glanced at her with a trace of an apologetic smile. "And no . . . girlfriend. Like I was kind of a loner."

Holly's heart was beating so unnaturally hard that she felt faintly nauseated. She had to try to tell him the truth again, beginning with how she'd assaulted him. Maybe he'd even believe her this time—and forgive her. But when she parted her lips, an image of Jessica and Robert Samuels swam into her mind. They were getting into a dark sedan with Treasure and Benji, and the kids were waving goodbye.

"Were you going to say something?" Cole asked.

"No." Heavens, the man had an uncanny knack for reading her mind, and his surfacing memories were putting her nerves on edge. "So you feel like . . ."

His gaze drifted over her, as if to make sure he wasn't making her angry. "Like I've been off somewhere by myself."

They were passing Mr. Berry's house now, and the lights from the decorated spruce shined in the semidarkness. Tree branches waved in the winter wind creating shadows on Cole's face, rattling against window panes. That same wind kissed Holly's cheeks, making her imagine the touch of Cole's lips, then it circled the cottages and sang a winter song, so low and melodious that Cole's voice could have sung it.

"I won't judge you, Cole," she said simply. In fact, she wanted him to remember for the sake of his own health. And then she was terrified that he would.

He shook his head. "Last Christmas, I know...I'm sure I was alone. I can see a building...a brownstone on a busy street." His dark blue eyes lasered into hers. "I wasn't here last year, was I?"

"No." Her heart was hammering hard, making her chest hurt, drying her mouth. She wetted her lips, knowing they'd only chap in this wind. "Can you...see anything else?"

He sighed. "I'm *positive* I was alone on Christmas Day. But nothing's completely clear, just the feelings."

Cole's feelings were of loneliness. What she didn't read between the lines, she could see in his eyes. Bittersweet emotions flooded her, her heart breaking because of the Christmases he'd probably spent alone, her heart singing because she knew he wasn't married.

And she felt a spark of anger, too. Because beyond the Joe Ray Stardust facade was a very real man. This man right in front of her who was far too special to be so alone. Suddenly, she wanted to cling to him the way her kids did.

"Holly, why did you say we'd skip church tomorrow?" Cole asked. "And cancel Sunday dinner with your parents?"

The questions came out of the blue. *Because someone at church might recognize you, and because my parents know you're not my husband.* She just wished Cole hadn't overheard her phone conversations. A sudden rush of fear went through her. Had he also overheard her speaking to her lawyer? Danice had called to remind her of Tuesday's court date—as if Holly could ever forget. Danice had also suggested Holly bring the kids.

"Holly?"

Fortunately, they were nearing her cottage and there wasn't time for detailed explanations. The kids and Stella were already on the porch waving for them to hurry. "Well," Holly murmured, "my folks will be over on Christmas Day, so we'll see them then."

Cole's lips set in a grim expression. "You needn't spare my feelings," he muttered.

Clearly, he assumed he wasn't on good terms with her parents because of the way he'd treated her. Holly nearly groaned aloud. Heaven knew, she already felt bad enough about the wrongful impressions he had of their supposed marriage. "I just thought we might like to have dinner..."

His eyes fixed on hers. "Alone?"

It wasn't what she'd expected him to say, and she tried to ignore how her heart fluttered. "Exactly." She managed a quick smile. "Just you and me."

"Please, Mommy, open the door," Treasure pleaded from the porch.

As if to illustrate their dire straits, Benji grasped the cottage's front door knob, only to have it slip beneath his mittened hand when he tried to turn it.

"Hold your horses." With a chuckle, Cole stepped lithely to the porch, pushed open the door, then shooed everyone inside.

"It was awful nice of you folks to have me down for dinner," Stella said, in a thin voice. "I can't wait to see how you've decorated the place. Now, where's that light switch?"

"I'll get it," Holly said. In the darkness, she surreptitiously slid Cole's yearbook into the closet. Just as she flicked on the overhead light, she inhaled a deep breath of the potluck dinner the neighbors had brought.

For a split second, even the rustling of usual house sounds seemed to cease. Stella's eyes narrowed, as if she sensed that something wasn't right. Then bright colors— snatches of sweaters and coats—bobbed around them as people popped from their hiding places.

"Surprise!" everyone shouted.

Irma quickly wheeled Mr. Berry out from the kitchen. Jumbo Stirling, who was too bulky to hide, followed with Linda. Joyce and Mac Ryan, the newlyweds, stepped another pace away from where they'd been crouched behind the settee. Other neighbors appeared from under the living room table.

An expectant silence fell.

"Surprise?" Stella pushed her glasses more firmly against the bridge of her nose, then stared toward the kitchen doorway. "Why, Irma, you know it's not my birthday."

Holly smiled over the top of Stella's head, taking in Jonathan and Maggie, who were standing nervously in front of the Christmas tree. Jonathan was in his mid forties, with wire frame glasses, a few extra pounds and thinning brown hair. He had his arm around his new wife, an energetic redhead with ringlet curls and a pretty, round face.

Behind the couple, the tree was gorgeous. Cole had placed Benji's collection of birds' nests in the branches, as well as the birds Mr. Berry had given them. He'd nestled pine cones, sprays of pampas grass, and even a few browned leaves deep in the pine needles. Lights and the paper chain ringed the tree countless times, and Holly felt as if she'd just come upon it in some enchanted forest.

Gingerly, Holly placed her arm around Stella and kissed her papery cheek.

"What do you say, kids?" Holly said softly to Benji and Treasure.

"Merry Christmas, Mrs. Lewis!"

Gently, Holly grasped Stella's shoulders and slowly turned her to face the Christmas tree.

"Me 'n Benji helped Daddy Cole call 'em," Treasure announced proudly.

Stella glanced downward. "Call who, honey?"

But the question remained unanswered. Because Stella glanced up again and this time her eyes filled with instant tears. "Jonathan and Maggie?"

Jonathan nodded. "Merry Christmas, Mom."

Blindly, Stella staggered toward the tree. She embraced her daughter-in-law, then hugged her son. Soon all of them were brushing tears from their cheeks, apologies tumbling from their lips.

It was Jumbo Stirling who broke the mood. "Pardon my French, kids," the big man boomed. "But damn if I'm gonna start crying, too." With that, Jumbo turned on Holly's tape player and "Jingle Bell Rock" flooded the living room.

Some people laughed with Jonathan, Maggie and Stella. Others applauded. Holly turned to face Cole and gazed into his eyes, her own brimming with tears.

"Now, don't you cry," Cole whispered.

"Reunions always get to me."

He lifted a finger and brushed away a tear as it fell down her cheek. "I know I look like a tough guy," he whispered. "But family reunions get to me, too."

There was no doubt about which family Cole meant now—theirs. For a moment, Holly suspended disbelief.

Just like Stella's family, Holly, the kids and Cole were a long-lost family, and they'd been reunited, too.

"Your secret's safe with me," Holly found herself saying.

And she meant it. There'd been a time when she'd been prepared to use his past against him. Now he was positive he wasn't married and didn't have children. But whatever secrets Joe Ray Stardust had hidden from the world would remain secrets. For all his outward charisma, he was a private man and Holly would never expose him. No matter at what cost to herself, she decided fiercely.

As she ventured another glance at Stella, Holly felt tears threaten again. Stella had the look of a woman whose faith in Christmas miracles had just been restored.

"Oh, Cole," Holly said, "you're so special."

"So are you, Holly berry," he whispered back. "So are you."

"MR. BERRY?" Holly had been just about to take the yearbook from the closet and sneak it upstairs when her eyes caught those of her landlord.

"Yes, dear?" he said.

"I've got a bit of a problem." Somehow, watching Stella's reunion with Jonathan and Maggie made Holly feel as though she could ask for help. She seated herself on a stair, so she'd be at eye level with the older, distinguished man.

"What can I do for you?" he asked.

"Well..." In hushed tones, Holly told him about the pending court case with the Samuels. Finally, she finished by saying, "So my lawyer, Danice, wants a character witness to be present for me. Will you come?"

Mr. Berry looked stunned. "Well, I..." When he saw her face fall, he flushed bright red and rushed on. "Don't worry, dear. Oh, of course I'll do it."

"Thanks so much," Holly said. And then, as soon as she could, she sent him a final smile, surreptitiously took the yearbook from the closet and headed upstairs.

Finally, she thought, entering her bedroom.

Shutting the door tight, she leaned against it for good measure. Feeling like a thief in the night, she ripped open the package.

Here goes. She slipped out the yearbook and began riffling through it. Giving up, she found an index. There were three page numbers listed after the name Cole Rayburn.

"Forty-three," she murmured, quickly thumbing through the slick pages.

It was him.

Cole Rayburn and the man downstairs were one and the same. Joe Ray Stardust's entire cover story *was* a lie—including his marriage.

She sank to the floor and pressed her hand to her chest. How long had her heart been racing like this? She glanced over the pictures—a small head shot, a close-up of him in a football uniform and a shot of him pulling a dove from a top hat during a school talent show. *I can't believe it's the same man.*

Suddenly, Holly's head jerked to the side. Was someone coming? She grabbed the envelope, leaped to her feet and scurried to the far side of the bed. Kneeling, she lifted the quilt's edge, then slid the envelope and yearbook under the mattress. Feeling Joe Ray's wallet, she flushed. If the poor man stayed much longer, she was going to run out of space in which to hide things.

Just as she dropped the quilt, the door swung open.

"Sweetheart?" Cole said.

Still kneeling in the floor, she glanced up, fighting the guilty color that rose to her cheeks. "Just looking for a more comfortable pair of shoes," she lied. "I thought I might have left some under the bed."

Cole shot her a devilish grin. "Maybe you and I better look under the covers."

He was available. She knew it. And the newfound knowledge was warming her blood. "But it's Christmas," she couldn't help but tease, "and we're supposed to be good."

Cole lay on the bed, then stretched his long body across the mattress. He began to caress her hair, pushing the long strands away from her face. "Guess what?"

"What?"

Cole's fingers tangled in her chestnut waves, until his palm slid around her nape and he gently drew her closer. "I don't really care what Santa thinks of me this year," he confessed huskily, just before his demanding lips claimed hers.

Holly shut her eyes tight. And for the first time, she reveled in the sensations, letting her tongue tussle with his, not offering the slightest protest. Because Cole Rayburn wasn't married—which meant he could belong to her.

"BACK IN A SECOND."

"I'll be right here," Cole said.

With a lazy smile playing over his lips, Cole watched Holly carry their chili bowls out of the dimly lit living room and into the kitchen. He couldn't have taken his eyes off her if he'd tried—not last night at Stella's party or tonight. Beneath Holly's long olive skirt, her full hips swayed and her matching ribbed top, so unlike her bulkier sweaters, clung to her upper body, accentuating her slender waist and full breasts.

With a start, Cole realized that the sheer voluptuousness of his wife's curving figure was making him think of having more kids. Sure, he desperately wanted to get back in her bed. But he wanted a family life, too. He and Holly were still young and Benji and Treasure weren't even in school yet, so there was still time.

Cole stood, shoved his hands deep in his jeans pockets and stared at the Christmas tree. The twinkling lights, the red and green candles on the living room table and the crackling fire in the hearth provided the room's only illumination. "It Came Upon a Midnight Clear" was playing on the radio.

Yeah, he wanted more kids. So many feelings had returned over the last twenty-four hours, and he was sure of it. His elusive past seemed so close that he could reach out and touch it. He'd been lonely for a long time. He knew that now. But why hadn't he turned to Holly and the kids?

You might never know, Cole.

Maybe he didn't care. He was home with his family now. As he'd strained for his lost memories, he'd gotten close enough to know that he'd missed years of the kids' mischievous giggles and playful chatter. He'd missed get-togethers with neighbors and quiet dinners alone with Holly.

As he stared, almost unseeing, at the tree, every last Christmas he'd missed suddenly tore at his heart. He could never express his emotions, not the way Stella's son had. But Cole was glad he'd made it home where he belonged. Now there was only one last hurdle to leap: making Holly love him.

When she reentered the living room, Cole caught her in an embrace, one hand sliding around her slender waist, the fingers of the other twining through one of her hands. When she settled a hand on his shoulder, the warmth of her palm seeped through his shirt, sending waves of awareness across his skin. Somehow, his own body seemed more lithe and nimble than it had in days. *Forget Joe Ray Stardust,* he thought. *I feel like I could give Harry Houdini a run for his money tonight.*

He sighed with contentment. As he began to turn Holly in slow, graceful circles, he glanced at her. "You know why I don't care about the missing pieces to the puzzle of my mind?"

Holly's chin tilted downward and her eyes narrowed, lending her an air of mystery, but making her emotions unreadable. "No, why?"

"Because your body fits against me so perfectly." The snug fit was making him feel hot, almost edgy.

When Holly hummed a response, he drew her closer, sweeping his lips across hers. At nothing more than that feathery touch, he heard her breath catch. Lacing his fingers even more tightly through hers, he curled her hand against his chest. Her other hand drifted from his shoulder in a soft caress, then glided down his chest.

For a long time, they danced. Wherever he led, she naturally followed, so he shut his eyes and rested his cheek against hers. All week, he'd felt so sure of her rejection that he'd fought his physical responses to her—until last night. She hadn't held back when he'd kissed her during Stella's party.

Or tonight. Had Holly forgiven him? Something had changed. In her every movement, he could sense it and he let her warmth flood him until closed channels of desire deep inside him started to open like gates. As he inhaled the deepest breath of her he could, the tape segued into "White Christmas."

"I never knew a woman could feel so good," he murmured. *Or so right when she moves with me.* They danced in perfect rhythm. No matter how they moved, their limbs interlocked like puzzle pieces. Against his chest, her breasts felt so soft and full that he longed, as he always did, to caress them with his hands and lips and tongue.

"You don't feel so bad yourself," she murmured.

"Your attitude's sure changed since yesterday," he said in a low, rusty voice.

"Ah, Cole, a lot's happened since yesterday."

She sounded so dreamy that he leaned back momentarily, just long enough to look at her face—her glowing skin, her perfectly shaped eyebrows, her alluring wide lips. She smiled, pressed her cheek against his chest and shut her eyes tight.

"Like what?" he asked right before his lips captured hers again, the warm spear of his tongue tussling with hers.

"Just things," she murmured throatily against his mouth.

They may have been married, but each nuance of her, including the way she kissed, seemed new to Cole. He'd forgotten how she most liked to be touched, and every time his tongue dived between her lips, he learned a lesson. Unlacing their fingers, he drew her arms around him until he felt her hands clasp again, this time around his neck.

Gliding his arms around her waist, he gave himself over to pure physical sensation, his drifting mind wishing they could simply, magically vanish together. Liquid heat began to rise in his blood, flowing to the most intimate part of him, stirring his desire until he felt himself get hard.

"So what happened yesterday?" he whispered, bending even closer, letting her feel the full length of his tall frame against her. Her thigh naturally fell between his, grazing his building erection through his clothes as they danced, chafing him, driving him mad with wanting her.

Biting back a soft moan, his hands guided her so that she pressed even harder against him.

Lifting her gaze, she looked into his eyes. Her skin was flushed with the awareness of the undeniable heat building between them, and her voice revealed her emotion. Catching with desire, her words were so soft he could barely hear them. "I...I'm falling in love with you, Cole."

So, it's been so bad between us that you'd quit loving me. He drew a deep breath, the air feeling cool as it passed his teeth. "Good," he whispered softly, the mere brush of his tongue searing her lips like a sword drenched in fire. "I want you to fall in love with me, Holly, over and over again."

As his hands dropped from her waist, molding over the firm contours of her backside, he grew harder still. When he pressed her fully against his erection again, she inhaled sharply against his lips. As she arched toward him, the tips of her breasts constricted against his shirt.

Cole leaned away, just far enough that through her clingy olive top he could kiss her breasts. Taking one into his mouth, then the other, he ignored the taste of cotton and bit the constricted tips ever so gently. Then, over and over, with excruciating, agonizing slowness, he sponged the taut nipples with the pad of his tongue—kneading them, teasing them through her clothes, wetting them through the shirt until Holly gasped.

As she leaned farther back in his embrace, Cole felt her body turn less yielding and start to tense with her growing need. She arched her back over his arm and her mound came flush against him. His half-closed eyes dragged hungrily over her body—over the sleek flatness of her belly, the full rounded curves of her aroused breasts, the wet spots he'd left on her shirt—until desire pumped through his veins like quicksilver.

When he spoke, his voice was rough. "You're beautiful."

Like some goddess who'd let a poor servant look his fill, she returned fully to his embrace, and the desire he felt was more overpowering than any he'd ever imagined. He felt pent-up, cagey, as if he hadn't had a woman in years. And with hard, demanding kisses, he further stoked the fire that had already burned out of control.

The music was forgotten. His limbs barely moved in the dance, and against her mouth, he raggedly said, "I feel like I've been on a shelf forever."

Holly's voice was raspy. "A shelf?"

He kissed her once, hard. Then he moaned against her lips. "You just took me down and dusted me off, sweetheart."

Her hands slid over his hips. "If you're lucky, I'll polish, too."

When his hard, hungry mouth claimed hers again, her hands drifted around his waist. Fingers crept lightly over his backside with such tender touches that the muscles in his abdomen clenched and he thought he'd burst.

Forcing himself to think only of her pleasure, he rained fiery kisses over her cheek and down the slender column of her throat. Then he swiftly caught one of her hands and slipped it between them, dragging it over his zipper, curling her fingers around the hard length of him. "Don't be shy with me, Holly," he said gruffly. "I'm yours."

"I never felt like this...." she murmured. "The way you touch me..."

"Keep touching me," he whispered, his tongue plunging between her lips again, his quick hands lifting her skirt and sliding between her thighs, beneath the elastic of her panties. The minute he touched the melting core of her, he knew there was no turning back. She was so warm and wet, they had to go upstairs. Now. When he withdrew his hand, she moaned, sounding utterly bereft.

"Upstairs," he said simply. "We have to go up."

She nodded. Somehow, her face seemed stark in the dim light. Her eyes were round and wide, her lips wet and glistening, her nipples still pebbled beneath her top. She didn't move, so he took her hand and all but led her to their room.

Once they were inside, he shut the door tightly. Because he couldn't wait to touch her again, he merely leaned against the door and blindly drew her to him in the dark. As his hand splayed across her belly, her behind pressed hard against his front, and he trailed scalding kisses on her neck.

"What are you doing to me?" she gasped.

"Performing my best sleight of hand, luv." He barely registered that a faint British accent had crept into his tone, or that Holly tensed in his arms. Tracing fire over her breasts with his dexterous fingers, he lifted her skirt again, and touched her until she rocked against his groin and he was kissing her deeply, catching the cries and whimpers that could wake the kids.

"Shh..." he whispered as his eyes adjusted to the darkness. But he was unable to stop the soft sighs that rose to his own lips as his famous fingers shot inside her with lightning rapidity, then traced the nub of her desire. When she came, she emitted small pants and his mouth covered hers again, catching them.

Then he half dragged her to the bed, sprawling her across it. Lying her on her belly, he settled on top of her. And as he shucked his pants and briefs, she turned to face him, grasping his shoulders, her eyes full of need. With an attempt at a smile that faded when she glimpsed his naked body, she brokenly whispered, "I guess your magic's back."

Her voice was a barely audible croak, and he didn't know what she was talking about. Desire had taken such a hold over him that maybe he didn't even care. He merely lifted her skirt, not even bothering to remove it. His eyes settled on her panties, which had got caught between her knees. "Hmm?"

"Magic..." she murmured raggedly. "It sure worked on me that time."

"And it's about to work again."

Holly pressed her still-quivering legs together. "Let's wait a minute..."

He would have laughed if he didn't need her so badly. Instead, he ignored her and slid her panties the rest of the way down from her knees and said, "We haven't even started yet." Feeling her shaking knees against his palms, he urged them apart, then he settled between her legs, the creamy, silken skin of her thighs teasing the hair-roughened lengths of his.

"But... we need a condom."

"No," he said almost gruffly, "I know I'm fine..." He wasn't sure how, but he did know that. "You're my wife...."

And he had to feel her skin against his. He had to feel the warm enveloping slick softness of her as he entered her. Before she could protest again, he'd slid inside her with one slow torturous thrust that made her pull him close and moan against his shoulder. At the sound, he became a sword on fire; burning, he buried himself to the hilt.

"I have—have to—" she began pointlessly, breathlessly.

He silenced her with kisses. Over and over he thrust inside her, with slow steady strokes, until she moved with him.

Her voice was a strangled sigh. "I have to tell...tell you things."

If she could talk, more power to her. But the lights in Cole's mind were fading fast. Plunged into the netherworld of his own darkened consciousness, he felt he was half awake, half asleep. Images flew by—of faraway places and people he should remember. But he shut his eyes tighter and concentrated on holding back, on making Holly come again and again. "I love you," he whispered. "Ask me for anything."

Her voice seemed far away. "Anything?"

"I want to give you the world."

Then darkness edged around his mind. Time and time again, he drove deep inside her, never wanting this to end. When her legs tightened around his waist and the small palpitations of her body squeezed him, he felt right for the first time in days.

Rising to his knees, he cupped her bottom and lifted her against him. Then, he let himself go, spilling into her with a moan he could barely suppress, burying himself deep inside her velvet softness.

He felt years of tension lift from him as he sank his full weight on top of his wife again, then wrapped her tightly in his embrace. He felt so. . . free. All the shut down channels in his body opened wide, unhampered blood rushed to his head, and feelings—raw and real—circulated through him.

And then, still holding Holly tight, he remembered everything.

Chapter Ten

It was magical lovemaking, so potent and powerful that Holly had promptly fallen asleep in Cole's arms. In her heated dreams, she'd relived his every caress—from the innocent, whispery flutterings of his eyelashes against her cheeks to the dangerous, hot, honied drizzle of his tongue over her breasts. She'd awakened to fantasies that became realities again the instant she realized Cole remained wrapped around her like a blanket.

None of it was a dream.

It was real.

Holly had forced herself to slip from beneath the covers and don her flannel gown and robe. She'd kissed Cole awake, first with nothing more than the soft, firm pressure of her mouth, then with the light, moist flick of her tongue. In a soft murmur, she'd suggested Cole hop into the shower, then she'd come downstairs, her well-loved body feeling swollen all over. She felt so full and complete that it was as if she'd found a lost piece of her life and snapped it into place.

"Oh, darn," she whispered now, realizing she'd burned a batch of pancakes. She tossed them out, stirred the batter, then started over again. After a night with Cole Rayburn, it was hard to concentrate. But she had to. Today was her first day at Country Casuals, and she wanted to make a good impression.

When Benji and Treasure ran into the kitchen and seated themselves, Holly tilted her head. Not only had the shower quit running, but Cole had already dressed the kids, which was good since they were all running so late.

"Ready for breakfast?"

Benji crinkled his nose. "Do we gotta have burnt pancakes?"

Holly chuckled. "Of course not. I just started another batch."

"I bet I coulda eaten 'em burnt," Treasure offered.

"Sorry, honey, but it's too late." Holly blinked, reminding herself to pay attention before she burned this batch, too. But it was impossible. She had two kids with Bobby—two wonderful kids that she loved more than life. Nevertheless, last night made what she'd had with Bobby seem like child's play.

She flipped the pancakes, then glanced through the kitchen window. More snow had fallen. There wasn't a footprint in sight, so it was as if a whole new world had appeared. *Today marks a new beginning,* she thought. *Cole, the kids and I are going to share our lives.*

They would all find such happiness. With Cole, every day would be Christmas. They would raise the kids, maybe even have some more together. Soon, she and Cole would be laughing together about the crazy way they met, with her conking him over the head like something out of an old screwball comedy.

No, there'd be no repercussions for what she'd done. A man who loved her the way Cole had last night would more than forgive her, and a man who bonded with her kids the way he had wouldn't just walk away. No, after last night there was no turning back. God, she'd never known this kind of love existed. Never dreamed it would be hers.

She was ready for tomorrow, too. Danice could tell Judge Selsa that she had a good job. Thanks to Cole, the rent was paid. And Mr. Berry had agreed to appear as her character witness. Smiling, Holly lifted the frying pan, carried it to the table and slipped pancakes onto the kids' plates.

"Can't you flip 'em in the air?" Benji asked.

"Mommy can't," Treasure said, "but I bet Daddy Cole can."

"Can what?"

It was Cole. Holly tried to wipe the telltale grin off her face, but she failed. Even though he was wearing a plaid flannel work shirt, faded jeans and boots, the silver strands in his hair gleamed in the soft light of the kitchen and lent him an air of distinguished sophistication. His dark eyebrows formed perfect crescents over his eyes; his expression remained unreadable.

The man sure had a poker face. Probably, it came from years of using his expressions—or lack of them—to distract crowds while he performed magical sleights of hand or prepared to vanish. *Well, he won't be vanishing again any time soon.*

She imagined flinging her arms around his neck and burrowing her face against that soft flannel shirt while he whispered sweet nothings in her ear, his deep voice and deeper kisses sweeping her far away. "I'll finish your pancakes, then shower while you eat," she said. "I don't want to be late for work."

He nodded. "After we drop off the kids, I can take you to the mall."

Whatever he thought about last night, there was no hint of it in his voice. But registering the easy domesticity of their conversation, she smiled. "You need the car?"

"When things get slow at the garage, I'll finish working on the clutch."

Was it her imagination or had he sounded curt? She squinted at him but couldn't discern any change in his features. "How many pancakes do you want?"

"Two."

She chuckled. "Well, I'm making you three."

"So, I had a choice?"

Something in his tone cut through her denial, and her heart fluttered in panic. *Last night, he said he loved me, that he wanted to give me the world. But he used the word luv, too. His British accent seemed to come back. Had it? Had he remembered?* "What's that supposed to mean?"

Just as he was about to respond, the kids started begging him to perform for them. "You want to see a magic trick?" Cole said.

Seeing his easy smile, Holly felt both foolish and relieved. *Don't sabotage this relationship by reading too much into Cole's every word. Bobby was completely devious, and it's made you paranoid when it comes to men.*

With a soft sigh, she realized that if she wasn't careful, the kids would notice the change in her and Cole's relationship. Treasure and Benji were emotional weather vanes—one small shift in the wind and they'd start spinning. Soon enough they'd know Cole was here to stay, but Holly wasn't quite ready for all their questions yet.

Suddenly she felt Cole's eyes on her back. She automatically ran her hands over her robe, smoothing the fabric over her hips. She gave Cole his pancakes, then slid the fryer into a sink of sudsy water. When she turned around, Cole had covered his plate with a bright red scarf.

Benji and Treasure watched him expectantly.

"Say the magic word," he said.

"Abracadabra!" the kids squealed.

Cole whisked away the scarf. Beneath it, his pancakes had somehow magically drizzled themselves with melting butter and syrup.

Holly moved around the table again, coming to a standstill behind Cole's chair, her belly pressed against the warmth of his back. She thought of the thousand mornings in their future where she would feel this content. "Looks like your magic really is back."

"Sure does."

It wasn't just her imagination. Under Cole's silken voice ran a thread of steel. Her mouth went dry. "Is something wrong?"

He shot her a disarming smile. "Yep. You're running late and my breakfast is getting cold."

But it was more than that. And no amount of smiling could deactivate the alarm bells that now sounded in her head.

HE WAS JOE RAY STARDUST. He knew that now. Oh, he was Cole Rayburn, too. In fact, thanks to the woman beside him, he felt more like Cole than he had in years. Barely perceptibly, his fingers tightened on the steering wheel. Call it ego, but if nothing else, he simply couldn't believe no one had recognized—and rescued—him before now.

"I *know* something's wrong," Holly said, clearly attempting to keep her tone light.

"Well, there isn't."

Except for the fact that he felt murderous. And that they were on a bridge above the Elk River. Just over a rail lay the Civic Center's icy, snow-patched parking lot and, in the distance, red and green lights on the trees near the Express Mall shone in the crisp, sunny morning.

Cole clenched his teeth, fixed his face into a granite mask and tried to keep his eyes trained on the road, but against his will, his gaze skated to the Civic Center lot, to the exact spot where Holly had clobbered him over the head.

Had she been trying to kill him? Or merely maim him? Feeling her eyes scanning his face, he somehow forced himself to casually drape an arm around her shoulders. He mustered his smoothest, most seductive tone. "C'mere, Holly berry."

A smile teased her lips. Playfully, she tossed her head, making her wavy hair fly over either shoulder. "I'm already next to you."

He smiled back. "I want you closer."

With a relieved chuckle, she scooted against his side. "You're *sure* nothing's wrong?"

He gave her shoulder a quick squeeze. "Positive."

Staring through the windshield again, he felt her curious eyes latch onto his skin like hooks. In spite of her attempts to appear unconcerned, those eyes pleaded and searched, sensing that something had changed between them. *Quit watching me, Holly,* he thought. *Just let me go.*

But where was he going?

He wasn't sure. Only one thing was certain. He had to get away from her.

Oh, he'd been biding his time. Last night she hadn't even left him a choice. Hell, with her naked, sweating, trembling body still clinging to him, he'd been powerless to move. She was so hot and wet, like a damp, warm cloth applied to the wound of his years of loneliness.

He'd lain awake while she slept, telling himself to leave her, feeling unable to go. And all the while, waves of sensation—her soft lips and warm breath, the pressure of her thighs—buffetted against him.

Even now he could remember how it felt to be inside her. Even with the bulk of their coats between them, he could shudder from it. But why had the woman who'd cried such needy whimpers against his bare skin assaulted him? Battered him with a club in a lonely parking lot? Lied to him about their relationship?

And who was she? Some crazed fan? An ex-journalist in hiding?

Cole squinted through the windshield, as if he were concentrating on driving. He knew her. He could swear to it. But where had they met? She wasn't from Weller's Falls, and she'd never worked for the Joe Ray Stardust Show. Not that his head trauma had anything to do with his inability to remember. This was the usual kind of forgetfulness.

Everything else had come back. He could see Holly swing that croquet mallet. Hear the crack as it hit his skull. Feel the trickle of blood on his forehead. He even remembered how she'd dumped him into her trunk and driven away.

But why? Who is she? And what does she want from me?

Without warning, a stab of pain cut into his soul. It dug inside him, gouging a hole so deep he felt hollow. He had to fight not to lash out at her in fury. *Damn you.* His jaw set so rigidly that the telltale angry muscle in his cheek started to tick.

Not that it mattered. When it came to hiding his emotions, he'd had years of stage practice. Creating illusions was his livelihood. He could disassemble and rearrange the mask of his face with the speed of light. And for a full third of his life, he'd lived a lie, too. Oh, yeah, he thought dryly. In a battle of wills and cunning and lies, Holly didn't stand a chance.

One by one, Cole relaxed the muscles in his face, his back, his limbs. By degrees, the sparkle returned to his eyes. He grinned down at Holly. "Car warm enough for you, sweetheart?"

She smiled. "You're warmer."

When she snuggled against him, curling her head against his shoulder and sliding a hand along his thigh until it rested on his knee, he nearly flinched. Through the worn denim of his pants, he could feel each of her long fingers. The touch of betrayal stung even as it aroused, and he hated how his blood warmed to it, but he imagined stripping off his pants, feeling those fingers gliding along the bare skin of his leg.

Damn her, he thought again. *Damn her straight to hell.*

In the past, had he done something to her that made her seek out this kind of vengeance?

Well, whatever her initial motives for the assault, she'd fallen in love with him. Even if she hadn't told him so, the way she clung to him last night would have said it. So would the pleading in her eyes this morning. She was in love—and terrified he would discover the truth.

Holly's fingers rubbed maddening circles over the threadbare fabric of his jeans, from his knee to his thigh. He forced himself to smile at her again.

She smiled back.

But her eyes were full of guilt. Even worse, they begged him to forgive her. Not that he would. As soon as she got out of the car, he'd return to her house and ransack it. Within the hour, he meant to find out exactly who she was and what she wanted from him.

For now he'd simply ignore her clean scent and close proximity. Soon enough, those fingers that were so ten-

derly stroking his thigh would vanish, so would the unmistakable, traitorous response of·his body. But for a few
more torturous moments he could let her act as if his body
belonged to her.

Hell, he'd even respond. Later, it would be easy enough
to douse the fire. To forget his physical craving for her all
he'd need to do was think of her lies. Not only had she
pretended they were married and that he was the father of
her children, but she'd made him feel guilty for an affair
he'd never had.

What had Glennis been thinking all this time? he suddenly wondered. No doubt, she was livid when he'd missed
the live taping of Thursday night's show.

Serves her right.

Icy rage suddenly coursed through him. If Glennis
hadn't been so hell-bent on seducing him, maybe none of
this would have happened. Probably, when Holly bashed
his head, his overtaxed mind had used the opportunity to
conveniently check out of his complicated life. What had
Doc Kester said? Cases of traumatic amnesia usually oc-
cur when the mind wants a rest.

"What are you thinking?" Holly ventured.

"Not a thought in my head, sweetheart."

"There must be one."

If there was, I'm sure you'd have clobbered it out. He
smiled. "Nothing—other than that you're the prettiest
woman in the world."

"So you're happy?"

"Yeah." *As long as I don't think of the kids.* And he
wouldn't. He simply couldn't think of Benji and Treasure. How could Holly have let him think those kids were
his? *Turn off your mind. Don't think about them.*

Holly sweetly pecked his cheek. "You can go to the in-
door garage. They gave me a parking pass."

Cole nodded, turned into the building, then pulled alongside the attendant's booth. As Holly leaned past Cole to flash her parking card at the attendant, his mouth went bone dry. He desired her more than he'd ever desired anything. There was no denying it. Lord, why did he have to crave some wild woman who'd clubbed him over the head and played him for a fool?

Cole sighed as the attendant nodded them into the lot. "Where's Country Casuals?"

"Level two," Holly said.

He forced himself to draw her against him again as he wound around the parking garage and slid into a space. Through the double doors of the mall's second level, he could see an ATM. *Good.* Holly had to have hidden his credit and bank cards somewhere. When he found them, he could come back here and get cash. Not to mention a plane ticket, he realized, seeing the travel agent's office next door.

Suddenly, Holly grabbed his sleeve and yanked it hard. The movement was so unexpected that Cole actually did flinch. "What?"

"I lost my bracelet!"

Liar. You weren't wearing a bracelet, he thought. But he didn't want her to know he was on to her, so he followed her lead and leaned down to search the floor of the car. What was her hidden agenda now?

If only he was a fortune teller, instead of a magician, he thought. Then he'd know what her motives were, as well as what was going to happen in the near future. Would he wind up legally prosecuting her? Or simply leave her, vanishing without a trace? Maybe he'd stay and make love to her—again and again, not leaving until he was positive it would break her heart. *Don't kid yourself, Cole. It'll break her heart now.*

Next to him, Holly's distress over the nonexistent bracelet was so exaggerated that Cole had to fight not to roll his eyes. A vexed groan escaped from between her lips. "I don't see it anywhere," she said.

Cole swept his hand under his seat. "Me, neither."

Glancing into her eyes, he realized the worst thing he could do to her would be to use his money and power to take away her kids. But was he that angry?

He wasn't sure. All he knew was that he wanted revenge. And he wanted the truth. God knew, he wanted her—but that was a closed chapter.

Holly lifted her head and peeked over the dashboard, then she sat up. Following her gaze, his eyes narrowed. Obviously, she'd been hiding from an older couple who'd just passed.

"I sure hate losing that bracelet," Holly said, watching the man and woman with worried eyes.

Cole stared at the couple. The auburn-haired woman wore a fur coat. From beneath the man's well-made hat, gray hair was visible. He carried a cane and his overcoat and slacks were of fine wool.

Cole wanted to know the identity of the couple, but he merely shrugged. "When I get to work, I'll look for the bracelet again. I didn't notice it before, so what did it look like?"

"Oh—" Holly blushed. "It's a thin gold chain, with a..."

Lies sure rolled off the woman's tongue. "A couple of small beads on it," Cole couldn't help but suggest.

Holly nodded.

Thoroughly enjoying her discomfort, Cole shot her another quick smile. "Oh, I remember now. It's that one I got you for your last birthday, right?"

Holly swallowed so hard he could hear it. "Er...right."

He stared at her for a long assessing moment.

"Cole, please tell me what's wrong," she said in a rush. "Was it . . . was it the lovemaking?"

"Lord, no," he said swiftly. At least that much was the truth. Looking at her again, he wondered how eyes that soft and vulnerable could belong to a woman who was so deceptive. What she'd done to him last week couldn't be an accident. Otherwise, she have run inside the Civic Center for help. Glennis would have been contacted. Before she'd hit him, Holly had known who he was.

"So, making love was . . . really okay?"

She looked so sincere. He tried to remind himself that the woman could be pure poison. "Making love was better than okay," he admitted, thinking he wanted to be—*had* to be—deep inside her, just one more time before he ditched her cold. "No one else—" irony suddenly laced through his words "—has ever made me feel quite the way you have."

She looked terribly pleased with herself. "Really?"

He nodded, then glanced around. The lot was empty. As he brushed his lips across hers, he surreptitiously slid his hands beneath her sweater. Tracing quick circles over her bra, he felt her nipples harden beneath his touch. Lord, but it was tempting to simply drive away with her and take her in the back seat at some Lover's Point as if they were still teenagers. He'd waited years to want a woman the way he wanted her. Hell, he'd waited more than years. He'd waited his whole life.

"I love you so much," she murmured against his lips.

Everything in her voice said she was now sure that things were right between them. His intimate touch had convinced her. Right before his lips captured hers in a hard, bittersweet kiss, he whispered, "I love you, too, Holly."

And with all his heart, he wished he was lying.

"YEAH, I KNOW, JACK—" As Cole wedged the phone receiver between his ear and shoulder, he halfheartedly feigned a cough. "I know you need me, but this cold just came on."

"You definitely think you'll be in the day after Christmas, though?" Jack Deegan said hopefully.

Not on your life. "Sure."

"Great," Jack continued, sounding relieved, "I know it's Christmas Eve, but that feller with the fancy sports car came back. You know, the one who came Saturday for gas and kept saying you looked like...whosit?"

This was so bad it was good. "Joe Ray Stardust?"

"Yeah," Jack said. "And he's somebody famous, right?"

"Right." Cole half listened as Jack started giving him a rambling description of the customer's troubled Jaguar.

While Jack talked, Cole found himself damning not only Holly, but every blessed soul in this lousy backwoods town who seemed to need something from him. No matter how he tried to deny it, the Pine Cottage Estates had been transformed since his arrival last week. Houses were decorated inside and out. From the roadside, the new sign gleamed. And eight hours on the job with Jack Deegan told Cole that the man needed a mechanic who knew late-model cars.

This was apparently the first morning of Benji's short little life that he hadn't dreaded going to day care, too. When Cole dropped off the kids, they'd flung their arms around his neck and kissed him as if they'd never see him again. *Which they won't.*

"Thanks so much for making me float, Daddy Cole," Benji had whispered before he'd merrily fled for the doors.

Cole's chest got tight. He had no idea how Holly had roped Benji and Treasure into whatever scheme she was trying to pull, but those poor kids needed a father so badly that they'd latched right on to him.

Don't you dare start thinking about those kids, Cole.

"So, Cole, what do you think?"

He sighed. "Hate to tell you this, Jack, but it's the transmission."

Jack groaned. "These newfangled cars. It's all electronics nowadays. Well, I'll just tell that feller you're comin' in the day after Christmas."

Cole didn't have the heart to tell the man otherwise. "Fine."

Hell, he realized as he hung up, he almost would rather work for Jack than Glennis. He'd always loved cars, and he hadn't seen the insides of a top-of-the-line Jaguar for years. He owned one, but he'd never once worked on it himself.

And he should have. He should never have let go of Cole Rayburn—that simple guy who loved cars and women and the woods. He knew that now. Just as he knew that Holly was the only woman he'd ever want.

Years ago, on that cold Christmas Eve night in Joe's Stardust Bar, she was the woman he'd been dreaming of. After he started his logging job up near Watertown, they were going to meet. He was going to build her a little cabin in the woods with his bare hands. And then they were going to settle down. Start a family.

Maybe he really had never seen Holly before. Maybe they'd only met in his dreams. Or in hers. He shook his head, remembering how she'd described their first kiss in the Christmas sleigh in the snow. It was nothing more than a fantasy. But it had felt so real. God, he loved magic. And he was good at it. But all he'd ever really wanted, he realized, was a simple life with kids and a woman like Holly.

"Not with a woman *like* Holly," he muttered. "With Holly."

Feeling furious again, he looked around. He'd explored every drawer and cabinet and he'd come no closer to figuring out why Holly had hidden him here instead of helping him.

He'd searched more meticulously than he wanted to admit, hoping to find something to exonerate her, hoping some altruistic motive had driven her to treat him the way she had. But this time, the master of illusion had been had. Cole hadn't a clue as to what in his relationship with Holly was true and what was lies. But he'd found damning evidence she was dangerous.

Upstairs, hidden under her mattress next to his wallet, were his high school yearbook and the Express Mail envelope she'd recently received. Conveniently, the Joe Ray Stardust roadie jacket had disappeared, so Cole had no idea what size it had been, or whether it belonged to Holly or someone else.

He shoved himself off the counter and headed upstairs for the last time. None of this made sense. A peek into her checkbook proved she really was broke. But if she was so dishonest, why hadn't she tried to use his bank or credit cards? Was she waiting for his memory to return, so that she could blackmail him? Or did she want to sell the information about his dual identity to one of the tabloid TV shows?

If so, she'd definitely find buyers, Cole thought grimly. There were plenty of bloodthirsty newshounds, people like Fred James who was always chasing Glennis. Reaching the top of the stairs, Cole headed toward Holly's bedroom again, hoping another trip there would turn up something new.

Our room. He tried to shove aside the thought as he crossed the threshold, but his eyes panned the bed. Reliving their lovemaking, he could see Holly fully naked, lying across the mattress, her skin damp with perspiration, her eyes dark with need.

Then, opening a drawer, Cole lightly traced his fingers over the men's clothes inside as if he were a psychic who could name the owner by just touching the cloth. No doubt, the clothes belonged to Holly's boyfriend or husband . . . to Benji and Treasure's real father.

Daddy Cole. He could hear Treasure croon the words. Who was the little girl's other daddy? Surely, whoever had worn these clothes was long gone. That's why they were musty, dusty and smelled of moth balls.

Quit torturing yourself. Abruptly, Cole shut the drawer. Then he snatched his wallet from where he'd left it on the mattress and shoved it into his back pocket. Leaning down, almost against his will, he leafed through the yearbook, recognizing faces he hadn't thought of in years.

And then he slammed the book shut. *To hell with this. To hell with pasts that are over. Cole Rayburn is history. And so is Holly Hawkes.*

"I'm outta here," he muttered.

But when he reached the kids' room, he stopped. His eyes scanned past the rabbit he'd given them, then fixed on Treasure's heart-shaped clock. Cole's heart wrenched. *You never did find out if she could tell time.* Suddenly, it seemed very important that he know. In the silence, he could hear the clock ticking.

Time's running out.

And so am I. He started walking again, this time toward the front door.

He'd given Holly every chance. He'd searched the house. And all he'd found was proof that she'd been researching his life in Weller's Falls. Whoever Holly was, she was dangerous.

He loved her. And yeah, he'd waited all his life for her. But he was Joe Ray Stardust. And he'd never let her destroy him.

FRED BREEZED INTO Glennis's office. "Are you sitting down?"

Glennis was reclining in her swivel chair, with her feet propped on her desk and her high heels crossed at the ankles. "What do you think?"

"That you've got the greatest legs in New York. Maybe in the world."

Narrowing her eyes, Glennis glanced behind her at the floor-to-ceiling windows that looked out over Rockefeller Center. It was early evening and the Christmas tree lights shone. Below, ice skaters circled the rink.

What was she going to do about Fred? He seemed as determined to win her affection as he was to expose Joe Ray. She told herself she was encouraging his flirtation, but only as damage control so she could better beg Fred not to expose Joe Ray if it came to that. And yet, she was starting to feel strangely drawn to Fred....

He came around her desk and seated himself on top of it. "I have a lead," he said.

Glennis sat up so quickly that she nearly knocked Fred aside. Ignoring his look of censure, she said, "A lead on Joe Ray?"

Fred nodded, looking none too happy about her reaction. "I think he's still in West Virginia. My research team had two phone calls saying he's been spotted working at a gas station."

"I don't want you pursuing your investigation of him, Fred," she said adamantly.

"Too bad," he shot back.

She sighed, feeling resigned and wanting any information Fred had. "A gas station," she repeated, knowing such a seemingly unlikely thing was possible.

"And get this," Fred continued, "we have a witness who says she saw an unidentified woman hit Joe Ray with a club in the Civic Center parking lot the night he performed."

Glennis gasped. Then she pummelled Fred with rapid-fire questions. "Was he injured? Is he all right? Did your staff call all the hospitals?" She realized Fred's expression was turning hard. "Why are you looking at me like that?"

"You keep forgetting that when I find Joe Ray Stardust, I intend to blow his cover story sky-high."

Glennis was afraid it would come to this. Over the past few days, Fred had guessed nearly everything—including the fact that Joe Ray wasn't really married. She reached out and gently caressed Fred's shoulder. "You can't," she murmured softly. "For my sake . . ."

"That's exactly why I'm doing it."

Glennis squinted at him. "What do you mean by that?"

"Without a career, maybe you'll start thinking of serious dating. And of someone other than Joe Ray."

Glennis crossed her arms. "Don't count on it."

"Just get your coat, Glennis."

She didn't budge. "Why?"

Fred sighed. "Between the way the snow's coming down and the fact that most of the airlines are booked, we probably won't get a flight out of here. Maybe I can win your heart by driving you down to West Virginia."

Glennis didn't budge. "I'm not going anywhere with you, Fred."

"Then I'll go alone. And, like I said, I mean to expose Joe Ray when I find him."

Glennis sighed, wishing Fred would quit playing hardball, and that she could find a way to protect Joe Ray. Then, glaring at Fred, she rose and grabbed her coat.

Chapter Eleven

When Cole dropped her off, it had been a close call, but now Holly didn't even care if she ran into the Samuels again. Her heart was soaring. She'd been wrong to suspect Cole was angry this morning. He loved her.

She had an hour for lunch, so she strolled through the mall toward a toy store, smiling and remembering how Cole had come on to her in the car. The quick heat of his demanding mouth and the agonizing flick of his fingers across her breasts had assured her he more than wanted her. The man couldn't live without her.

And she couldn't live without him.

Fighting a flush, she forced her mind off Cole and the sensations his suggestive touch aroused. The owner of Country Casuals had given her a partial advance on her first check, so she could buy a few more things for the kids. Since Pretty Pets was always open on weekends, they were closed on Mondays even during holiday seasons, but tomorrow Holly could get Benji's puppy.

Hearing a sudden squeal behind her, Holly turned and caught a glimpse of big hair and bright bracelets. Two teenagers were seated on a bench.

"Should we go back and get his autograph?"

"I don't think it's really him, so you have to ask."

"I *know* it's Joe Ray Stardust. And I'd faint if I asked. You ask. C'mon, he's standing right by the money machine."

Holly's heart pounded hard. Automatically, she smoothed her red sweater over her skirt, then readjusted the strap of her shoulder bag, as if gaining complete control over her outfit might help her master the situation with Cole. *Don't panic. He came back to take me to lunch, that's all.*

But deep in her heart she knew better. Cole—a.k.a. Joe Ray Stardust—had found out the truth. She felt it with the terrifying force of a revelation.

It's all over, Holly.

With raw-boned fear nipping at her heels and a surge of adrenaline rushing through her blood, Holly sped her steps to a near run. Tears stung her eyes and everything blurred—silver and gold tinsel, red and green bulbs, the faces of passersby and the lights and ornaments on the tree in the mall's center.

She backhandedly swiped her cheeks and tried to take a deep breath, but her heart kept beating too hard, hammering in her chest. Everything seemed too loud—the conversational chatter, the Christmas carols pouring from a music store. *Please, I can't lose this man!*

Rounding a corner, she froze. Panic made the blood in her veins turn to ice. Even from this distance, she could see that Cole was still at the ATM and that a stack of bills was shooting from the machine. She watched in horror as he scooped up the money, slipped it into his clip, then retrieved a bank card.

His cards were under my mattress.

Her heart still thudding dangerously, Holly inched backward, needing to think. There were countless stores between them. Should she confront him—or run? Clearly,

Cole's memory had returned, and he'd searched her house, finding his belongings. But how long had he been deceiving her? And had he returned to the mall only to use the ATM or to see her?

She'd almost backed around the corner when he glanced up—and right into her eyes. Nearly tripping over her feet, Holly flung out her hand, but only caught the air. Even as she steadied herself, she knew she'd never really regain her balance. Not with those midnight eyes piercing her soul.

Maybe he thought, "abracadabra." Because, as if by one of his sleights of hand, the mall vanished. Nothing more than clean, gleaming reflective surfaces surrounded Holly. And in all that white light she saw only those eyes.

They were such a deep blue they were nearly black—like the midnight sky lit by a million stars, or sapphires surrounded by razor sharp diamonds. They carried such a look of calm fury that Holly's knees turned liquid. *Take the upper hand, or you'll lose him.*

"He's so dreamy."

It was one of the teenagers. They were behind Holly again. She'd better get to him before they did. Better to be on the offensive than the defensive.

Lifting her chin, she strode decisively toward Cole, her eyes drifting over his open navy coat and his broad chest. She wanted nothing more than to press her face against the worn, soft flannel of his old plaid shirt. *He loves you. He said he loves you. If it's true, nothing will change that.*

But the closer she got, the more veiled those eyes became. By degrees, the fury left them, until they were as blank as a moonless, starless night, as black as coal.

He said he loved you, but he's not even going to give you the benefit of the doubt. At the realization, her temper flared. Heaven only knew what he was thinking about her and the kids.

The fact that he didn't bother to move, but merely waited for her was unsettling, too. So were those watchful eyes and the wry quirk of his mouth. Well, two could play at this game. Stopping in front of him, she lightly tossed her hair over her shoulder, looking not the least surprised that she'd caught him using his bank card, as if she'd suspected he'd known the truth for days.

"There are two young women behind me," she said coolly. "I think they want your autograph. So..." She trained her gaze away from the darkened bruise and stitches on his forehead, jerking her head toward the mall's double doors. "Maybe we should go outside to talk."

He arched an eyebrow. "To the parking lot?"

The reference to the Civic Center lot was clear. As much as she fought it, angry warmth flooded her limbs. Why didn't he simply ask her for the truth? She'd never meant to hit him. She met his gaze dead on. "The parking lot," she repeated. "That's what happens to be outside."

"Oh." His lips twisted into a quick, cynical smile. "I just figured you took all your victims to parking lots."

"That too," she snapped. Given his inability to hide his anger, his memory must have returned after he dropped her off this morning. She guessed every blessed missing piece of it had come back, too. She lowered her tone. "I guess you really think I'm some sort of..."

"Bruiser?" His gaze drifted over her, trailing slowly from her face, down her red sweater to her skirt—and it burned everywhere it touched.

When his midnight eyes returned to hers again, her lips parted in frank astonishment. "I really didn't mean to hit you."

"Joe Ray?" one of the teenagers called out.

His eyes never leaving Holly's, he shook his head. "Afraid you've found a look-alike. I'm not your man."

As the disappointed girls turned away, Holly thought, *He's my man.*

And to keep him, she'd somehow have to control her angry temperament. If not for her innate disposition, maybe she never would have reached for that mallet in the first place. Maybe she'd have had a meeting of the minds with the Samuelses, too.

The Samuelses. Glancing around, she tried to hide her sudden panic. "I simply refuse to have this conversation here."

Cole's humorless chuckle gave her absolutely no comfort. His eyes dared her to move, and his voice became a near drawl. "Trying to avoid someone?"

He'd read her like a book. Maybe the telepathy he'd displayed on stage was real. Or else she hadn't been as clever in the car this morning as she'd thought. "I have nothing to hide."

He glared at her. "And I do?"

Righteous anger welled within her as she thought of the mansion in Connecticut that was so probably empty, and of the adoring public he'd deceived. "I'd say so."

"Do you intend to blackmail me?"

So, this was what Cole really thought of her. Momentarily forgetting that she *had* considered resorting to blackmail, she lifted her chin a haughty notch. "Excuse me if I'd rather not make a public scene."

"My, my," he returned dryly, giving her the once-over, "haven't you turned imperious?"

She surveyed him. "Maybe."

With a soft grunt, Cole pivoted very deliberately on his heel and strode toward the double doors leading outside, leaving Holly to stare slack-jawed at his retreating back. Lord, but she was sorely tempted not to follow him.

Everything in that infuriating, leisurely gait said she wasn't worth so much as a backward glance, and each of his long-legged steps tweaked her temper. She told herself she didn't know which she felt more—anger over his condescending manner or fear because she might lose him. Fear won out. She trotted after him, hating herself for doing it, but feeling terrified he'd vanish.

She swallowed hard. If he did disappear, she'd never find him again. Right now, seeing him in his threadbare sexy jeans and old work boots, he almost looked like a regular, if unusually handsome, guy. He was simply Cole—the man she wanted, the man she loved.

But he was also Joe Ray Stardust. He was rich and famous, and the studio could keep him completely insulated from the public. The man probably lived under lock and key, in an unknown place as hard to penetrate as the boxes from which he escaped.

No, if Joe Ray Stardust didn't want company, he didn't get it. Never taking her eyes from his back, she watched his agile steps fly across the shiny tiled floor, then she pictured herself trying to call him. In her mind's eye, an imaginary telephone rang and rang.

Her heart ticked like a clock counting the milliseconds until he left her. Where did the man really live? she wondered. Certainly not alone in that huge stone mansion. No, the location of his real home was top secret. Even employees, such as Bobby, had believed what was apparently a bogus public relations biography. If Cole walked away from her, there was no address, no phone number, no mutual friends to call.

Up ahead, he pushed through the double doors that led outside—and she gasped. Her feet took flight and she broke into a full run, her pride forgotten. He couldn't vanish from her life. She needed him. Her kids needed him.

As if she were dying, the life she'd lived for the past week with Cole flashed before her eyes. She felt the heat of his naked skin burn down the length of her, saw the passion in his eyes light up her darkened bedroom when he kissed her, and heard the gentle timbre of his voice when he told her he loved her. She could see the decorated tree next to Mr. Berry's house, the new sign, the smile on Stella's face when she saw her son.

Damn it, her whole world had changed because of Cole Rayburn. Lover and magician, he'd brought her back to life, reawakened her emotions, levitated her and made her float on clouds. And while she'd robbed the man of his memory, he'd slowly but surely restored hers.

With every fiber of her being, Holly now remembered her own need to love a man, to love *him*. She longed to be held and caressed, to feel Cole's lips in her hair, to hear his soft voice murmur ever gentler words of desire. And for a terrifying, heart-stopping second, with nothing more than the sound of her own feet pounding hard in her ears, Holly was sure she couldn't catch him.

As she burst through the double doors and into the parking garage, an arctic blast hit her full force, reminding her that her jacket was inside Country Casuals.

But Cole was still here.

And that was all that mattered.

But does it matter to him? Holly stopped in her tracks. Cole was ambling casually toward her car; it faced an interior garage wall and was squeezed between a concrete column and an old blue Cadillac. It was a tight fit, and as Cole edged along the Cadillac toward the driver's door, she realized he had only come to the mall to use the ATM.

He's leaving me. Rage such as she'd never felt pumped through her. "He knew all along," she muttered. "Maybe he even lied when he said he loved me."

A tempestuous wind swirled around inside her—shaking her, not letting her go. Feeling irrational, she started running again. This time, she didn't stop until she'd stormed between her car and the Cadillac. As Cole slid the key into the door, she stared at him. "Were you even going to tell me you were leaving?"

Cole barely bothered to look at her. The cool disdain in his eyes told her the gentle, good-humored man she loved had vanished. In his stead had come someone else—this strong, silent man, this rich, powerful stranger.

"Sweetheart," he said in a deceptively gentle tone, "I just hate long, drawn-out goodbyes."

"Well, you're not going anywhere," she assured. "Because I mean to have this out."

"Do you, now?"

The long British vowels of Joe Ray Stardust's speech had reemerged. At any other time that voice would have lulled Holly into a state of blissful, sensual fantasy. Now it sent a shudder down her spine. When Cole left the key dangling in the door, backed away a pace and turned to face her, she realized she was in trouble. She'd gotten so dangerously close to his body that she could smell his pine-scented skin, the faint mustiness of Bobby's old shirt.

Inadvertently she'd blocked the driver's side door. Now, Cole couldn't get in the car. Nor could he return to the mall unless he squeezed past her, which was impossible. Realizing she'd trapped him, her mouth turned dry.

She inched backward, becoming aware of the frigid air. Her nipples hardened painfully against her red sweater. Whether it was from the cold or Cole's close proximity, she didn't know or even care. All she knew was that Cole noticed and that his eyes lingered on her breasts without apology or regret, but in a frank, assessing, mildly curious way that made her cheeks sting as if she'd been slapped. She quit moving, freezing against the driver's door, as that infuriatingly lazy gaze drifted over her breasts a final time, then shifted to the car keys.

His voice turned frosty. "Do you mind?"

Holly crossed her arms over her chest, wondering if he was referring to the focus of his gaze or his use of her car. Either way, her answer was the same. "I most certainly do."

At the challenge in her tone, he tilted his head and surveyed her. "Why?"

"That's my car." Fighting not to leap back when he advanced, she held her ground. How could he have this effect on her? She felt faint and furious, hot and cold. Even in her angry confusion, her eyes lingered on his mouth, longing for a kiss. Heaven help her, but she felt aroused even though he hadn't even touched her. Yet, she thought. Everything in his eyes said he was about to lay his nimble-fingered hands on her—for good or ill.

Somehow she kept her voice steady. "Did you think I'd let you simply get in my car and drive away?"

He shrugged. "You've been letting me drive it for a week."

"But now you're leaving."

"Maybe." He shrugged again. "Actually, you don't know where the hell I'm going."

He was right. She didn't have a clue. Though it wasn't in her to plead with a man, she'd try reasoning with him. "Look, we've... both been in the wrong."

He grunted softly. "What?"

"You heard me."

In one swift movement, he was right in front of her, squeezing her between the cars, then pinning her against the door. When she tried to wrench away, his body moved flush against hers. *Oh Lord,* she thought in panic, *I'm not the only one who's aroused.*

At the frank realization, she gasped and the sharp intake of winter air hurt her lungs, making them ache and burn. Feeling the hard, ready heat of him at the juncture of her thighs, both anger and raw need stirred her blood. "Get away from me," she demanded venomously.

He didn't budge. What woman in her right mind would allow a man to toy with her this way—entertaining arousal even as he was leaving her? Suddenly, the mere whisper of his warm breath against Holly's cheek made her want to scream. Her eyes darted around the parking garage, but passersby were hauling bags and boxes, oblivious to her plight.

Cole's voice was murderous—his breathing shallow, his words ragged. "You assaulted me."

"I didn't mean to."

"I was suffering from memory loss and you took me to a crackpot."

"Dr. Kester's a good doctor!" She tried to squirm from the grasp of Cole's thighs, but there was nowhere to go and at each desperate movement, the lower half of his body only nestled nearer. As if only now registering her desire to escape, Cole leaned more of his weight against her.

"Holly, you let me completely misconstrue my relationship to you. And your kids." His voice was laced with threads that bound her as surely as his thighs.

Now his sculpted face turned so hard that the chiseled bones could have cut diamonds. Her knees were failing her again, and she could barely find her voice. "I tried to tell you the truth."

He stared at her as if she were beneath contempt. "You could have tried harder."

"But Dr. Kester said you had to remember on your own and—"

Something in Cole's face stopped her. Everything was about to blow sky-high. The hurricane brewing in those dark eyes made her want to run for cover. A muscle ticked in his cheek that reminded her of time bombs.

"Let's get back to what you think I did wrong," he said.

She shivered. Sucking in a breath, her teeth tingled. "You deceived the public," she said.

"Go on."

"You..." She could barely meet his eyes. Whatever he'd done, he probably had reasons. But so did she.

His lips thinned in a bloodless smile. "Yeah?"

"You don't really live in Connecticut." Her voice rose. "And you're not really married, the way people think."

A cynical chuckle came from between his lips. "You're sure about that?"

She stared at him, her eyes widening.

His derisive laugh didn't meet his eyes. "Oh no, Holly," he assured. "You were right. No wife." His dangerous, stormy eyes turned a full shade darker. "No *real* wife."

Or kids.

Only his eyes said it. And they said it with raw-boned pain. *Don't back down, Holly,* she thought, hoping sympathy didn't get the best of her. She'd spent years convincing herself that Bobby wasn't a liar and a cheat. Shouldn't she quit making excuses for men? Cole had lied to the public about who he was, where he lived and his marital status.

And damn it, he's been lying to me.

"How long's it been since your memory returned, anyway?" Her jaw set as rigidly as his. Anger gripped her again and her tone turned into a faint singsong. "'You're my wife,'" she mocked, "'so, why won't you sleep with me?'"

"That's rich," he muttered. "You think I used you?"

"Did you?"

"No," he returned roughly, "but I think I'll start."

With that, Cole grabbed both her hands. Reflexively, she sidestepped, but with lightning speed, he wedged one of his legs between her parted thighs, further trapping her. He was so close that locks of his hair brushed her forehead in the wind. "Who are you?" he demanded. "And what do you want from me?"

With all her being, she fought not to squirm, to ignore the agonizing, magical touch of his body. Through the fabric of her skirt, she could feel his erection, feel his muscles working in his thighs. He brought his lips right next to her ear.

"When I saw you in the parking lot last week, I recognized you from somewhere," he said tersely. "Are you a reporter, a fan? C'mon, Holly, what do you want?"

"I don't want anything from you!"

Suddenly, willfully, he shifted his body, pressing himself hard against her, warming her core. "Oh, is that right?"

Blood rushed to her face.

His voice became a soft taunt. "What if I *was* married?"

"But you weren't," she growled. Realizing she'd said the words in the past tense, as if it no longer mattered that he wasn't married, her heart broke. Cole didn't even want to know why she'd acted as she had.

Even worse, his unforgiving eyes said it was over between them. She found her voice. "Look, I came out here to talk to you."

"So talk."

"But you don't want to hear what I have to say."

"You're damn right about that." For a moment, h simply stared at her. And then his mouth—hungry, angr and relentless—crushed down on hers.

She was helpless against his anger, overpowered by hi sensual assault. He kissed her without mercy, his tongu forcing open her mouth, plunging deep between her li Any fool would have known it was useless to fight. But flamelike, heated spear of her tongue tried valiantly, ing with his until he mastered her defiance. Agai again, heat surged through her, searing straight to he

When a rough hand slid behind her neck, rakin her skin, she moaned. Everything inside her had tu hot she could barely stand it. All was forgotten—th gerously cold weather, the crowded parking garag eyes of strangers. All she felt were Cole's fingers, ing furious fistfuls of her wind-tangled hair.

With a tug, he forced her head back farther, s arched against him. Then he renewed the kiss that w claiming, so demanding. Never had a man kissed her such hungry fire. Cole hated her. And he loved her.

And all she could do was respond to his passion, k ing him back just as wildly. Biting and nibbling, seek out his mouth whenever he moved. Maybe she would lose him, after all. Maybe he would stay. Maybe—

A hard rap on her car trunk brought her back to realit Her head snapped away from Cole's, and she stared in th direction of the sound.

It was Robert Samuels.

He was standing near a taillight, his cane still raised from where he'd rapped it against her car. "Ah," he said, "so this must be the man I hear you've been shacking up with."

ᴛHE STRANGER BE DAMNED, Cole thought. This was one
ɑrgument he didn't intend to have interrupted. Anger
ɔoursed through him again, but this time, the man was the
ᴛarget. Cole couldn't care less who he was or what he
vanted. All he knew was that the man was leaving. And
vhen he did, Cole was going to kiss Holly with a ven-
ɡeance. "Who is this guy?"

Holly inhaled sharply. "He's—"

"The owner of this mall," the older man said with
barely controlled fury. "Now, who are *you?*"

Cole narrowed his flinty gaze. No one took that tone
with Cole Rayburn—or Joe Ray Stardust. In fact, maybe
he should announce he *was* Joe Ray, which might take
some wind out of the man's sails.

Suddenly, Cole realized this was the man Holly had
hidden from this morning. The woman in the fur coat was
no longer with him, so Cole hadn't recognized him. Now
his eyes drifted over the man's well-made clothes. What
did Holly have to fear from him?

"Please, Cole, let's go," she whispered. "We've got to
get out of here."

He wasn't about to turn tail and run. "Who I am—"
Cole pinned the man with his gaze "—is none of your
business."

"Is that so?"

Cole nodded. "Besides, Holly's a woman, and she can
entertain whoever she likes."

The man's lips curled away from his teeth. "Is that what
you call it...entertainment?"

No man was going to make lewd insinuations about
Holly. Cole tensed. "Get away from the car or I'll move
you bodily."

"Oh, please," Holly whispered.

"So, you *are* the one who's been staying with her."

"What of it?" Cole said coolly.

"And with her kids?"

Whoever the man was, he knew Holly and probably meant her harm. But Cole would protect her. His voice turned as cold as his eyes. "We're consenting adults. And we do whatever we please."

The man shot Holly a victorious smile. "Well, I guess that seals your coffin. You can't hold a job, you can't provide a decent home for the children and you sleep around...."

"Why don't you place the blame where it belongs," Holly burst out. "That's not *me* you're talking about! That's your *son!*"

The man's derisive smile looked strained. "We'll see about that in court tomorrow."

Court? As the man spun around and strode toward the mall, the word was still echoing inside Cole's head. "Holly, what's happening here?"

She wrenched away from him and stormed out from between the cars until she was in the open, near the trunk. There were tears in her eyes when she whirled to face Cole. "Get away from me!"

He stared at her. Why was she crying? "Who was that?"

"Robert Samuels." She spat out the name as if Cole should have known. "My ex-father-in-law."

"Samuels..." Cole murmured. Then it came flooding back. "Bobby Samuels..."

"My ex-husband. If you'd ever bothered to ask."

That's how I know her. Cole's mind reeled with the memory. Last year, at the Christmas party, he'd had to fire Bobby Samuels. Only afterward had Cole seen a snatch of a red velvet dress in a darkened hallway and realized Bobby's date had probably overheard.

Now he knew the date had been Bobby's wife. Hell, Holly hadn't even heard the half of her husband's transgressions. At least she'd been spared that. But she'd left the party immediately. And from his office window, high above Rockefeller Center, Cole had watched her go.

He'd never seen her up close. But from afar, his eyes drank her in, roving over each inch of the lovely, lone figure in the gorgeous red cape and party dress. No wonder that dress had seemed special when he'd seen it in her closet. That night, as she'd squared her shoulders and hailed a cab, he'd felt drawn to how quickly she'd acted on her emotions, letting her gut instincts guide her. Just as he'd decided to follow her, she'd stepped into a cab.

In that fleeting instant he'd thought she was a woman he could love. Now he knew it was true. He could love her. He *did* love her. How she could have wound up with Bobby Samuels, he'd never know. Not that he'd say it.

He sighed, shrugged out of his coat, then held it to her on a crooked finger. "Here."

"I'm not cold."

It was a lie. She was obviously freezing. "Put it on."

"No."

"Fine." All week, she'd been lying to him, so what was she mad about? Still visualizing her in the red velvet dress she'd worn a year ago, Cole found himself thinking of the clothes in her closet, of how regular garments mingled with more expensive ones. After Holly left him, Cole guessed Bobby didn't bother to take care of her. "Holly," Cole said with insight, "I'm really sorry I had to fire him."

Angrily, she swiped away her tears. "You should be."

His temper flared again, and he shrugged back into his coat. "Your husband couldn't do his job."

"But you didn't have to ruin my life!"

He gasped. "I ruined your life?"

"When Bobby left, I didn't have anything."

"You had Benji and Treasure."

"And now you've gone and taken them away from me, too!"

"What?"

"The Samuelses want the kids, and I have to go to custody court tomorrow. And you—you—" Her voice broke. "You just gave them everything they need to take my kids away."

Warring emotions tore Cole apart. He'd told Holly he loved her. Didn't she know how much he'd come to care for the kids? All along, she'd been in serious trouble, but she'd never once turned to him for help. Instead, she'd lied and hidden him in her house.

"Holly, whatever Bobby Samuels did to you isn't my fault." Cole thought back to his first night at her house, when she'd unloaded on him, accusing him of doing things Bobby had actually done. Somehow, he kept his voice calm. "Nor is what's happening with the kids." She had to understand that much.

But she didn't. "Just get away from me!"

"You help other people," he said, "and someday you're going to have to let them help you."

She stomped her foot. "I said, go away!"

He'd had it. When he raised a hand and snapped his fingers, an envelope magically appeared. Slowly, he turned it, so Holly could see his plane ticket. "I'm on my way," he said simply.

Lithely passing her, he headed for the mall, thinking he'd find a taxi near the front entrance. Just as he reached the doors, he heard her behind him, her steps pounding on the concrete.

Not that he cared. He'd waited for a woman too long to be toyed with like this. He was leaving her for good. She'd never find him again. And it was her loss.

Decisively, he pushed through the glass double doors, then Cole did what he did best—he vanished.

Chapter Twelve

Holly's eyes settled on Judge Selsa. He was scrutinizing the kids, who were seated on either side of her. Fortunately, they were dressed in their best clothes, even if Benji's bruised eye gave him a rakish air.

Don't look scared and don't cry, Holly. Cole was gone and her heart was breaking, but she knew she had to stay strong for Benji and Treasure. "Oh, Danice," she whispered, "I can't believe this."

The lawyer glanced apologetically over the top of Benji's head. "This was supposed to be a simple, informal hearing," she returned grimly, patting down her iron-gray suit in such a perfunctory manner that it could have been a knight's battle armor. "If I'd known the Samuelses were going to play hardball, I wouldn't have advised you to bring the kids."

But it was too late.

Benji and Treasure had already heard their Grandpa's graphic account of the kiss he'd witnessed between Holly and Cole. After Robert Senior stepped down, a woman Holly had never seen took the stand. She was probably in her twenties, and she had short curly brown hair and green eyes.

"Yes..." The woman nervously addressed the Samuelses' counselor. "I saw a man who answers the description of Holly Hawkes's...boyfriend. And...well, I'd been shopping at the mall, so I only saw them from the road. They were in the Civic Center parking lot last week and she hit the man with some sort of long-handled club."

"She?" Judge Selsa cleared his throat. "Can you identify her?"

The woman raised an accusing finger and pointed at Holly. Holly's heart beat a rapid tattoo. It wasn't in her best interest to appear defensive, but she couldn't help but cross her arms.

"That will be all, ma'am." The counsel for the Samuelses turned to Judge Selsa. "Unfortunately, your honor, Holly Hawkes's boyfriend, the victim of this brutal, vicious assault, could not be found for questioning."

The last thought reverberated in Holly's mind. *Cole can't be found.... Cole can't be found.... Cole can't be found....*

She shook her head as if to dislodge the words and tried not to notice that this hearing was turning into a trial. She squeezed the kids' small shoulders reassuringly. Not that it helped. Benji and Treasure were about to cry.

"So Holly assaulted a man, then he left her because of it." Jessica Samuels tossed her auburn hair over her shoulder and sniffed as if she'd expected nothing less. "In light of this evidence, I wonder where my grandson got that black eye?"

The blood drained from Holly's face. How could Jessica imply that Holly would hurt Benji? *Am I going to lose my kids?*

As if sensing their dire circumstances, Benji yelled, "Nicky hit me at day care!"

"Gran'mama," Treasure called in a quavering voice, "you better leave Mommy alone or else!"

Judge Selsa slammed down his gavel.

Unable to take any more, Holly rested her elbows on the table, shut her eyes and pressed her fingers to her temples. Immediately, a vision of Benji's puppy leaped into her mind. She'd left a message for Mr. Warring saying she'd pick up Hot Dog today. So, no matter what else happened, at least her son would have the Christmas he deserved.

Just hang on to that thought, Holly. And push Cole out of your mind or you'll never get through this travesty of justice.

"Mommy?" Benji whispered.

Holly sat up and squared her shoulders. Leaning close to her son, she whispered, "What, sweetheart?"

"Why couldn't Daddy Cole come and help us?"

Benji's soft-spoken words were like knives piercing her soul. How could she tell the kids that Daddy Cole wasn't coming back? And how could she live without the man?

Don't give in to your emotions. Stay strong for the kids.

"We don't need help, Benji," Holly whispered brightly. "We've got lots of good things on our side."

Even as she said it, Danice rose to her feet. "Judge, we'd also like to present a character witness at this *informal* hearing."

Judge Selsa nodded. "Go ahead."

"Mr. Silas Berry," Danice called.

Just hearing the name, relief flooded Holly. As Mr. Berry wheeled his chair down the center aisle of the courtroom, Holly felt sure she'd told Benji the truth. Everything would be fine. Mr. Berry looked incredibly distinguished in his gray suit and navy tie. He was so well-spoken and commanded such respect. Surely, he'd convince Judge Selsa that she was of sound mind and character.

Without warning, Holly's heart wrenched. *Cole was right about you, you know.* She was too proud to ask for help. And maybe that *was* a kind of selfishness. If not for her pride, all her neighbors would have come to her rescue today. So would her parents. So would Cole.

But she'd only mustered the courage to ask Mr. Berry for help. And now she might lose her kids. *Oh, Holly, you've got no one to blame but yourself.*

"Thank you so much for coming, Mr. Berry," Danice said after she'd established the relationship between Holly and Mr. Berry. "Although this hearing is informal, I'd like to remind you that there's quite a lot at stake. Could you please give the court your assessment of Holly Hawkes's character?"

Mr. Berry said nothing. His hands were poised right above his lap and, even from where she sat, Holly could see that they were trembling. Something was wrong!

Danice cleared her throat. "Mr. Berry?"

He shifted uncomfortably in his wheelchair. "Before this week, I *guess* I would have said Holly was a nice woman...."

Danice masked her surprise. "Thank you," she said quickly. "That will be all."

Judge Selsa leaned forward. "I'm sorry, but I think I need to hear this. Please continue."

At the judge's prompting, Mr. Berry's words poured forth. "Recently Holly took up with a man none of us had ever seen before. He's been living with her and the kids. Now he's left her. I guess because she assaulted him. She also had a . . . well, a real wild party this week."

"The p-party we gave Stella?" Holly stammered.

Mr. Berry stared into his lap. "Yes."

"No…" The blood in Holly's ears whirred, so she could barely hear herself think. "That wasn't a wild party! That was—"

"Please watch that temper of yours, Ms. Hawkes," Judge Selsa said, turning to Mr. Berry again. "Please proceed, sir."

"There've been odd goings-on. One night I saw Holly and the stranger through the window, and it looked as if they were fighting. I think Holly threw him out, but then he sneaked back inside with some Christmas carolers."

"Christmas carolers?" Holly burst out. "Now, that's truly suspicious!"

"Please, Holly!" Danice whispered in warning.

But Holly knew it no longer mattered. Her kids were lost.

The judge cleared his throat. "It's clear that Holly Hawkes's residence at the Pine Cottage Estates may not be the best home for these children."

"Judge Selsa!" Holly exploded. "It may not be the best home, but it's *their* home."

The judge didn't bother to respond.

Cole had left her. Her kids were all she had left. Holly's grip tightened on Benji's and Treasure's shoulders. The Samuelses had betrayed her. So had Mr. Berry. It was all she could do to keep her voice from breaking. "How could you all do this to me?"

Mr. Berry looked up—and Holly realized his eyes were red-rimmed. "Jessica," he said, "you can't make me do this."

Holly's head jerked toward her mother-in-law. "You put him up to this?"

"She most certainly did!"

This time it was Stella. Flanked by Jonathan and Maggie, the birdlike woman flew right down the center aisle of the courtroom. Irma was close on her heels, followed by Joyce and Mac Ryan, then Linda and a very lethal-looking Jumbo Stirling. After that, Reverend Starkey came down the aisle with countless parishioners and people from day care, including Nicky Chamberlain and his mother. "And Jack Deegan?" Holly murmured in shock.

"Look, Mommy," Treasure said in wonder. "Every body's come to help us."

"'Cept for Daddy Cole," Benji whispered.

No, Cole wasn't here. But tears of gratitude sprang to Holly's eyes. Somehow, she managed to blink them back as Zeke Harden and Dr. Kester passed by. *My parents, too?* Holly was so shocked to see them, she couldn't speak.

Her mother was wearing a winter-white suit she usually reserved for church. She ran toward Holly, kissed her and the kids, then stepped back and wrung her gloved hands. "When you called and canceled dinner, I *knew* something was wrong. Why didn't you tell us?"

Holly's father, looking stiff and uncomfortable in his starched shirt and sport coat, did his best to smile. "You and the kids have never once missed a dinner, honey."

"I didn't want to worry you," Holly murmured.

"Worry us?" Her mother draped an arm around her. "Holly, that's what we're here for. That's the spirit of love...the spirit of Christmas."

And it was. The spirit of Christmas wasn't just about giving. It was about receiving, too. But why did Holly have to find that out now—when it was too late, when Cole had vanished?

If only she could turn back the clock—and turn to Cole. He'd gladly have helped her. He'd loved her. And she'd missed her chance.

Around Holly, everyone was talking at once. Words overlapped in a general outpouring of emotion that brought fresh tears to her eyes.

"When I broke my hip," Irma was saying to Judge Selsa, "it was Holly who did all my shopping and errands...."

"Mac and I've been trying so hard to have a baby," Joyce Ryan said. "And Holly's been so encouraging...."

Linda squeezed Jumbo's waist. "This big ole lug would never have proposed to me if it weren't for Holly...."

"And her rent's paid up," Zeke said.

Jonathan stepped forward dramatically. "My mother might have starved to death," he proclaimed, "if it weren't for Holly Hawkes."

"Every night since Thanksgiving, she's taken my mother-in-law dinner," Maggie explained.

Stella sniffed. "And now my family's reunited. Why, Holly threw us the most wonderful party...."

Judge Selsa's eyes narrowed, and he scrutinized each person in turn, as if judging them just by looking at them. Finally, his gaze landed on Mr. Berry. "Why have you been disparaging Holly Hawkes?"

The clear pain in Mr. Berry's eyes made Holly's heart ache for him. "Mr. Berry?" she ventured.

He swallowed hard. "If I can't pay the January taxes, they're going to take the Pine Cottage Estates away from me." He drew his hand into a fist and pressed it against his mouth. "Jessica said if I did a little spying, she'd help pay..."

Holly sighed. "How do you know my mother-in-law?"

Sadness crossed Mr. Berry's features and his voice turned wistful. "We used to belong to the same country club, back in the old days when..."

His voice trailed off and Holly's heart filled with sorrow at the unspoken words. *Back when his wife was alive and he still had the use of his legs.*

"If I—I lose that place—" His voice broke.

Stella sidled close and patted Mr. Berry's shoulders. "If he loses the place, every last one of us will be evicted, and he knows some of us will have trouble finding new homes. Especially people who're on fixed incomes, like me and Irma."

What a dilemma. Not wanting to see all his tenants turned out into the cold, Mr. Berry had decided to help Jessica.

Slowly, Holly turned toward her in-laws. "How could you put Mr. Berry into such a position?" She shook her head. "I've always wanted you to be a part of Benji's and Treasure's lives, but through them, you can't fix what's happened to Bobby." Holly glanced at her neighbors, then at Jessica. "All of us might be facing the new year without roofs over our heads," she found herself saying, "but I'll tell you one thing."

Jessica's composure was fading fast. "What?"

"Christmas is at my house this year. And if you want to see the kids, that's where you'll have to come." Holly's eyes darted to Judge Selsa's. "I can keep my kids, can't I?"

"Yes." His gavel slammed down. "And have a very merry Christmas, Holly Hawkes."

Everyone cheered—the Pine Cottage residents, the Reverend and parishioners and parents from day care.

A moment later, a stunned Holly realized the Samuelses had vanished. Turning to her mother, she said, "How did everyone know to come here?"

"A man who said he was a good friend of yours called," her mother said gently. "His name was Cole Rayburn."

Even now, from behind the scenes, Cole's nimble fingers remained at work. Holly clutched her mother's arm. "Did he say where he was? Where he was going?"

Her mother shook her head. "No, only that he was leaving town."

He's really left me. Holly glanced at her neighbors again. How could this much magic surround her, when the magician himself was gone?

"Is Gran'mama and Gran'pa Samuels gonna hate us?" Treasure asked.

Holly glanced at the kids in the rearview mirror. "No one could ever hate you. They're just mad."

Only now that the kids were safe and sound could Holly allow herself to remember the old days as they really had been. After all, the Samuelses had been like a second set of parents to her until Bobby's fast living had broken their hearts. Now they were grasping at straws, trying to find something other than their only son to bring meaning to their lives.

"If Gran'pa makes Gran'mama come over for Chris'mis," Benji ventured, "do we gotta be nice?"

A wry smile touched Holly's lips. She was sorely tempted to indulge a taste for revenge. "You sure do," she forced herself to say. "In fact, because it's Christmas you'll have to be extra nice."

Treasure sighed. "I just wish Daddy Cole would come home."

"We told Santa we wanted him for Chris'mis," Benji reminded her.

At that, Holly's eyes stung and she trained her gaze on the road. A glum silence fell inside the car. Outside, wet snow was falling, not that Holly's lousy old umbrella

would be of much use. She listened to the hypnotic pass of the windshield wipers, then flicked on the radio.

Nothing happened.

It was a sore reminder that her car was falling apart. *And that I need Cole.* Cole, who was so good at fixing the little mechanical things that plagued her. She thought of his elegant fingers, of their fascinating, agile movements. And of how they touched her body—teasing, arousing, satisfying. Heaven knew, that magic touch had prepared her mind and heart to travel with him. She'd packed her bags, ready for a long life's journey to places she'd never been.

And where she and Cole would never go now.

Biting back tears, Holly made a turn in the road. She'd just have to bring her old powers of denial into play and not break down in front of the kids. Up ahead was Pretty Pets, and as soon as she dropped off the kids with Irma, she'd come back and get the puppy. Stella said she'd keep it until tomorrow morning.

"Mommy!"

At Benji's sharp, sudden cry, Holly's eyes darted to the rearview mirror again. "Honey?"

Treasure was unbuckling her seat belt and scrambling across the back seat. "Stop!"

Holly lifted her foot from the gas pedal. "Wha—"

"Hot Dog's gone!" Treasure shrieked.

With a gasp, Holly pulled next to Pretty Pets. Sure enough, the window where Hot Dog had been was empty. Only his doggy bed, with its red-and-green plaid pillow, remained. The canned snowflake lettering that had carried Mr. Warring's holiday message was wiped away.

Feeling sick, Holly realized that Mr. Warring had probably done his best. He'd lost the sale of that puppy countless times because of her. And it was wrong of her to have

expected him to wait. Her heart breaking, Holly watched the tears well in Benji's eyes. *Oh please don't cry, baby.*

Her son's brave little voice filled the car. "I betcha Santa came and got 'im."

Treasure's jaw set stoically. "Sure he did."

But he hadn't.

And they all knew it. Feeling bone weary, Holly looked at the other window. It was empty, too.

The red train was gone. So was the miniature town. And yet, Holly could almost see the fancy display—the train's little red cars puttering along the winding track, passing the tiny houses and pines and boxwoods that were nestled on their cottony blanket of snow. Somehow, in her mind, that small imaginary world merged with the Pine Cottage Estates and her eyes blurred.

Staring into those empty windows, Holly felt exactly like them.

EVERY DAY'S THE FIRST DAY of the rest of our lives. And that's especially true on Christmas. So, don't worry, kids, we'll wake up to a whole new world tomorrow.

That's what Holly had told Benji and Treasure.

Not that they cared. Daddy Cole was gone, their grandparents had confused them, and they'd heard things in court about their mother that it had taken hours to explain. Instead of reading "'Twas the Night Before Christmas," Holly had admitted she was responsible for Cole's memory loss and convinced the kids he was better now.

Always more perceptive than her years, Treasure had screwed up her adorable face. "If Daddy Cole can remember now, why does he gotta leave and forget us?"

"He could never forget you," Holly had whispered.

Then the kids had kissed Fuzzy good-night, and Holly had turned out the light. For a long time, she'd sat in the room, watching her babies in the darkness. They'd slept immediately, as if the Sandman, rather than Santa, was to come tonight, to sweep them into a blissful netherworld of forgetfulness.

While she'd watched them, Holly had craved her own sweet dreams—those dreams where the phone would ring. Or Cole's knock would sound at the door. Dreams that would never come true.

She glanced around the living room. The few gifts were under the tree. Only the croquet set and *One Magic Christmas,* neither of which she could bear to look at, had remained hidden in her trunk. Mostly she'd done simple things. Filled the stockings with oranges and quarters and candy canes. For Treasure, she'd found a gold jewelry box in the shape of a treasure chest. But with all her heart, she still wished she'd gotten that puppy. It would have made Benji so happy.

Her eyes drifted over the lit tree, the fireplace, and the stool Cole had set next to the chimney. On it, beside a tall glass of milk, Benji and Treasure had left a plate of the cookies Cole had made.

This has been the best Christmas of my life, Holly thought. *And the worst.* And now, with the gifts under the tree and the kids asleep, Holly allowed herself to do what she'd wanted to ever since yesterday.

She broke down and wept.

"Mommy, Mommy!"

The kids sounded distant. Closer, Holly felt their tiny, insistent hands trying to shake her awake. At least that proved her limbs were still intact. So were her head and heart, since both ached from last night's crying. She opened one itchy, swollen eye.

Benji and Treasure, still clad in their pajamas, peered back.

Holly mustered a smile. "Merry Christmas, kids."

Treasure grabbed her hand and tugged. "Get up!"

"He came!" Benji exclaimed.

"He came?" Holly bolted upright in bed, her heart accelerating, her breath catching. "Cole came?"

Treasure shot her a stricken look. "Uh—no, Mommy."

Holly squinted. "So, who came?"

Benji stomped a sock-clad foot. "Santa!"

Holly masked her disappointment. Apparently, the kids had peeked at the tree downstairs. As she stumbled from bed and slipped into her robe, she noticed the time. "It's nearly ten," she said, her voice rusty.

Her parents would be here shortly, but they wouldn't expect the kids to wait to open their packages. Maybe Jessica and Robert Samuels would come and make amends, too. "Well, I guess we overslept," she murmured, thinking that she and the kids had never slept this late on Christmas.

"But we're awake now," Treasure said. "So, c'mon!"

You self-indulgently cried your eyes out last night. Now don't you dare ruin their Christmas. Still wishing Hot Dog was under the tree, Holly forced herself to smile. And when Benji and Treasure reached up, grabbed her hands and pulled again, Holly made a show of stumbling from the bedroom and down the hallway. At the bathroom, she stopped. "Want to head down and wait for me?"

Benji and Treasure shook their heads, clearly wanting to witness their mother's awed expression when she saw Santa's handiwork.

Holly quickly brushed her teeth and splashed water on her face, reminding herself to look surprised. Then, she let the kids drag her downstairs. She was actually standing in the living room before she realized something was... different.

Treasure's voice was solemn. "Look what Santa did."

"We musta been pretty good," Benji whispered.

For a second, Holly thought her roof had opened and that it had snowed inside her living room. Then she realized a white cotton throw dusted with gold glitter covered her entire floor. Boxes tied with thick red velvet bows were stacked sky-high, their green and gold paper gleaming.

Holly's heart swelled, feeling too large. And then she saw it. Perched atop a raised platform was the little red train. As it puttered around its twisting track, high above the magical, miniature town that had once been inside the window of Mr. Warring's shop, she could almost hear Cole's voice say the words aloud again. *I want to give you the whole world, Holly.*

And this Christmas, he had. Her throat closed tight. Especially when she saw that above the train and town was a huge open umbrella, the kind that would always keep off snow on a cold winter's day. On the outside, the umbrella was printed with rain clouds. But inside, it had a silver lining. Feeling sharp tugs on her robe, she glanced down.

"There really is a Santa Claus, Mommy," Treasure whispered.

"Yes, Treasure," Holly whispered back. "There really is."

And when Holly raised her gaze again, she knew she'd never believed it more than at that moment. Because Cole stepped from the kitchen into her living room.

"Daddy Cole!" Treasure shrieked, running for his open arms.

Benji nearly tripped over her heels. "Daddy!"

When Cole's eyes met hers and he lifted the kids into his embrace, Holly believed in magic. Santa Claus—the real

Santa Claus—had come. Wearing his bright red velvet suit, he'd shimmied down her chimney. And that wise old man with the white curling beard and twinkling eyes really did know what everyone most wanted and needed. He never forgot anyone on his list—and last night he'd delivered it all.

She blinked back tears and watched Cole put down the kids. *Don't jump the gun. You don't know why he came back. Maybe it's just to see Benji and Treasure.*

"Can we open our presents?" Treasure squealed.

"Can we?" Benji echoed.

Holly nodded, then heard wrapping paper as Cole strode across the room, over the gold-glittered flooring. He stopped in front of her, and a tear fell, splashing her cheek.

Cole chuckled softly as he brushed it away. "Good thing I got you an umbrella for Christmas," he said huskily.

Holly mustered a smile. "Don't you know it's bad luck to open an umbrella inside?"

His midnight eyes looked veiled. "With you in my life, I could never believe in bad luck."

A trace of a British accent touched his voice, sending tremulous thrills through her body. Did this magic man mean to stay with her? Should she ask? "Cole...I—"

Treasure squealed. Just as she glanced toward her daughter, Cole slipped his arm around Holly's waist. *Oh, please, Santa, let me keep this man for Christmas,* Holly thought, leaning against his side. Then she followed his gaze back to Treasure, who looked like an angel, standing barefoot on the white, gold-glittered carpeting. With a smile, Treasure held up the treasure-chest jewelry box. It had been wrapped in Christmas tree print paper, which now fell, unceremoniously, to the floor.

"Now, Treasure," Cole said lightly, just as she began to open the lid, "Santa told me that's a big gift."

It wasn't, though. Holly had put nothing inside at all. But as Treasure opened the lid, she looked stunned. Clutching the box, she staggered toward Holly and Cole.

"Santa gave me a diamond," Treasure whispered in shock, holding the open box out to Holly, who peered inside.

Sure enough, nestled on the satin was a silver chain. From it, hung a heart with a tiny diamond chip. Over the top of Treasure's head, Holly stared at Cole. How had he known that Treasure's wrapped gift contained an empty jewelry box? *Maybe Santa was here, after all,* Holly thought. *Or else Cole really is magic.*

Treasure stood as still as a statue while Cole gently fastened the necklace. "Thank you, Daddy Cole," she said softly. Then she all but floated to the tree again, looking as if all her earthly wishes had been fulfilled.

"You shouldn't have," Holly murmured.

"It's just a chip," Cole whispered.

"A diamond's a diamond," Holly murmured wistfully.

"A diamond is as a diamond does," Cole countered. With that, he raised his hand in the air and snapped his fingers. A small wrapped box appeared and he held it out to Holly.

Somehow, her trembling fingers managed to get past the paper—to the small, black velvet box beneath. Inside was a simple ring with a magically sparkling diamond. Gazing into Cole's eyes, Holly was barely able to trust what it meant. *Oh, please, Cole . . . please say it.*

He leaned and brushed his moist, warm lips across hers. "Will you marry me, Holly?"

"I love you," she whispered.

"Yeah—" he smiled "—but that's not what I asked."

Just as she parted her lips, a commotion sounded, one she thought was internal—the thundering of her heart, the whirring of her blood, the beating of her pulse. Then she realized the sounds were from outside. Horns blared, then car doors slammed. Holly's eyes darted from Cole to the window. "What in the world..."

"Glennis," Cole returned levelly.

And then someone shouted, "We know Joe Ray Stardust is in there."

THE LAST THING Cole needed right now was for Glennis to profess her undying love. Or to be harassed by reporters. What Cole needed was an answer to his outstanding proposal.

But through the window, he could see a strangely bedraggled Glennis trudging through the snow, her usually neat French twist unrolling around her face. Television news vans were parking in Holly's driveway and reporters with mikes and paper pads were climbing from the vans. Even worse, Fred James—tabloid news hound extraordinaire—was in the crowd.

"Cole?" Holly whispered with worry.

Cole shot her a grim smile. "I don't know if Bobby mentioned her, but the blonde is Glennis, my producer."

"He mentioned her," Holly said in shock. "And I recognize Fred James."

Cole's gaze swept over Fred's tailored coat and salon haircut. Somehow Cole wanted to protect Holly from this unexpected encroachment of his other life. After all, he really was Cole Rayburn, not Joe Ray Stardust. And he belonged here with Holly—in the mountains, with the fresh air and the kids. Would she refuse to marry him because of his New York life?

Tightening his arm around her waist, Cole wished he knew a magic trick for making every last person outside vanish. He needed this time alone with Holly, needed to hear her answer, needed to know if his lonely days were over.

"Look, Holly—"

Holly's tone turned practical. "We'd better see what they want."

Cole's whole side felt bereft as she slipped away from him and into a pair of shoes next to the door. She shrugged into his navy coat, which was long enough to hide her robe. Frowning, Cole watched the perfunctory manner in which she placed the jewelry box on the stair step. Somehow, she didn't look like a woman who was about to say, "I do."

Her concerned gaze met his. "Cole, I want to hear everything they have to say."

Was Holly standing beside him as his future wife, or as a friend? He didn't have time to find out because she opened the door. They both stepped onto the porch.

Glennis charged toward them. The walkway wasn't shoveled and her high heels sank repeatedly into the deep, damp drifts of snow. "Say a word to those reporters, Fred," she shouted over her shoulder, "and I swear I'll kill you!"

Abruptly, in midstride, Glennis came to a standstill, as if afraid to proceed further. Over the expanse of snow, she shot Cole a guilty glance, while the rest of the crowd, Fred James included, strode right past her.

"What's happening?" Holly said.

Cole sighed. "I think my career's over."

"What?"

Cole glanced down. Holly's stricken expression said she thought this was all her fault. "Holly," he said softly, "I don't care about the 'Joe Ray Stardust Show.' I just want you to marry me."

Before Holly could respond, Fred James strode into earshot. Cole looked past him at Glennis. They'd had a long, fruitful relationship. One that had made them both rich and famous. Had Glennis carried through with last week's threats to create a public relations story about Cole's supposed divorce in the hopes that he'd begin to date her?

If Glennis hadn't, it was definitely time Cole ended this charade himself. He loved performing magic. But far more than a career, he wanted an honest life with Holly.

Cole raised his voice. "Go ahead, Glennis." *Expose me if that's what you want to do.*

Glennis gasped. "I could never really do that!"

"I could!" Fred whirled around and addressed the reporters who had gathered in a semicircle around the porch. "Joe Ray Stardust is a fraud. The Connecticut mansion in which he supposedly resides is empty. He's not really married, nor does he have children."

So this is how it's going to end. Strange, but Cole had wondered about this moment for so many years. The cameras were rolling. The reporters looked excited. No doubt, finding both Fred James and Joe Ray Stardust in a place like the Pine Cottage Estates on a Christmas morning would get some press.

Fred continued, "Absolutely nothing in this man's biography is true. From start to finish, his life is a public relations hoax."

Glennis angrily shoved strands of hair away from her face. She shouted, "Why are you doing this, Fred?"

Fred glared at her across the snow. "Because I love you!"

Glennis stomped her foot. "I love you, too, Fred!"

"You do?"

"Of course I do."

"I don't believe this—" Cole gasped. Joe Ray Stardust's public relations cover had just been blown sky-high because Fred and Glennis had somehow fallen in love. Cole watched in shock as Fred strode through the snow, swept Glennis into his arms and then slammed a hard, claiming kiss on her lips.

Meantime, questions were being hurled at Cole from every side. "Mr. Stardust, is this correct? Are you living a lie?"

Cole cleared his throat. "Well, I—"

"Is it true you don't have a wife and kids?"

Holly's side brushed his as she stepped forward. "I've been married to this man for years," she said.

Behind Cole, the door swung open.

"Joe Ray Stardust is my daddy!" Treasure squealed.

"And he's my daddy, too!" Benji called out.

Cole had never felt so touched. Holly and the kids had come to his rescue, wanting to protect him. But he would never let the woman he wanted to marry—or the kids he'd come to think of as his own—live a lie. And he wanted to be an honest man again.

Near him, the reporters were murmuring among themselves. "Well, the kids are the right ages," said one. "They answer the descriptions in their bio. So does she."

For the first time in many years, Cole remembered asking his father why'd he'd lied about there being a Santa Claus. Now, he could almost hear his father's voice. *Because sometimes you have to lie in order to tell the truth.* In some strange way, he realized, Holly *was* telling the truth. She was his wife, in body and soul, and maybe that was why the reporters believed her.

Not that Cole could continue the charade. He held up his hand. "What Fred James just said is true. My real name is Cole Rayburn. I'm from upstate New York and I'm unmarried." Cole turned to Holly. "But I hope not for long."

"Oh, Cole . . ." Holly murmured.

"I want us to be ourselves," he said simply. Gazing into her eyes, he was vaguely aware that Glennis and Fred had now approached the reporters, and that Glennis, with her knack for PR, was now doing damage control, while the reporters took notes. And it sounded like Glennis, who was something of a magician herself, would actually make things come out right in the end.

Cole thought back to that long-ago night in Joe's Stardust Bar. In a heartbeat, his whole world had changed. But while life as Joe Ray Stardust had been magical, Cole knew a life with Holly and the kids would be even better. "Let's get inside before you freeze," he whispered, pulling Holly inside.

Disengaging himself from the other reporters, Fred shivered and tugged the bedraggled Glennis into Holly's living room. "For another kiss, do I get the TV exclusive?" Fred asked.

"Only if you interview Joe Ray—I mean Cole," Glennis returned. "And if you promise to play the story exactly as I say."

"It's a deal," Fred said.

Holly chuckled. "Go on upstairs you two," she said. "In the bedroom at the end of the hallway, you'll find dry clothes. Help yourselves to whatever fits."

Just as Fred and Glennis vanished, a loud bark sounded.

"Hot Dog!" Benji yelled, bolting toward the boxes.

"Hot Dog," Holly murmured moments later, as the dog hopped out from behind the packages into Benji's arms. Watching the dachshund puppy lick her son's face, tears sprang to Holly's eyes again. "Oh, thank you," she whispered softly, so only Cole could hear.

He smiled. "You didn't really think Santa forgot, did you?"

She smiled back. "He's been known to forget things on occasion."

"But he could never forget you," Cole murmured, brushing his lips across hers again and gazing deeply into her eyes. "I just wish I could put into words all the things I want to say."

"Try," she said raspily.

"I was thinking it seems right to be with you on Christmas, because it's the time of year when we remember the world as it never really was, but how we always want it to be." He drew her closer, wrapping his arms around her waist.

She chuckled throatily. "The way I told you about our first kiss that never really was?"

Cole nuzzled his cheek against hers. "The one in the sleigh?"

When she nodded, her lips swept across his again. "In the snow..." Suddenly Holly drew in a sharp breath. "Oh Cole, I didn't get you anything for Christmas. With all that's been going on, I—"

His mouth captured her last words, his tongue moistening her lips, then diving between them. "Holly," he whispered against her mouth as he drew away, "don't you know all I want for Christmas is you? Please, will you marry me?"

"Of course I will. I love you."

"Then put on the ring."

A soft smile lifted the corners of her lips. "It's already on."

Cole leaned back, narrowing his midnight eyes. Somehow, she'd secretly removed the ring from the box and slipped it onto her finger. His mouth quirked. "How did you do that?"

Holly shot him a wicked grin. "Mr. Rayburn, I do have a little magic of my own."

"You sure do, Mrs. Rayburn." Cole's voice caught and turned husky as he threaded his fingers through her hair. Then, tilting back her head, his lips parted hers for a kiss that was both brand-new and yet long remembered. A kiss of magic and miracles, it meant so much to him. And she meant the entire world.

Epilogue

"Mind opening more champagne, somebody?" Jumbo Stirling called out.

"Sorry, my hands are full," Fred said as he carried another tray of vegetables and dip into Holly's crowded living room.

"I'll get it," Cole said.

Holly glanced around the crowd in the cozy cottage. It was New Year's Eve and everybody had shown up: her folks, the neighbors, parents from day care and people from the parish. Her eyes settled on her husband, who was seated next to her on the settee.

Just yesterday, Reverend Starkey had married them in a much-publicized ceremony. Treasure was the flower girl, Benji the ring bearer. And Irma, Stella, Joyce and Linda were maids of honor. Glennis, of course, had used the opportunity to rally the press in Cole's favor.

Not that it was necessary. Right after Christmas, Fred James had interviewed Cole. Cameras had been set up in front of Holly's tree, and Cole had talked honestly and openly about that long-ago Christmas when he'd lost his family, and about the lonely years he'd spent living a lie.

Admiring his willingness to come clean, the public had forgiven him. Cole would remain the special man who brought magic into their homes every week.

Holly shifted her weight on the settee, then glanced past Cole toward the lit hearth. Her parents were joking with Zeke, while Stella had joined Maggie and Jonathan. Irma and Mr. Berry were deep in lively conversation. Judging from the twinkle in Irma's eye, Mr. Berry might even be flirting, Holly decided. On the mantel was an antique clock—a wedding gift from Glennis—and the face now indicated it was nearly midnight.

Cole smiled. "You look so serious."

"Serious about you." Her eyes took him in. His stitches had been removed and his forehead was healing nicely. So was Benji's eye. Somehow, that seemed significant, as if they were all heading into the future with clear heads and vision.

Cole reached for the champagne. Dressed in casual gray wool slacks and a red sweater, he looked more elegantly attired than usual, but his magical hands were as deft as ever. He removed the cork and nestled the bottle in an ice bucket. Then Jumbo Stirling grabbed it, filling Linda's glass.

"Well, Glennis." Cole dunked a celery stick into the dip and crunched a bite. "Are you and Fred really going to live in that old mausoleum?"

"Holly—" Glennis put her arm around Fred "—could you please make Cole refrain from calling my mansion a mausoleum?"

Holly merely shook her head. This week's sale of the Joe Ray Stardust estate to Glennis Gaynes had made headlines. "Sorry," Holly said, "but I wouldn't marry a man who didn't have a mind of his own."

Cole looked hurt. "I thought it was my body you were after."

"That, too." When Holly snuggled closer, he draped his arm around her shoulders.

"I think we'd better cuddle," he said in a stage whisper.

"Just thinking about that old Joe Ray Stardust mausoleum gives *me* shivers," Holly agreed.

Cole leaned closer. "I want to give you all your shivers," he teased.

She grinned. "We do have to figure out where to live."

Cole glanced around the crowded cottage. "For now I can fly to New York on Thursdays. But if we have more kids..."

Holly's mouth quirked. "And if the Samuelses keep visiting..."

Jessica and Robert had come by on Christmas, apologies tumbling from their lips. Maybe it was because Bobby had called. He'd checked himself into a twenty-eight day rehab program, and it looked as if he meant to stick it out.

Or maybe the Samuelses had had a change of heart because the spirit of Christmas had touched them, just as surely as it touched so many people this year. The Samuelses had even helped Mr. Berry pay his taxes. After that, Cole had quietly bought the Pine Cottage Estates ensuring that no tenants would have to move in the future.

There were so many bright things in their future, Holly thought with a sigh. Because Cole had come clean in front of the entire nation, they'd gotten a prompt call from Dorry Connery asking that Cole bring the family to Weller's Falls for his fifteenth-year High School reunion.

Yes, Glennis had a real knack for troubleshooting. It was why she was known as a top-notch producer. It even turned out that her car mechanic wanted to relocate, so after the new year, the man was signing on with Jack Deegan. In spite of Glennis's surface cool, she had as much heart as know-how. And Treasure and Benji had taken to "Auntie Glenn" immediately.

"Holly?"

She grinned. "Cole?"

He chuckled, nodding. "Irma wants you."

Holly glanced up.

"Should I get the kids?" Irma asked.

Holly glanced at the clock. "I guess you'd better. I think they're in their room."

A moment later, just as Glennis poured glasses of juice for the kids and champagne for the adults, Hot Dog bounded downstairs, then pranced into the room.

"Wait up, Hot Dog," Benji demanded, stopping on the stairs.

"He never waits," Treasure said with a giggle.

In the background, Holly heard Jonathan ask Stella if *she* might want a dog. "Why, yes," she said. "Now that I've met Hot Dog, I think I might."

Cole waved the kids down. "C'mon," he called indulgently, "it's nearly midnight."

Even from here, Holly could tell the kids were sleepy. But they'd begged, and she and Cole had finally agreed to let them usher in the new year.

Treasure skipped into the room. "Can we really have some kids' stuff from the mausoleum house, Auntie Glenn?" Her hand shot to her chest and she touched the heart charm on her necklace, as if it might have disappeared since the last time she'd checked.

"You sure can," Glennis said. Since she and Fred were moving into the Joe Ray Stardust Estate, Glennis had promised Benji and Treasure the toys there. "As soon as

Uncle Fred and I get to Connecticut, we'll send you everything.''

Of course, no gift could top Cole's most recent one to Benji and Treasure—the bequest of a small attaché case that contained Cole's very first magic set. Already the kids could make Hot Dog's doggy biscuits magically appear.

Somehow, all the gifts made Holly worry a little. But she, Cole and the kids had the most important gifts of all— a love for family, friends, neighbors and each other.

"Soon enough they'll be back in day care," Cole whispered as if reading her mind.

She smiled. "And starting school." Treasure would go next fall. Curling her head against Cole's chest, Holly sighed.

And then the clock on the mantel chimed.

At that first stroke of midnight, everyone fell silent. Hot Dog didn't even yelp.

While she listened to the lovely old clock, Holly gazed from the kids to Cole. With each new chime, his midnight eyes seemed to grow darker and deeper. At the twelfth stroke, his rich voice filled the air.

"Happy new year," he said.

"Happy new year," everyone shouted.

Then Cole's eyes settled on Holly's. "Happy new year, sweetheart."

Her cheeks grew warm. Around her, everyone was kissing—her parents, Glennis and Fred, Joyce and Mac, Jumbo and Linda. Maggie and Jonathan jointly planted smooches on Stella's cheeks, and Irma leaned solemnly and kissed Mr. Berry.

"Happy new year, Cole," Holly whispered.

His lips settled on hers for a quick, familiar kiss that made her feel as if she were home to stay. When he drew away, she glanced toward Benji just in time to see him kiss his sister's cheek.

Suddenly, so low she barely heard it, then gaining in tempo, Cole began to hum "Auld Lang Syne."

Holly's mind filled in the words. *"Should auld acquaintance be forgot, And never brought to mind? Should auld acquaintance be forgot, And auld lang syne?"*

Cole lifted his champagne glass and handed Holly hers. The kids found their juice glasses and raised them.

"To auld lang syne," Cole said.

All around them, glasses were raised.

"Here, here," Irma said.

"Here, here," said Stella as those who were still seated rose to their feet.

"For auld lang syne," Holly said. With her glass raised, she gazed deeply into Cole's eyes, roughly translating the words. "To the good old times."

"And to all the good old times that lie before us," Cole whispered softly.

"May we never forget them," Holly whispered back.

Then with a musical, magical clink, Cole touched his glass to hers and sipped his drink. And with warm, champagne-moistened lips, he kissed her tenderly, as he would every New Year's Eve at the stroke of midnight for so many, many years to come.

HARLEQUIN®

A M E R I C A N ◆ R O M A N C E®

A HOLIDAY RECIPE FROM THE KITCHEN OF

Jule McBride

Here's one of my favorite recipes. It's a special Christmas tradition in my family. Enjoy!

JULE McBRIDE'S ALMOND BARK CANDY

2 cups Rice Chex
2 cups Corn Chex
2 cups Wheat Chex
2 cups broken-up pretzels
2 cups salted mixed nuts (I use Spanish nuts with the skins)
1 package (1lb) Almond Bark Candy

Mix cereal, pretzels and nuts in a large bowl. In a double boiler melt the Almond Bark Candy. Combine melted candy with cereal, pretzels and nuts, coating the mixture well. Then spread the mixture on waxed paper. When it's cool, break into pieces and store in airtight containers.

This holiday munchie is great for gifts, and the recipe makes a bunch. Deliver to friends in mason jars tied with bright red ribbons, glittered shoe boxes, or stripped-down shiny silver paint cans decorated with holiday bows and stickers.

**Don't miss Jule McBride's
Harlequin Intrigue debut!
IN #418 May 1997 HER IMAGINARY HUSBAND?**

Free Gift Offer

With a Free Gift proof-of-purchase
from any Harlequin® book, you can receive
a beautiful cubic zirconia pendant.

This stunning marquise-shaped stone is a genuine cubic
zirconia—accented by an 18" gold tone necklace.
(Approximate retail value $19.95)

Send for yours today...
compliments of HARLEQUIN®

To receive your free gift, a cubic zirconia pendant, send us one original proof-of-purchase, photocopies not accepted, from the back of any Harlequin Romance®, Harlequin Presents®, Harlequin Temptation®, Harlequin Superromance®, Harlequin Intrigue®, Harlequin American Romance®, or Harlequin Historicals® title available in August, September or October at your favorite retail outlet, together with the Free Gift Certificate, plus a check or money order for $1.65 U.S./$2.15 CAN. (do not send cash) to cover postage and handling, payable to Harlequin Free Gift Offer. We will send you the specified gift. Allow 6 to 8 weeks for delivery. Offer good until December 31, 1996, or while quantities last. Offer valid in the U.S. and Canada only.

Free Gift Certificate

Name: _____

Address: _____

City: _____ State/Province: _____ Zip/Postal Code: _____

Mail this certificate, one proof-of-purchase and a check or money order for postage and handling to: HARLEQUIN FREE GIFT OFFER 1996. In the U.S.: 3010 Walden Avenue, P.O. Box 9071, Buffalo NY 14269-9057. In Canada: P.O. Box 604, Fort Erie, Ontario L2Z 5X3.

FREE GIFT OFFER   084-KMFR

ONE PROOF-OF-PURCHASE
To collect your fabulous FREE GIFT, a cubic zirconia pendant, you must include this original proof-of-purchase for each gift with the properly completed Free Gift Certificate.

084-KMFR

HARLEQUIN®

A M E R I C A N ◆ R O M A N C E®
®

It happened in an instant, but it would last a lifetime.

Suddenly

For three unlikely couples, courtship with kids is anything but slow and easy. Meet the whole brood as three popular American Romance authors show you how much fun it can be in a "family affair"!

#647 CHASING BABY
by Pam McCutcheon
September 1996

#655 MARRYING NICKIE
by Vivian Leiber
November 1996

#664 ROMANCING ANNIE
by Nikki Rivers
January 1997

a Family

SAF

You're About to Become a *Privileged Woman*

Reap the rewards of fabulous free gifts and benefits with proofs-of-purchase from Harlequin and Silhouette books

Pages & Privileges™

It's our way of thanking you for buying our books at your favorite retail stores.

Harlequin and Silhouette—
the most privileged readers in the world!

For more information about Harlequin and Silhouette's PAGES & PRIVILEGES program call the Pages & Privileges Benefits Desk: 1-503-794-2499

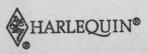

HARLEQUIN®

HAR-PP20